AURORA'S HEART

Suzanne Cass

Aurora's Heart

Storm Cloud Press, Perth Australia

Copyright © 2026 by Suzanne Cass

Cover by Vikncharlie

All rights reserved.

ISBN: 9781764485807

To Gary, Kyle and Arran, you are my everything.

CHAPTER ONE

Aurora sighed and rubbed a hand across her eyes, then peered at the clock on the wall. Still another four hours left on her shift. She hated manning the front desk. It was a thankless task, filled with endless report-writing, fielding numerous phone calls from *concerned* citizens about the dog that'd been barking for hours next door, or the teenager on the e-scooter riding without a helmet on the footpath right past their house, while also taking down a multitude of details from people who walked in off the street to report a lost phone or a stolen bicycle. But as the newest rookie in the Luleå police department, she didn't get a lot of say in where she worked. Her only consolation was that Mårten, her older and supposedly wiser partner, was also taking the day to complete reams of paperwork under the chief's orders.

She really shouldn't grumble; the past six months had flown by, and now her probation was finally over, and as of two weeks ago, she was considered a fully fledged constable. Mårten had helped her get through it all, giving her a stellar evaluation report, and she was eternally grateful for his knowledge and calm presence. She knew some people in the force considered her a little too intense, a little too much of a perfectionist, and Mårten had helped her smooth out some of her *"sharp edges"* as he called them, and help her become more adept at taking things in her stride instead of freaking out at every little thing she couldn't control.

Aurora dipped her head and stared at the document on the computer screen; an incident report form collating all the stolen cars in the area over the past month. Thrilling stuff. God, she hated paperwork. No one warned her there would be this much paperwork when she'd first signed on to the police cadet school. If they had, well maybe she would've… Nah. She gave a quiet laugh, because she knew she wouldn't have listened if they had. She'd been all starry-eyed and so full of earnest excitement at how she was going to make a difference in this world that she would've waved any warnings away as a mere trifle. Paperwork, smakerwork, that's what she would've said; a nuisance, yes, but an essential part of policing. Now, she wasn't so sure. She wanted to be out there doing real policing. Maintaining law and order, solving crimes, guarding public safety, and all the other things it said on the police mission statement that she'd learned so early on by heart.

She tapped her finger restlessly on the desktop. If only she could be tracking down one of these stolen cars instead of listing their details on yet another interminable form. Her mind refused to focus on the screen, and she sighed heavily. She was so tired she could lay her head down right here on the desk, close her eyes and—

"Hi, Aurora." She heard a door closing behind her, but didn't need to turn around to know who was speaking. Her shoulders tensed as he came to stand at her elbow.

"Hi, Erik." She pretended to be typing on her keyboard, not lifting her gaze to look at him. There was a moment of awkward silence as he continued to stand next to her. "What can I do for you?" she asked politely, disguising a sigh under her breath. He was staring at her, she just knew it, and Aurora wasn't really in the mood for Erik this afternoon. He was one of the two IT specialists in the building and was harmless enough. Tall, blond, with strong Nordic cheekbones and bright blue eyes behind his frameless glasses. Erik had a crush on her; it was written all over his face every time he looked at her. It was in the way he fawned over her, bringing her coffee first thing in the morning, or walking casually past her desk at least ten times a day when he clearly had no reason to be there. It was kind of cute, but also kind of annoying.

"Oh, yes." Erik seemed to shake himself out of his reverie. "Inspector Tuckburg asked if I could look into a job for him. He wants me to upload a file to the system, but it seems the video evidence of that gas station robbery he needs isn't listed." Erik shoved a stack of papers in front of Aurora. "You and Mårten supposedly logged the USB stick with the footage last week, so I was wondering if you know where it got to?" Aurora met his gaze at last and she studied him from below lowered lashes, her mouth forming a thoughtful pout as she considered his request.

Inspector Tuckburg was close to retiring, and while Mårten said he'd been a good cop back in his day, he was now spending more time in the office, *putting his skills to other uses*, as he put it. Tuckburg was great at doing the deep dive research, all that background checking that other cops detested. He could spend endless hours reviewing CCTV footage to track down an assailant, and had been known to spend days sorting through phone records to find a single incriminating text that helped to nail a criminal for fencing stolen goods.

Aurora knew Erik's errand could've waited until she was back at her desk. They'd caught the guy who'd committed the robbery at the gas station weeks ago, and Tuckburg was just crossing the t's and dotting the i's to make sure they had an airtight case when it finally went to court. It was nothing urgent, and she had to tamp down a surge of irritation. She wished that Erik wasn't so…transparent. Not that she wanted someone to play hard to get, not at all. But did he have to be so obliging? So gullible?

A reflexive stab of chagrin hit her in the gut. Back when she'd first started working here, she'd been the one to have a crush on someone. On Mårten. Now she looked back at that time and knew her feelings had been more to do with her insecurity at being the brand-new rookie trying to impress. He'd been assigned as her partner, and he was an absolute dish, with all that silver-flecked dark hair and the lightest blue eyes she'd ever seen—even if he was a bit older than her. She'd been drawn to his solid, rock-steady character; someone who was also a good man, a kind man, one with honor who wasn't afraid to uphold the law. She learned a lot from him in those first few months and felt as if they'd become very close.

But then Summer had come onto the scene, and it was clear that Mårten had fallen hard and fast for her, even while he was helping to protect her from a crazed man intent on kidnapping her. And Aurora had got over her crush in a hurry; she wasn't one to lust after another woman's man. Now, Aurora counted Summer as one of her best friends. The two of them had so much in common.

She refocused on Erik, who was still waiting for an answer.

"Can I look at it later?" she asked. "I've got a pile of stuff to get through here." She waved a hand in the direction of her computer. She was pretty sure she'd registered the USB stick correctly, but perhaps she'd punched the wrong storage number into the system. "I'll go down to evidence tomorrow when I'm not on front desk and sort it out," she finished, giving Erik a quick—hopefully mollifying—smile, before turning away.

"Oh, okay, that'd be great." He was still standing there, and she silently wished he'd leave. But she knew what was coming next before he even opened his mouth.

"Oh, and, Aurora..."

Her shoulders hunched upward as her fingers thumped the keys a little harder on the keyboard.

"Have you had time to consider my request yet? You know, for dinner? With me?"

"Umm," Aurora scowled at her screen before swiveling in her chair to face him. This was the second time Erik had asked her out, and she still didn't have a definitive answer for him. Yes, Erik was good-looking, in that clean-cut, athletic sort of way. So maybe she should consider him. Maybe she was being too picky. Being uncharitable by hesitating. She'd dated his type before, back when she'd worked at the homeless shelter in Gothenburg. He was a safe bet, and with Christmas only two weeks away, it might be nice to have someone special to take her out on a few dates. She stared at him, hoping to feel some kind of spark, something that made her heart flutter. Damn it, why didn't her heart flutter?

The main front door flew open, admitting a blast of arctic air and saving her from her predicament. A man with desperation written all over his face ran up to the counter. Panting heavily, he took a few seconds to gain enough breath to be able to speak.

"I need help," he huffed.

"Yes, sir. Calm down. That's what I'm here for. Can you explain what the problem is?" Aurora used her most soothing voice; she'd become used to fielding questions from near-hysterical civilians, and found the best way to treat them was with cool composure. Usually, there was an easy solution. Something about this guy had her adrenaline spiking, however. He wasn't kidding around; he was truly scared, she could see it in his eyes. He spoke English with an American accent, clearly not a local then.

"My father is missing. He's out there in the snow somewhere. I need help finding him. Quickly." He tugged off his black beanie and ran an agitated hand through his hair.

"Okay. Can you tell me where he went missing? And how long ago?" Aurora began typing, even as she asked more questions, logging a new case and entering the details as he answered.

"We were on some Lapland tour thing. We came in on the cruise ship last night, and this was one of those extracurricular day trip things." The man waved a hand in the direction of the harbor. "Oh, God." He bent down and leaned his hands on his knees, sucking in more air. "It's all my fault. I should've stayed at the lodge with him and drunk akvavit, and not gone out to do that stupid ice plunge. I should've listened to my gut and not to that idiotic tour guide, who told me my father was on the second bus and not to worry."

The guy sounded legit. And if it was true, then something needed to be done sooner rather than later. An old man lost in the freezing Norrbotten County wilderness wouldn't last long.

"You need to stay calm, sir," she said, peering over the edge of the desk at the top of his head. A head full of thick, dark, wavy hair that curled enticingly over his forehead as he leaned down.

"I'm trying," he replied, but it was obvious he was struggling to breathe. He was going to hyperventilate if he wasn't careful. And that was the last thing she needed—a civilian passed out on her reception floor.

With what seemed like herculean effort, the man regained control and straightened up slowly, fixing her with eyes as dark as the bottomless ocean. Wow. A girl could drown in those eyes.

She was suddenly aware that Erik still hovered at her elbow. "Erik, could you ask Inspector Viskten to attend the front desk, please?" This case might need more than her rudimentary expertise, and Mårten had good knowledge of the local area, including all the tourist traps and activity centers.

"What?" Erik had been staring at the man, watching with fascination as the drama unfolded. She guessed he didn't get much action hidden away in the bowels of the building, sitting at his desk and staring at a computer all day. "Oh, yes, of course." He left without further comment.

"Sorry," the man apologized, standing up straight, obviously having pulled himself together. "What else do you need to know? We have to start looking for him straight away." He cast a quick glance over at the window by the door, then banged his palm down on the countertop. "The sun's gone already. This bloody northern winter, it gets dark in the middle of the bloody afternoon. I can't believe I agreed to come on a bloody northern exposure cruise. I hate the snow." These last comments seemed to be more directed at himself, so Aurora ignored his hand still resting demandingly on the countertop and moved on.

"Of course. Can I ask your name and the name of your father?"

"I'm Jiro Nashimori. My father is Kenichi Nashimori. We're both American nationals, and we were taking this cruise together. It was his idea, said he wanted to see the Arctic Circle before he died." Jiro blew out a breath and looked at her expectantly. When he stated his name, it confirmed her first thought that he was of Japanese descent, even if the olive skin, dark hair and slightly tilted eyes hadn't already done so.

"Do you know the name of the place where your tour bus took you?" There were many tourist adventures and experiences to be had around Luleå. They'd sprung up around the town for exactly the reason Jiro had stated. Because of the lucrative cruise industry. It brought hordes of tourists here year-round; winter was just as popular as the summer months because people could experience the polar north from the comfort of a luxury boat. The tourists were fooling themselves if they thought they could embrace the real Sweden with one quick sled ride and a meal of reindeer cooked the traditional way on the open fire. It was a farce, but it brought much-needed income to this otherwise isolated town way up north. Aurora kept all her thoughts hidden behind a bland look as she waited for his answer.

"It was something like Luleå Adventures. They had activities like dog sledding, reindeer interactions, an ice plunge, you know, all those sorts of things." Jiro didn't know it, but he'd just described about half of all the tourist places within thirty miles of the town. Most of them were family-run small businesses.

As Jiro finished reeling off the list of activities, the door opened behind her, and she breathed a quiet sigh of relief as she felt Mårten enter. Without looking up, she knew his assessing gaze would be taking in everything about this distressed man at the front counter, and it took only a second for her partner to understand the mood in the room.

"I'm Inspector Mårten Viskten." He reached a hand across the desk and introduced himself. "I'm sorry to hear your father is missing. Let's see what we can do to find him." Mårten peered over her shoulder, reading from the notes she'd taken. Then he stood and fired a few pertinent questions at Jiro regarding where he last seen his father, what sort of mood his father had been in, if he was appropriately dressed for the cold—which Jiro assured him he was, as the tour had supplied them all with proper clothing—what was his father's level of fitness, exactly what activities had his father partaken in, and was there anything Jiro could think of that might make him want to miss that bus? All things she would have thought of to ask, eventually. But it just reiterated how much she still needed to learn from Mårten's experience and knowledge.

Jiro answered Mårten steadily, although she could see that he didn't like the tone of the questions as his face hardened and his lips firmed into a thin line. But he must've realized Mårten was only doing his job, and he held onto his temper, which put him up a notch or two in Aurora's mind. A lot of people—men especially—got angry when their motives were called into question.

At last, Mårten said, "Luleå Adventures. Hmm. I know the man who owns that place. Let me give him a quick call." Aurora felt some of the weight shift from her shoulders now that Mårten had stepped in and taken control. He would know what to do. Like he said, he knew people around here. While he hadn't been born in the town—much like her—he'd moved here as a rookie cop and stayed on to continue his career, rising up through the ranks to Inspector over the past twelve years, he'd become quiet well known amongst the locals.

She watched Jiro, his dark gaze fixed on Mårten as he picked up the phone and made the call. He was no longer breathing hard, seemingly recovered from his mad dash into the station—had he run all the way from the docks where the cruise ships came in? It was a good couple of kilometers, but a fit person could do it in around ten minutes. And he looked very fit.

Wearing a dark- blue Patagonia-branded torso-hugging puffer jacket that he'd unzipped when he entered the building, and black insulated pants, she could tell he had an athletic body underneath the cold weather gear. Tall, at least six feet, she put him in his late twenties. Beanie still in his hand, she noticed he wasn't wearing gloves, and unless he had them stuffed in a pocket somewhere, that might need to be remedied before he went back out into the cold. The temperature had peaked at -5C today, but as the sun set, it would only get colder, down to -20C at least. Tourists didn't seem to understand how profound the cold was up here, and how quickly it could affect a person. It affected fine motor skills first, and often took away their ability to think clearly, even before the first signs of frostbite or hypothermia set in.

She heard Mårten asking pointed questions to the guy on the phone in the background, but couldn't hear the reply. Jiro began to pace around the small reception area. He glanced up at her, spearing her with his dark, questioning gaze. Sudden heat shot through her as their eyes met, and she quickly averted her gaze, opening an Internet page on her computer instead, to do a search for tourist places in the area, in case they needed to contact them all to find this missing father. He went back to his pacing.

Unable to help herself, she peeked at him once through lowered lashes. He wasn't her type at all. He was too… Handsome. Confidant. Too American. Admittedly, she didn't know many Americans personally but the few she did know here in Luleå had all been overly optimistic and assertive, loud and taking up too much space—apart from Summer, who went against the stereotype and was none of those things. She just wasn't into all that testosterone-fueled self-gratification. She much preferred the quieter, contemplative type. Men who had a sensitive side, like Erik.

Mårten was suddenly at her elbow, breaking her reverie. "Right. I've talked to Dávvet, and he has confirmed they ran a tour for the cruise ship this morning. They had one-hundred-and-twenty-two people listed on the tour. Two buses dropped them off around ten a.m. this morning, and they left again at one p.m., around two and a half hours ago.

But the farm never does an official headcount, so he can't comment on whether anyone didn't make it back onto the bus after the activities. That is the cruise ship's responsibility, he said. There are no tours booked for this afternoon, and as far as he's concerned, the place is empty, just him and his staff, and no one was left behind."

Jiro opened his mouth to speak, but Mårten held up a hand to stall him. "I trust this man. He's one of the best tour operators in the area. Some of the others can be a bit… cavalier when it comes to people's safety, but Dávvet's not one of them. So if he says your father isn't there, then I believe him. But he's going to start a search straight away. He'll call on his surrounding neighbors to help as well. Dávvet is Sámi, so he knows what he's doing. He knows the country, and if your father is there somewhere, he'll find him."

"Good, good." Jiro nodded with relief. "So when can we get out there?" He left his implication that the police would join the search hanging in the air.

Mårten looked at his watch before answering. "It's already dark. I'm not sure there's a lot we can do right now." Mårten was apologetic, but even Aurora was a little taken aback. She had yet to be involved in a full-scale search and rescue and so didn't know the exact protocol. Perhaps it made sense not to search in the dark, as they might miss something important.

"What. No! You have to do something. You have to mount a search."

"We will," Mårten raised a hand to placate the man. "But it'll take a couple of hours to get everything organized. I think you might underestimate the severity of a winter night up here. People would be putting their lives at risk to search for your father," Mårten replied. "And at the moment we only have your word that your father is missing. We need to be one-hundred percent sure he didn't just return early and isn't on the boat somewhere."

"He's not." Jiro slapped his beanie against his thigh in agitation. "I checked our cabin. He definitely hasn't been back since we left this morning; I'm sure of it. And I checked most of the obvious places on the ship, it's not a big boat, you know."

Aurora knew that the ships that made it all the way north into Luleå harbor were much smaller, but also more opulent, than the enormous cruise ships you got in the Caribbean. They were designed to be able to break through sheets of ice if need be, all the while keeping their customers toasty warm as they watched the winter wonderland float by in the lap of luxury.

"He's not answering his phone either," Jiro said, nearly shouting now. He held up a hand and apologized. "Sorry. I know you have to ask these questions, and I know there's a procedure to follow. But if my father is lying somewhere in the snow…" He left his sentence unfinished.

"If he is, Dávvet will find him," Mårten assured him. "I'll mobilize a team to set up a base at the property to coordinate the search. They'll be heading out soon."

"Okay." That seemed to mollify Jiro a little. "Can I go out with this team of yours, then?"

"I'd like you to accompany us to the ship first, if you don't mind. It's due to leave the harbor in a few hours, and I want to make double sure your father isn't on it somewhere."

"What? The boat would leave without us?" Jiro seemed shocked at Mårten's revelation.

"I'm afraid so. I'm sure they made it very clear to you that if you missed the departure time, they wouldn't wait." Aurora knew the cruise lines had very strict policies about this. They had to, otherwise they'd constantly be running late waiting for passengers to re-board because they got sidetracked by a pretty souvenir, or decided to stay an extra hour to sit and sip cocktails in an ice bar.

"Yes, I remember hearing that. But surely this is different. My father is missing. He didn't just get carried away and forget the boarding time." Jiro's chin jutted forward, his eyes flashing with anger. "They can't just leave without us."

"I'm sorry, but they will," Mårten replied, pity written in the downturn of his lips "So I think we should go and talk to the ship's captain, as well as the crew, to make sure no one has seen him this afternoon, and then conduct a thorough search first before we head out to the property."

Jiro stared at Mårten as if he couldn't fully grasp what he had just been told. Aurora felt a surge of sympathy for the man. He obviously cared about his father deeply, and wanted him back safe and sound. What would it be like? To have a bond that strong with a parent? To love someone that much, you'd do just about anything to get them back? Aurora pictured her own father and felt the familiar anxious crawl in her guts when she did so. What Jiro had with his father seemed to be the polar opposite of what she had with hers.

Mårten tapped Aurora lightly on the shoulder. "You want to come?" His question caught her off guard. She'd been expecting to stay here and continue to cover the desk. "I'll get the chief to assign someone else out here. You're needed in the field," he added.

"What? Oh yes please." She was out of the chair in a flash. If Mårten said it was okay, she didn't have to be asked twice. Anything had to be more interesting than sitting here for the next four hours. And Jiro was definitely interesting, she mused as she watched him pull on his beanie over his curly hair and zip up his jacket impatiently. Her interest had been piqued, not only by him, but by the case he presented. A missing elderly man, possibly lost in the snow and ice, with time running out to rescue him before he succumbed to the elements. Aurora had to tamp down the curl of adrenaline that spiked through her body. It always happened on the cusp of a new case. It was one of the reasons she loved being a cop.

CHAPTER TWO

Jiro stood behind the tall cop, fuming, as he listened to the captain of the cruise ship answer his questions. "The passengers have been warned time and again that if they are late for an embarkation, we will not wait for them. They also know they are free to join us at the next stop if they would like." Captain Charbel Germain stood with his hands behind his back, only half concentrating on what they were saying. The rest of his focus was directed out of the large windows toward the activity on the dock below. He was clean-shaven, younger than Jiro thought a captain of such a large ship would be, but stoney-faced, with hard glittering eyes the color of a glacier below the peak of his snow-white captain's hat. Jiro hadn't liked the look of him the moment they stepped onto the bridge; he knew he would get no sympathy from this man, but it rankled him nonetheless.

"That's just not bloody well good enough." The words exploded from Jiro's mouth before he could stop them, frustration getting the better of him as he stepped around the inspector to stand face-to-face with the captain. "An old man is missing out in the freezing snow and ice and all you can do is shrug your shoulders and say, *See you at the next port?*"

Captain Germain had the sense to let concern furrow his

brow as he turned to face Jiro, finally giving him his full attention. "I'm not saying that I am not worried about your father," he replied. "But we have rules in place. I have two-hundred other passengers I have to think about. And unless it is something like a death on board, I'm bound to stick to my schedule."

"Don't give me that bullshit. You could change the bloody schedule if you wanted to. You're the bloody captain." Jiro knew this was true, but he also knew he was being harsh. A missing passenger wasn't the captain's problem, not really. And what he said about having a duty toward the other passengers was also true. It didn't mean he had to like it, however. And it also didn't mean that the captain wasn't an egotistical prick.

"This is bullshit," he repeated, but the heat had gone out of his words, and it was more a case of sheer defeat than thinking he could sway the captain to his cause.

Up until this point, Jiro had been enjoying the cruise immensely. Even the name of the boat was impressive, Le Commandant Charcot, named after a French polar scientist. His father had chosen this cruise because it was something he'd wanted to do all his life, and he couldn't hold back his excitement as they'd walked up the gangplank to board the ship on that first day. "This boat is the world's first luxury polar exploration vessel. It's capable of sailing into the heart of the ice. It can go where other ships just can't." His father had almost done a little skip of joy. It was the first time in as long as Jiro could remember that the sensible frown that always weighed down his father's face was replaced by a smile. Jiro had decided it was a good omen for the trip. They'd had five days of enjoyment, a sort of détente really, and Jiro had begun to lose his wariness around his father, dropping the emotional shield he'd held in place for so long. Now, it seemed like he'd been wrong. Dead wrong. Rather, he should've seen his father's out-of-character upbeat mood as a bad omen, not a good one. Perhaps he should've realized on the day they boarded something else was going on.

"Hmm, I know, Papa, you've told me all this before," Jiro had replied with a good-natured smile. And didn't he know it? Once he'd agreed to the cruise, his father had been like a child waiting for Santa to come, bombarding him with phone calls and emails about the various activities they could do and the amazing things they would see. His father had used the strongest motivator he knew—guilt—to get him to agree, telling him that the trip was to celebrate his upcoming seventieth birthday, as well as a Christmas present to himself, and it was the one thing he wanted to do before he died. He was desperate for his youngest son to accompany him, but had been a little vague on the reasons why.

When Jiro had asked why his older brother, Taro, wasn't also invited, he was met with more vague replies. Taro was too busy expanding another new business enterprise. Of course, the golden boy was too busy. Papa thought the sun shone out of Taro's ass, and he'd never been able to see past Taro's charm defensive and his flashy lifestyle to the dark underbelly beneath. Jiro knew his older brother wasn't the perfect son Kenichi thought he was, but his father refused to hear his words of caution, instead trying to push Jiro to take up a position in Taro's ever-expanding company; to be more like his older brother. So Jiro had stopped bringing up the subject many years ago, instead choosing to follow his own dreams of working in animal conservation and moving to San Diego to get away from it all.

The unusual contact with his father had been surprising at first—Jiro rarely heard from his father under normal circumstances. But ever since Jiro had agreed to go on the cruise, it was as if Kenichi was a different man. Perhaps age was finally getting the better of him. Perhaps he was finally mellowing after all these years. But Jiro had decided that he wouldn't take anything for granted. And it seemed he'd been right not to.

"They have a team of specialists on board," his papa had continued as they climbed the gangplank. "Scientists who will give lectures about the areas we sail through. We can learn more about the ocean. More about the environment." Jiro had to admit he was nearly as excited about that part of the cruise as his father. He was eager to learn more about this Nordic country too, its habitats and ecosystems, both marine and land-based. It was one reason Jiro had decided to overcome his skepticism and accompany his father on this trip, to find out more about this fascinating destination. Perhaps this time his father would be so distracted by the beauty of the place that he'd forget all about the constant reproofs, forget how much Jiro disappointed him on a daily basis.

And for the past five days Kenichi had indeed been a changed man, exclaiming with delight over the dolphins as they frolicked at the bow of the ship and tipping his head back in awe to watch the amazing lights of the aurora borealis washing the night sky with green and blue as they watched from the special viewing platform on the top level of the boat. That was until last night, when the stern, uncompromising father he knew had returned with a vengeance. Jiro was still to understand what had caused the transformation; all he knew was that Kenichi had received a phone call while they'd been sitting at dinner. He'd stood up and left the table to take the call, but the second he returned, Jiro could see the dark mood written all over his face. He refused to talk about it, and so they had spent the rest of the night eating in silence, until Jiro had excused himself and gone back to his cabin alone. His father had been no better this morning, a scowl on his face even as Jiro collected him from his cabin to join the tour out to the reindeer farm. And Jiro had known he would have to endure this tour with a fake smile and gritted teeth.

The inspector moved in closer behind Jiro, jolting him back to the present. "We understand you have rules you need to follow," he said, taking over the conversation again. What was his name? Inspector Viskten, or something like that. Jiro preferred the young constable. She seemed much more sympathetic to his situation. And a whole heap better looking too. Not that he'd had much headspace to contemplate more than the fact his father was gone. But the small, red-blooded male part of him that wasn't all-consumed with finding his papa still noticed her. As soon as he'd approached the front desk, even while he was still struggling to breathe, he was aware of her big, brown eyes, almost too large for her face. Dark auburn hair pulled back in a bun at the nape of her neck, but with a few fetching wisps left to drift free around her heart-shaped face. A slightly pouty mouth, and a cute way she had of tilting her head slightly to one side as she listened to him while she took notes.

"I presume you have no problem with our team searching the ship, then?" The inspector asked briskly.

"Not at all." The captain lifted his chin and squared his already square shoulders. "But my crew have already done that, and they have found nothing."

"Good. I presume you will also allow us entrance to all the restricted areas as well?" Viskten said, already turning on his heel and indicating the constable and himself to precede him out of the room.

"Yes, of course." The captain replied with more than a hint of irritation. The cop was clearly getting under his skin, but at least he couldn't brush him off as easily as he had done to Jiro. "I need you to disembark the boat no later than five p.m. sharp," Germain said to their disappearing backs. "We leave port at five-thirty, and you cannot be on the ship when we do so."

Jiro got the feeling neither of the cops liked the captain any better than he did as no one bothered to reply as they marched down the steps leading away from the bridge.

After visiting his father's cabin one last time, just to convince the cops his father really wasn't there, he waited for an interminable hour in a private lounge area, while Viskten and four other officers searched the ship. The female constable remained as his companion—or perhaps she was really his guardian—probably to make sure he didn't suddenly disappear as well. She stood by the window staring out at the partly frozen ocean, mercifully staying quiet, while he paced back-and-forth across the carpet. He couldn't bear any more platitudes right now. His nerves were worn so thin, he might just explode. It was hot in here, and even though he'd flung off his thick winter jacket and hung it over the back of a chair next to the constable's uniform jacket, he was still sweating inside his thermal shirt and fleece. They kept all the rooms on the cruise ship at a very comfortable twenty-two degrees, but right now, as overheated and stressed as he was, he would welcome a blast of the frozen air from outside. He unzipped his fleece and threw it on the chair next to his jacket, then continued pacing. The constable never even moved a muscle; only her eyes followed him as he walked.

It suddenly dawned on him he didn't even know her name.

To give his mind something else to do apart from turning scenarios of his father lying freezing to death in the snow over and over in his head, he said, "I'm sorry, I didn't catch your name back at the reception desk."

"Oh, yes. Constable Aurora Karlsson, at your service." She stood at attention, clicking her heels together, her formal manner bringing a reluctant smile to his lips. An unusual name, but it suited her. Named perhaps for the northern lights that people from all over the world come and see up here? She seemed very…enthusiastic. Eager to be of help. And when she fixed those enormous dark eyes of hers on him…well, it sent a prickle of awareness through him. That dark-blue uniform, the way it hugged her legs and backside, following the curve of her breasts, and the navy-blue peaked hat that sat jauntily on her head; it was more than a little sexy. He'd never really thought of a woman in uniform as being sexy before, but now…

When he'd first rushed through the main door of the police building, he'd thought her to be incredibly young, sitting there behind the large desk—even though she'd been highly efficient, he couldn't fault her on that—and he assumed she was a green rookie straight out of cadet school. Now that he had a better chance to really look at her, he could see she wasn't as young as he first thought. Probably closer to his own age, in her late twenties. But she deferred to the male cop, who was obviously her senior, which made him think that perhaps his first assessment of her being a rookie cop was correct. Perhaps, rather than coming to the force straight out of school, maybe she'd taken a few years to come to the decision and joined up a little later in life.

To get his mind off the attractive woman in the dark blue uniform, he said, "Do you know how much longer this is going to take?" Jiro was normally a fairly patient man. Working with the wolves at the rehabilitation centre, spending hours quietly surveilling them from a distance had taught him how to be still, how to remain focused and not let small irritations get to him. But this was altogether different. It felt like his insides had become a washing machine, swirling and tossing around so much that he might even throw up. It was almost impossible to stand still.

"It shouldn't be too much longer now," she replied, a typical cop answer, and he wanted to growl that he didn't need platitudes, he needed action. Almost as if she could see he was about to lose it, she added, "Maybe you could fill me in on exactly what you and your father got up to at Luleå Adventures. That might help to narrow down our search area if we know exactly where you both were."

Was she hoping to distract him? He'd already told the inspector that his father had stayed back at the barbecue lodge while he'd partaken in some of the other activities on offer, but he guessed it couldn't hurt to give more details. Fine, he'd play her game, if only to keep himself distracted.

"The place was pretty well organized," he admitted grudgingly—he still wasn't sure how the owners hadn't realized one of their visiting tourists had failed to rejoin the party and board the bus, and he wasn't about to forgive any of the staff before he'd talked to them first. Surely someone must've seen his father in the hour before they boarded the bus to return to the ship. He had to allow that the place had been well run, tidy, and the animals had seemed well-cared for. Not like some of the other run-down, barely scraping by tourist attractions he'd been to in the US.

"They took on a reindeer experience first, introduced us to their tame herd, and we got to feed them and pat them," he continued, remembering his joy as he warily stroked the fur of the mythical creatures—almost as if he was waiting for the animals to leap into the air and take off pulling Saint Nick's sled. But his father's bad mood remained like a wet blanket around his shoulders, sucking away the delight he felt and replacing it with disappointment. Disappointment with his father for reverting to his predictable, surly self. And disappointment in himself for allowing his father's bad disposition to affect his own.

"We both decided to do the dog-sled ride next," Jiro said, stopping his pacing long enough to stare out of the window as memories returned. Sitting next to his father, who said nothing for the whole ride, Jiro had relished the feel of the icy wind brushing past his cheeks, and the sound of the joyful yips from the huskies who obviously loved their job. The huskies reminded him of the wolves he tended at the centre on the outskirts of San Diego. Their yellow, omnipotent eyes that seemed to look right through you. That aura of restrained menace, a feeling of wilderness kept leashed just below their skin. Huskies were domesticated dogs, however, and even though they were bred to work and live in the snow, they still welcomed a human touch. The wolves, on the other hand, could never be trusted. They would always remain a wild animal, which suited Jiro fine, because that's where they belonged.

"After we finished, everyone returned to the barbecue hut for lunch and a hot coffee to warm us all up." While Jiro could've kept riding that dog sled forever, his sense of duty made him take his father back into the hut so that he didn't get too chilled. "Later, I decided to take the ice plunge challenge, while my father remained behind to drink mulled wine. He said he might go back and pat the reindeer one more time, but he was done with the cold for now." Jiro didn't tell her that he'd used the activity as an excuse to get away from his father. The ice plunge had been a shock to his system, the frosty water only one or two degrees above freezing, sending an immediate, painful ache deep into his bones and making his balls shrivel to the size of raisins. But he was glad he'd done it, as he chatted with the other brave souls who had also completed the challenge back in the thawing warmth of the sauna. He should've stayed with his father instead, and that was why the guilt was now eating him alive. It was his fault Kenichi was missing. Instead of being the obedient son and staying by his side, in a fit of pique he'd gone off to have more fun, leaving his father alone and unguarded.

"Hmm." The constable pouted with that pretty mouth of hers as she mulled over Jiro's revelations. "So you don't know whether he went back to the reindeer enclosure?"

"No. I left him sitting on a chair drinking his wine." Jiro didn't add that his father had sat alone at the back of the hut for a reason. Not one for making easy conversation, Kenichi hadn't encouraged anyone to sit with him and hadn't made any friends on the cruise, preferring to stay within the bubble of his son's presence. So it wasn't a complete surprise that no one seemed to have noticed him leave, or known where he went afterward.

"So there would be no reason for him not to want to return to the ship?"

"No, none. He was looking forward to our next stop across the gulf in Oulu, Finland. We only had another three days left on the cruise, and he wanted to make the most of each and every day" Well, he had done up until that phone call had altered everything last night. Had his father changed his mind? Did he not want to continue the cruise? Jiro didn't know the answer. And then there was the strange voicemail from his brother left on his phone this morning. If Jiro didn't know better, his brother had been trying to warn him about something, but it was unclear exactly what the threat entailed. He hadn't had time to return the call, and he hadn't wanted to broach the subject with Papa and ask if he'd also heard from Taro; any mention of his older brother always brought tension to the room, as if there wasn't enough tension already. Even if he didn't say it, his father's common mantra would hang in the air like a bad smell *"Why can't you be more like your brother?"* leaving Jiro to feel less-than, unworthy, like a second cousin. But perhaps he should've screwed up his courage and done so anyway.

Should he tell Aurora about his misgivings? Jiro remained undecided. He was making his papa out to be perfectly content on this cruise; a man who was enjoying every moment of life. If he told her about the phone call and his father's sudden change in mood, she might think he was being overly dramatic. She'd want to know why, and she'd probably want to dig deeper into his past to look for any guide to his switch in demeanor, and he wasn't prepared to reveal his childhood traumas to this woman. But if he didn't tell her, might they miss a vital clue that would help them find Papa?

Why was he hesitating? Any normal, loving son would be giving up every detail, no matter how small, in the hopes of helping in the search. If his mother were still alive, Jiro knew he would be doing everything in his power to find his father right now, for her sake. But she'd died eight years ago and taken any vestiges of humanity her father might have harbored with her.

Guilt warred with a sense of duty inside Jiro's head. Kenichi Nashimori was all about duty and responsibility, and had drummed into both his sons how important it was to respect their elders and their tradition and culture. But Kenichi Nashimori was also a hypocrite in Jiro's eyes. He demanded respect but never gave any back in return. For most of his life, Kenichi had been a bully and a tyrant, pushing his boys to succeed at all costs. Taro had used his father's driving forces and thrived, following in his father's footsteps, starting up an umbrella business selling antique and second-hand furniture, to run alongside the highly successful Nashimori's Furniture Company. But Jiro had rebelled, going in the complete opposite direction to study conservation at uni, and his father had never got over the disappointment. But he couldn't let his father die. He would never live down the self-condemnation if he did. And Taro would never let him live it down either. He had a responsibility to tell everything he knew.

Just as he opened his mouth to tell Aurora all that he knew, however, the door to the private sitting room flew open and Inspector Viskten strode in. "You are correct; there is no sign of Kenichi Nashimori aboard this ship," he said without preamble. "I checked with the security officer, and he has confirmed there is no electronic register of your father coming back on board."

"Right," Jiro replied slowly. He hadn't thought about it at the time, but of course every passenger scanned their key card whenever they disembarked or re-boarded the ship, so they would have an electronic record of who was on board at all times. Not that it was fail-safe; he was sure people could slip on and off without scanning, but they would only do that if they were trying to avoid detection. Had his father been trying to avoid detection?

"I'm sorry, but we will have to let the captain sail this evening as per his schedule. You might want to grab your things from your cabin if you want to stay and help with the search," the inspector added, and Jiro nodded glumly.

Then he raised his head and said, "So, when can we get back out to the reindeer farm?"

Viskten flicked a quick glance at Aurora. So quick, Jiro might've missed it if he wasn't staring directly at the man.

"What?" Jiro demanded. "What's going on now?"

After a moment's hesitation, Viskten said, "I've been called back to HQ for another priority matter. And Constable Karlsson is due to finish her shift in half an hour. So, unfortunately, we will have to hand you over to another team. Inspector Dalström will be taking over from here. He and his partner, Constable Moreau, have been briefed and will be waiting for you back at HQ."

Jiro felt as if the wind had been knocked out of him, and his shoulders deflated. They were abandoning him already? No, that wasn't right. They weren't abandoning him; they were handing him off to someone else, but it still didn't feel right. It was an irrational thought, he only met the two cops less than a few hours ago, but for some reason they felt like a lifeline between him and his lost father. Now he would have to start telling his story all over again to a brand-new set of ears. What else could be higher priority than a missing seventy-year-old man?

Jiro stood mute, his confusion and anger making it impossible to speak without saying something he'd regret.

"Oh, but…" Aurora spoke for the first time, staring at Jiro with her big eyes, confusion and some other cryptic emotion flitting across her face. Then she turned to Viskten. "I'd like to continue with this case, if that's okay?"

Jiro's heart stuttered in his chest. He didn't know why she wanted to stay; all he knew was he was suddenly desperate to have Aurora remain with him. But would the inspector agree?

CHAPTER THREE

Aurora was almost as surprised as Mårten looked when the words left her lips and she asked to be allowed to remain on the case. She hadn't known she wanted to stay and help with the case until he said it would be handed over to Dalström. Her spontaneous request had been on instinct. It would mean doing overtime, which Mårten would have to ask Rydberg to approve. And it would also mean she'd have to get someone in to make sure her father got his dinner. Drat, she hadn't thought about that when she'd opened her mouth. Nevertheless, she stood at attention, not letting any emotion show on her face as she waited for Mårten's reply.

Aurora had watched as Jiro had paced around the small room, working out his agitation with movement. She knew how he felt; she was also one who needed to keep busy, was constantly on the go, had been told more than once by her teacher when she was in school that she needed to learn to sit still. A strange swell of pity had overtaken her as she studied him. Pity and something else that she couldn't quite put her finger on. She hadn't been surprised when he'd suddenly removed his fleece and thrown it on the chair next to his jacket; it was boiling in here. The surprise had come when she found she could barely drag her gaze away from those wonderful muscular shoulders, every contour revealed beneath a skin-tight thermal undershirt. Aurora had never been one to drool over a man before, but heavens above, he was quite yummy. With his dark hair falling over his forehead and his equally dark, tilted eyes flashing with concern, he was like no other man she'd ever seen before.

"If that's what you want, Aurora," Mårten replied, snapping her attention back to him. "I can work it out with the boss. I'll let Dalström know you'll be joining his team. I'm sure he won't mind another pair of eyes to help with the search, especially seeing as how you have firsthand knowledge on this case for now."

"Thank you." She eased out a breath. This was good. Now she was keen to get going. Keen to get out there and start searching.

"I want you to keep me updated. No matter how late it gets," he said, placing a hand on her shoulder as she turned to retrieve her jacket. She wanted to protest that she would be fine; she knew what she was doing. But she understood she was still his responsibility, and he felt a duty of care toward her. It was probably a small miracle he was letting her do this on her own. But he knew how much she chafed at the bit with wanting to be a *proper cop*, and he was giving her a chance. He would also know it was an opportunity for her to learn useful search and rescue skills, which was possibly why he'd asked her to come along in the first place. She wondered what important job had called Mårten back to HQ, but didn't want to ask in front of Jiro, so she went to take another step toward the door. Jiro was still messing about putting his puffer jacket on over on the other side of the room.

"Be careful out there, Aurora. Please." Mårten's tone held a slight edge that had Aurora swiveling her head to look at him. His Arctic-blue eyes flashed a warning at her. Then he leaned in and said quietly into her ear, "There's something strange going on here. I'm not sure he's telling the complete truth. Keep an eye on him." That made Aurora take a mental step back. Mårten hated the term gut instinct. He didn't believe in feelings or intuitions, only cold hard facts, and the wisdom of hard-fought knowledge. So if he was telling her something wasn't right, she would definitely listen. What was it that Mårten thought Jiro wasn't telling them? When he'd been detailing their movements out on the farm, she hadn't sensed he was making any of it up. It felt authentic. But now that she thought about it, there had been a kind of strained tension around him whenever he mentioned his father. She'd reasoned that away as pure fear for what might have happened to his father, but perhaps there was more to it than that. Maybe she'd have a chance to figure it out better once they got to the property.

"Okay." She nodded her agreement just as Jiro joined them, holding out her jacket for her.

"Are we going?" he asked impatiently.

Mårten shot him an unreadable glance. "Yes," he replied simply, then led them out of the room. Aurora ushered Jiro through and followed behind, staring at the back of his head as he replaced his beanie, Mårten's words still rolling around in her mind.

* * *

The police cruiser snaked down the darkened road, the headlights creating a false bubble of light around them. Outside of that bubble, it was pitch black on either side, even though it was only just past six p.m. A large storm had blown in last week, bringing with it the first real winter blast. And it'd been big, dumping six feet of snow, at least. The road had been plowed recently, and the drifts on each side were piled high. A light snow had started to fall, and Dalström had turned on the windshield wipers, their soft swishing sound the only noise to break the silence inside the car. Endless forest stretched out on each side of the road, but it was so completely black out here that if Aurora hadn't been familiar with this road, she would never have guessed what lay outside the headlights. Jiro sat next to her in the rear of the vehicle, staring out into the blackness. He'd hurriedly stuffed clothes into a bag in his cabin, then followed her and Mårten off the ship without a backward glance.

No one had spoken in the twenty minutes it'd taken to drive out to the reindeer farm. She could tell Dalström wasn't all that happy with her joining the team; Mårten had been wrong on that count. The detective inspector's silence told her everything she needed to know. She got the feeling Dalström might regard this mission as a waste of time; beneath his capabilities. Which surprised her, she'd always thought he was a fairly honest cop. A family man for sure; he liked to be home on time so that he could sit down and have dinner with his wife and children. Perhaps that was it. Maybe it was as simple as his not wanting to have to do any overtime on this dark, wintry night, only a few weeks out from Christmas.

She wasn't regretting her decision to stay on the case, but she found herself wishing that Mårten had been able to take the lead on this one. He would've been much more proactive, and made it feel more of a teaching experience for her. She missed his solid presence, but she guessed she needed to learn to stand on her own two feet if she ever wanted to become a proper cop.

Earlier, as they'd driven out of the underground car park at police HQ, she'd furtively sent a flurry of texts to her next-door neighbor. Millie was an older lady, recently retired, who'd taken Aurora under her wing when she'd heard she was to become a carer for her father. Millie had always said she would help with him whenever work took Aurora away from her duties at home. Aurora wasn't sure what she would do without Millie. All she knew for sure was that she couldn't keep relying on the older lady. But she wasn't sure what other options she had. Her younger sister, Astrid, was of no help, as she still lived in Malmö, an eight-hour drive away. Aurora couldn't really blame Astrid for staying away. Aurora was the one who'd moved from their hometown up north to Luleå. Astrid had stayed and built a career for herself in journalism, working her way up the ladder and was now employed at Sweden's second largest newspaper. She was proud of her little sister, even though she could be exasperating and selfish at times. At least she'd carved out a life for herself. And at least she seemed unaffected by their traumatic childhood. Probably because Aurora had taken the brunt of their father's angry outbursts, but she didn't begrudge her sister for that.

Aurora turned to look at Constable Moreau, who sat directly in front of her in the passenger seat, staring straight out the windshield at the falling snow. He'd seemed affable enough when they's first all got into the car, but when it became clear his senior partner wasn't up for a conversation, he'd closed up as well. Up until now, Aurora hadn't had much to do with Moreau—a level five constable, and her senior, who'd been on the job for six years now. He had a young family and was a solid cop by all accounts. The other women at HQ all swooned over Moreau, and Aurora supposed his wavy, brown hair, dark-blue eyes, and pronounced cheekbones could be considered handsome if you liked that sort of thing. Supposedly he'd inherited his good looks from his French father, as well as his French accent. Even though he'd been born in Sweden, he'd spent quite a few years in his youth traveling between the two countries.

Jiro sat quietly in the backseat beside her, his head turned away, and she wondered what he was thinking. His mind was probably focused on only one thing. Finding his father.

His shoulders were square and taut, his chin lifted, and he was surrounded by a tense aura of holding himself back, of remaining rigidly still. She thought back to his pacing on the cruise ship and in the reception area and knew it must be hard for him to stay immobile even for this long.

All of a sudden, the vehicle slowed. "I know it's up here somewhere," Dalström muttered to himself. Sure enough, a faint light appeared out of the dark, illuminating a sign that said *Luleå Adventures - experience the heart of Sweden*. The detective inspector swung the car left onto a long driveway, and now they all got a good look at the surrounding forest as the car cut along the snowy road. Someone on the farm must grade this road every day to make sure it was possible for tourist buses to traverse. Lofty snowdrifts piled up on each side, and she could see how deep the snow was underneath the forest trees. Back in town, the streets were icy and slippery, but the townsfolk remained insulated from the full brunt of the deep winter deluge. Now they were outside the city limits, however, the extent of the snow coverage was evident.

Aurora soon made out well-lit huts and scattered buildings set in a clearing nestled in a thickly forested area and at least a dozen cars parked up in a flat space between the trees—a couple of them police cruisers—with many people milling around in the shadows. It was a hive of activity. This must be base camp. Her heart rate accelerated. It was time to get to work. Time to find this missing man.

"Right, we're here," Dalström growled as he pulled up next to another cruiser and switched off the engine. "Currently, the owner of the property, Dávvet Lindgren, has been coordinating the search. But I'm going to take command once we get inside." Aurora had expected nothing less. It only made sense to have someone from the law directing everything. Mårten would've done exactly the same thing.

Dalström swiveled in his seat to stare back at Aurora, and she almost recoiled at the intensity of his gaze. "I want you to stick to this guy like glue. He's your responsibility, got it?"

"Yes, sir," she replied hastily.

"And you," the detective inspector pointed an imperious finger in Jiro's direction, "I don't want you getting in anyone's way. And I don't want you getting lost either. Stay here; don't wander away from the main farm buildings. Do as you're told, and this will all go smoothly. Hopefully, we can have your father returned to you in the next few hours."

Aurora was a little shocked at the tone Dalström had taken with Jiro. He was a victim here, but the detective inspector was treating him as if he were a suspect. Or at the very least, a problem that needed to be solved. And his insinuation that they were going to find the missing man easily made Aurora's skin crawl with worry. The owner of the farm, Dávvet, had been searching his property for nearly three hours now with no sign of the old man. Mårten had been sure that if he was to be easily found, then Dávvet would have already done so. Which meant the search needed to be extended past the outer limits of the property. But it was dark and freezing, and the logistics of balancing the need to keep the people who were searching through the snow safe against the need for quick action was immense. This was not going to be an easy task, and she wondered why Dalström thought it would be. Although Aurora had only had a few interactions with him over the past six months, she'd thought she'd liked Dalström. He had never been anything less than convivial around the office and had been helpful more than once when Aurora had needed an experienced eye to look over her reports when Mårten wasn't available. Now, she was seeing a whole new side of him.

"As long as you do your job properly and find my father, then I'll do as I'm told," Jiro replied coldly. The detective inspector narrowed his eyes at Jiro, and for a few seconds, Aurora thought Dalström might react to his veiled insult, but he pursed his lips and turned back around, pulling on his gloves.

"Let's go," he commanded, stepping out of the car, everyone following suit.

Aurora made sure she stuck close to Jiro's side as they approached a large hut. This was where most people seemed to be either entering or leaving, and she guessed it was where Dávvet had set up his temporary command post. At least Jiro had grabbed a pair of gloves from his cabin earlier, which Aurora noticed thankfully that he was now wearing. Inside the barbecue hut, it was hot, and Aurora had to resist the urge to rip off her jacket. Many people milled around, sitting at tables and chairs or lined up on stools along a long wooden bar, drinking glasses of what looked to be hot mulled wine. Dalström headed straight toward a hulking man over by the bar speaking into a two-way radio. Jiro followed close on his heels, and Aurora had to hustle to keep up with both men.

She arrived beside Jiro just in time to hear the big man say in Swedish, "Right. Come on in then. See you in twenty minutes." Dávvet wasn't just tall; he was more like a man mountain, sporting a thick, dark beard and somber, gray eyes.

Dalström introduced himself, and they shook hands. Then there was an exchange, all in Swedish, which became more heated as they talked, and Aurora's heart sank. Jiro looked to her to translate, and she bit her bottom lip; it wasn't good news.

"There is no sign of him so far," she started. "It seems Dávvet has made the decision to call off the search, at least until first light. It's getting too dangerous out there. The snow has started to fall in earnest, and there's more on the way, he says."

"What? No, he can't." Aurora had expected his passionate reply and felt deeply sorry for him, but under the circumstances she understood. She held up a hand to stop any further remonstrations.

"Dalström doesn't agree, however. He thinks the men should be sent out again. Let's just wait and see," she suggested. She wasn't sure who she wanted to be right. It was a hard thing to do, to weigh up the life of one man against the risk for dozens of others. The detective inspector was digging his heels in, almost shouting now, and a couple of people turned from their mulled wine to stare at the arguing men. This didn't bode well if the two people in command couldn't even agree on a plan of action. Aurora knew who would win in the end. Apart from the six Luleå police officers, the bulk of the people out searching were all locals; they would listen to Dávvet. He was Sámi and knew the terrain and the countryside better than some town cop. Knew when to keep going and when to call it quits. Again, Aurora wished Mårten could be here with his calm demeanor and considerable negotiating skills.

It suddenly went quiet, and the two men glared at each other across the table. Then Dávvet laid the hand piece of the two-way radio carefully down on the countertop, took two steps away and headed for the door, stopping only to pull on a jacket before he exited. The fight had been won and lost. Dávvet refused to let the locals continue their search, and when Dalström demanded that he was in charge now and people would do as he said, Dávvet let his feet do the talking. One by one, the other others left their tables and chairs and followed him out the door.

"I take it that didn't go well," Jiro said into the ensuing silence.

"No," Aurora replied, watching the detective inspector's face turn an interesting shade of red.

"Right, assemble all the other officers in here. We'll continue the search alone if we have to," Dalström ground out from between clenched teeth, taking up the position Dávvet had so recently vacated.

"But, sir, we don't even know what areas have already been searched," Moreau asserted. "We need that man's help." He pointed to the closed door Dávvet had disappeared through. "We can't just go out blind; we could be covering the same areas and wasting precious time and resources." Moreau's relaxed stance changed as he stood up straighter, his arms going stiff at his sides. He was taller than his boss by at least three inches.

It seemed like Dalström wasn't used to his junior partner arguing with him, because he turned on him with a look of surprise that soon morphed into undisguised displeasure. But Moreau didn't quail at his superior's withering glare, instead, standing his ground, and saying, "I'll bring all the officers back in," Moreau agreed, "But we need to have a better plan of action before we send them back out again." Aurora suddenly liked the constable a whole lot better.

Jiro tugged on her sleeve to get her attention. "What now?" he asked. His face had drained of all color as he stared at her, sick with worry and desperation.

"Let's go and sit over here," she suggested, taking him by the arm and towing him away to the far corner. He didn't need to hear the lead detective arguing with his partner, and she didn't want him to get involved in another dispute with Dalström either, who clearly didn't like his authority being challenged. She'd been told to stick to Jiro like glue, and that was what she intended to do. There was going to be no active searching done until Dalström could sort out the mutiny within his ranks, and so Aurora decided to do what Mårten had always taught her to do; if in doubt, take time to regroup. Sit down and look at things from all angles to make sure you hadn't missed anything. Find any weak spots.

At first, Jiro resisted until she said, "I know you feel helpless, but there's nothing else we can do right now. We can't go out and search alone without backup. You'll be of no help if you—we—get lost or hurt out in the wilderness too. You need to wait until a decision is made. But maybe we can look at things from a different angle." She thought back to Mårten's words just before they'd left the cruise ship. He didn't trust Jiro because he thought he was holding something back. Well, maybe now was the time to try and get the truth out of him.

Reluctantly, he followed her. "Let's do some brainstorming. See if we can come up with any new angles," she said as she pulled out a chair.

"Okay, okay," Jiro replied reluctantly, his gaze fixed on Dalström and Moreau over by the bar, who were still debating, although now they'd both lowered their voices, suddenly aware how this might look to the son of the missing man. Unprofessional to say the least.

"So let's concentrate on things we know for sure," Aurora started, and Jiro finally turned his focus to her. She pulled out her notebook, flipping it open to a blank page and writing a heading at the top with a recently sharpened pencil. Mårten had taught her to take notes. Especially this early in her career, it helped to keep track of everything she heard and saw.

But before she could form her first clear thought, he said, "Drat, it's so hot in here." He stood and removed his jacket, gloves, and beanie, slapping them on the table before retaking his seat. She wanted to do the same, but she was more used to these constant changes in temperature. Going from a warm house out into the freezing weather and then back into a warm car, out into the cold again to get across the parking lot, and then into another warm building was part of life here in northern Sweden. It was a continual game of hot, cold, hot, cold, and most locals got to the stage where they left their jackets on inside unless they intended to stay for a long period, otherwise they would be constantly stripping off, putting back on, stripping off, putting back on. Compromising, she took off her gloves and beanie, quickly averting her eyes from Jiro's nicely muscled shoulders, revealed once more by the stretch of his thermal shirt. But even as she did so, there was a strange twisting sensation in her gut, like butterflies trying to beat their way out from the inside. Drat, why did he affect her like this? She had to keep reminding herself this man was a victim and needed to be treated with calm efficiency, not viewed with some kind of strange, baseless lust.

"We know for sure that you left your father in this hut when you went out to do the ice plunge. And that's the last time you saw him. Correct?"

"Correct," he replied.

"What time was that?"

Jiro gave a shrug. "I wasn't checking the time. But there were twenty of us doing the ice plunge, and so it probably took an hour or so. The buses left straight afterward at two p.m., but I didn't have time to go back to the hut and collect Papa because we were running late by that stage. I just assumed my father would be boarding the bus with everyone else. I asked one of the tour guides if she'd seen him, and she said she was sure he must've got on the other bus. God, I wish I'd checked myself instead of believing her." He clenched his fist on the tabletop.

"So the last time you saw him was probably around one p.m. then?" Aurora asked, hoping to keep him on track. Wanting to blame someone else was not going to help.

"That sounds about right," he admitted roughly.

"And you didn't report him missing to the police until

around four-thirty. So he was unaccounted for for at least three and a half hours before anyone was alerted," Aurora mused.

"Again, that is correct. But I'm not sure why this all matters." There was exasperation in his tone.

"I'm just setting a timeline," she replied. "Like I said, we need to document everything we know for a fact." Aurora flicked her gaze back to the two police officers at the bar. Moreau seemed to be losing the argument, and he was now replacing his hat and stalking to the door, probably going to round up the other officers and bring them inside so Dalström could brief them. Was he going to send them out on a fruitless search? She would have to wait to find out, and in the meantime she and Jiro could continue to think this through logically.

"Dávvet Lindgren began a search almost straight away after we contacted him, using his staff and locals from the area. We arrived nearly three hours later, after we'd talked to the captain. And by that stage, Lindgren was pretty sure your father was nowhere to be found on the property."

"Yeah, how can he be so adamant that Papa's not here?" A deep frown creased Jiro's forehead. "Three hours doesn't seem like a long time to search such a large property and be so sure."

Aurora tended to agree, but then the Sámi people were different from normal Swedish locals. They were more attuned to the country. This was Dávvet's traditional land, owned by generations of his family, so he would know it like the back of his hand. Would know its every mood, every tree, every rock, every crevice.

"And if he's nowhere obvious on this property, then where else can he have gone? He can't have walked far in this snow and ice. Right?"

"Hmm," Aurora agreed.

Before she could frame her next question, however, Jiro shrugged and said, "The only other option is for him to have fallen down a crevasse or somehow been swallowed up whole, never to be seen again. Is that a possibility?"

"Or a lake," Aurora commented, then immediately wanted to slap a hand over her mouth. She needed to learn to keep her thoughts to herself, and not add to Jiro's distress.

"Shit, I hadn't even thought about frozen lakes. He could've fallen through the ice, and now he won't be found until the thaw." Jiro's dark eyes went wide in his expressive face. "We need to talk to the owner. He'll be able to tell us if there are lakes on his property. We can search them first." He went to stand, ready to go out into the cold and look for frozen lakes, not realizing they would need specialist teams if that was indeed what'd happened to his father.

"I'm sure Dávvet has already checked that. He would've said something if any tracks had been found on or near a lake," Aurora placated, laying a hand on his arm. She instantly regretted touching him, as a frisson of awareness passed over her. Slowly, so as not to look like she was reacting as if she had just been branded, she took her hand away and laid it calmly on the table.

"I guess so." Jiro re-took his seat. "God, this is just so…" He waved a hand in the air, his face crumpling as he suddenly looked close to tears. Aurora noticed the shadow of stubble forming on his chin and lower jaw, and it made him seem more defenseless somehow. "I can't find words to describe how this feels. Like I'm helpless. I've never felt this helpless before. I don't know what to do next."

"Hmm," Aurora murmured sympathetically, not really knowing what to say.

"And if he's not lying out there in the snow, then, I mean, what else could've happened to him?" But even as he said the words, he sat up a little straighter, a light of apprehension entering his eyes. "We need to talk to the owner," he said suddenly.

Aurora didn't disagree. There were a million questions, a million small details that might make the difference in this search, and Dávvet was the man who might hold the answers. She didn't understand why Dalström hadn't kept him here to answer those questions. This was the first time she'd seen one man's pride get in the way of an investigation. Working with Mårten had perhaps shielded her from other people's egos; he was always fair-minded and aboveboard as far as she could tell.

"I'll ask the detective inspector if we—"

"No!" Jiro's reply was emphatic. "You know he'll come up with some reason why we can't."

"Why is it suddenly so important to talk to him?" she queried, wondering what might have occurred to Jiro to make him so intent all of a sudden.

"I need to find out if it's possible for someone to enter his property without his knowledge."

"What do you mean?" Aurora tilted her head to the side, but she was already processing this new train of thought. Was he talking about an abduction? Why would anyone want to abduct an old man?

"The only other way for him to have left the property would have been in some sort of vehicle. Either a car or a snowmobile. Yes?" he continued.

"It's possible," she agreed. "But if that were the case, any tracks or signs of a vehicle would've been lost by now underneath all the other foot traffic and vehicle tires of the searchers." The hair on the back of her neck was standing at attention. This was a whole new train of thought, one that she didn't think had really been considered. As far as they were concerned, this was a case of an old man wandering off and getting lost in the snow.

"Which is another reason we need to talk to the owner. If he knows this property as well as you say he does, then he'd be able to tell us that sort of thing." Jiro stared at her, waiting for her answer.

"If you think he's been abducted, then it's important we tell Dalström straight away." While she was beginning to dislike Dalström, she wasn't about to stretch protocol that far by withholding vital information. She stood, looking over at her superior. He was speaking into a mobile phone, half turned away from her, but the look on his face was thunderous. What would he do if she took this new information to him? Would he follow it up or ignore her? But he was the lead on this case, and she had to follow the chain of command.

Jiro reached for her arm, tugging on her sleeve to stop her. "No, please don't," he pleaded. She turned to face him and was arrested by the intensity of his dark gaze. He was leaning in so close, she could almost see the individual pinpricks of stubble on his upper lip. She was caught between duty and wanting to help him. Between the pull of the appeal in his eyes and the tug of responsibility. Before she could make a decision, Moreau clomped noisily back into the room, followed by five other police officers, all rugged up in jackets and beanies and covered in snow, stamping their feet trying to get warm. They crowded around the detective inspector, muttering between themselves. He finished his phone call, jutting out his chin and standing up taller.

"Come over here." He beckoned imperiously to Aurora and Jiro, waiting until they stood at the back of the crowd before he spoke again. It looked like she'd missed her opportunity to speak to him. For now. But at least they were hopefully going to find out what the next move was.

"That was the chief on the phone. The search has been called off until first light. There's more snow forecast tonight, which will hamper any efforts, and we can't take the risk of anyone else getting lost out there." Dalström spoke with authority, as if this had been his idea all along, as if he hadn't just been about to send them all back out into the freezing snow. Moreau, who was standing beside her, gave a quiet sigh of relief.

She'd believed that his partnership with Dalström had been a good one; an equal one. But now she had another insight into their dynamics and decided that Moreau must be very good at handling his superior's mercurial moods and downplaying any repercussions. She felt a little sorry for him. Everyone had to handle difficult people at one stage or another in their career, but it must be hard for Moreau to keep a smile on his face with a partner like this. Perhaps this was an aberration. Dalström was clearly used to getting his own way, and on any normal day it was probably easy to keep him happy. Perhaps Moreau was used to this and took it in his stride. He was definitely more easygoing than Aurora, and maybe that was the way he handled things most of the time. Except this time he couldn't let things pass.

"So, you're just going to leave my father out there to die in the cold?" Jiro pushed his way between two officers, and Aurora's focus snapped back to her charge. Jiro might not have understood much of the Swedish conversation, but he clearly hadn't missed the underlying message.

"We don't want to call this search off any more than you do." Surprisingly, Dalström answered in English, with cool equanimity, for once staying in complete control, and even sounding slightly sympathetic. "But the facts can't be ignored. It's snowing hard out there now." He gestured to the other officers still shaking snow off their jackets. "It's dark, and the temperature will drop to at least -20C tonight. You could walk right past him if he were lying in the snow and not even know he was there."

Jiro put his head in his hands and let out a moan. "And what if he *is* lying in the snow in these freezing temperatures all night? Do you think he could survive that?"

Dalström didn't answer.

Aurora made a quick decision. It was now or never. She owed Jiro this much at least. If no one else was going to help him, then she would. It was out of character for her to act so impulsively. Yes, she was always eager to take on any job, to learn as much as she could about policing. But she always did it in a considered manner. Some called her a perfectionist, but she liked to think of it as being meticulous; she needed to have every detail straight in her head to make sure she was making the best decision. There was no time to think this through, however.

She stepped forward to stand shoulder to shoulder with Jiro. "Sir, can I have permission to take Mr. Nashimori back to town in one of the cruisers? He will need a hotel to stay at. I'd like to make sure he's safe and comfortable," she spoke in English and kept her voice level, making sure her request sounded completely reasonable, not letting on she had an ulterior motive.

She wished Mårten were here. She missed his evenhanded guidance. Right at this exact moment she realized how lucky she'd been to be partnered with Mårten as a rookie cop. He was everything an honorable cop should be, and he showed her daily how to do the job with integrity. He wasn't afraid of using force when it was required, but she was learning the valuable lesson from him that subtlety usually got you farther than violence. Mårten was good at considering every angle before he made a decision, so that he was sure he knew what he was doing. He never stormed the front door of a house to arrest a drug dealer unless he knew the back door was also guarded. If they attended a domestic abuse call out, he would always sit down to hear the victim's story first, but he never jumped to any conclusions until he'd also spoken to the perpetrator. And he was teaching her to do the same. But right now, in this situation, and without Mårten's advice, all she could do was follow her gut. She really hoped she wasn't fucking this up.

Dalström's sharp gaze landed on her. His features softened slightly as he studied her, finding no guile in her blank gaze. "Yes, why not? I will allow that," he replied in English for Jiro's sake.

"Thank you, sir." Aurora let out a quiet breath. She took Jiro by the elbow to lead him out the door.

"Oh, and Constable." Uh oh, was he going to change his mind? The detective inspector waited until she was facing him once more. "I'm sure Inspector Viskten will have work for you to do tomorrow. I can't see that we will need you again. Thank you for your help." Dalström dismissed her with a magnanimous flick of his hand.

If Aurora hadn't had another plan in mind, she might well have spat back a retort. She was known for her caustic comments while on the job; she'd never suffered fools gladly. But this time she held her tongue. There was no way she was going to be shuffled off this case without a fight. But she would leave that fight until tomorrow.

"Yes, sir," she replied, head held high, and steely eyes fixed on the door. "Let's get out of here," she muttered to Jiro.

CHAPTER FOUR

Jiro warmed his hands on the mug of coffee as he watched the big man take a seat at his kitchen table. Jiro had been impressed when he'd first been introduced to Dávvet Lindgren by the tour guide as they descended from the bus this morning. In Jiro's head, he was everything a Swedish mountain man should be. He must be six foot five if he were an inch, and his blond beard, and long blond hair pulled back into a man bun made him look imposing. Now, seeing him close up, he was even more impressive. He must lift weights because his biceps were enormous, threatening to bust through the flimsy fabric of his long-sleeve undershirt.

Jiro and Aurora had sat in the police cruiser pretending to look at her phone until all the other cops had left the scene. Then he'd followed her as she strode through the dark forest to Dávvet's house, and once they'd determined the lights were still on, she'd knocked on his door and sweet-talked their way in. Dávvet had reluctantly agreed, but asked them to be quiet as his wife was getting their three young children ready for bed upstairs, reminding Jiro that it was still early, only just past eight o'clock. He felt that it should be much later; these long winter nights really screwed with your head.

He glanced over at Aurora and wondered how many rules

she was breaking by talking to this guy without strict instruction from that asshole detective inspector. He was glad she was helping him, don't get him wrong. But he wondered why she'd decided to withhold Jiro's suspicion that someone else may have been involved in his father going missing from her supervisor. To stay behind and follow up with his request, when all she probably wanted to do was go home to her warm house and have a hot meal.

As he stared at her, Jiro was distracted by the tiny silver, heart-shaped studs Aurora wore in both ears. He'd never thought about whether female cops wore jewelry or not before. But on Aurora, the dainty earrings made her look… more feminine? No, that was probably too blunt an observation, and also quite sexist. Perhaps it was more that they gave an extra edge to her beauty. She was beautiful in an unconventional way. He suddenly wondered what it meant that they were heart-shaped? Was she a closet romantic at heart? Or was it something more mundane like a boyfriend had bought them for her? He shifted in his seat, aware that thought made him uncomfortable. He shouldn't care whether Aurora had a boyfriend or not. She was here to render assistance, to help find his father; that was all. He shouldn't be viewing her as anything else but another Swedish police officer doing her job. A means to an end. So why was he so interested in what sort of earrings she wore?

"You have questions for me?" Dávvet said, breaking Jiro's reverie, and bringing him back to the present. Concentrate on finding his father, not on some irrelevant silver earrings, he reminded himself.

"Yes, if that's okay with you," Aurora replied, pulling out the small notebook and pencil from the top pocket of her vest. She'd done the same earlier this evening as they'd been sitting in the barbecue hut; keeping notes on the case, which he found strangely endearing.

"Sure." Dávvet shrugged his enormous shoulders. "I'd much rather speak to you than that inspector detective or whatever he was. He didn't have a clue." Dávvet grunted. "I was wondering when one of you would get around to asking the right questions."

Their conversation was conducted in English so Jiro could understand. Even now, it still surprised him that almost everyone in Sweden could speak fluent English.

Aurora ignored his first comment, probably not wanting to admit there was dissent in the ranks, or how much of an idiot Dalström really was. Instead asking, "We're trying to set up a timeline for when Mr. Nashimori was last seen by anyone. Did you or any of your staff see him sitting either with his son or alone at a table near the back of the hut straight after lunch?" Aurora lifted her head from her notepad to stare intently at the reindeer herder.

"I was only in the hut for a short time after I brought everyone back from the sleigh rides. My waiting staff are very competent; they don't need me hovering over them. I left almost straight afterward to look after the dogs. Feed them, put them back in their kennels, that kind of thing."

Aurora nodded, indicating he should continue.

"But after I got the phone call from your Inspector Viskten, I went back to the hut to do exactly as you suggested. The staff were just finishing up for the day, and I asked if anyone remembered seeing the Japanese man and his son. Tory—she works behind the bar—said she thought she remembered him." Dávvet tilted his head in Jiro's direction. "Probably because she has a peculiar fondness for good-looking Asian men, and was checking you out." He spoke directly to Jiro this time. "No harm in that," he added, when Jiro sat back in his chair, dumbfounded. That'd not been what he'd been expecting to hear.

"No, no harm in that," Aurora replied, shooting Jiro a

quelling glance. "But does she remember his father?"

"Yes, she definitely saw the pair of them. Right at the back, they were. She even pointed out the table they were sitting at. The older one wasn't bad looking either, she said, if you were into older men." Again, Jiro tried to hide his shock. He hadn't thought of his father as anything more than old for a long time. At least since his mother had died, anyway. The idea of his father with another woman was unacceptable, and the idea that he might be attracted to a woman, or be attractive to them was just not on his radar. Jiro couldn't see past the man his father had become, couldn't see past his resentment to even acknowledge that he and his brother probably got their good looks from his father. The idea was anathema to him.

"Tory is one of my best," Dávvet continued. "She's quick, efficient, keeps the place tidy and is a good observer. She keeps an eye on all the patrons. She can often tell me if someone has had too much to drink even before I notice."

"Okay, that's good to know. What about afterward? Once the good-looking son had left. Did she remember the father sitting by himself?" she prompted, with a wry smile in Jiro's direction.

"Yes, she did," Dávvet said slowly, and Jiro's heart did a double-tap. This was good. This was something solid he could grasp onto. Like Aurora said, now they could start a proper timeline. He was about to ask if Tory could pinpoint what time that was exactly, when Dávvet threw a hand-grenade into the conversation. "But he wasn't alone for very long."

"What?" Jiro's heart did another double tap, but this time it was accompanied by a sliver of ice running through his veins. Who would've gone to talk to his father? It wasn't inconceivable that someone had seen him sitting alone and felt sorry for him. But it was highly unusual that Kenichi would've welcomed company; in fact, he would have actively discouraged it. Wouldn't he?

"Do you know if this person was one of the cruise passengers?" he asked, his words tumbling out in a rush.

"As far as we could tell, he was, yeah. On the days when we have busloads of tourists booked in from a cruise, we are full to capacity and so we shut to the general public. Tory seemed to think he was also wearing one of those cruise-issue jackets. You know, the dark blue ones they give to all the passengers."

Jiro nodded to Aurora to show that he did know the jackets. When he'd entered his cabin way back on the first day of the cruise, he'd seen the well-padded waterproof coat folded neatly on the bed, the ship's logo front and center on an embroidered patch on the left-hand side. It was part of the company's duty of care to all its passengers to make sure they were appropriately clothed for the cold weather. The captain recommended all passengers wear the jacket whenever they disembarked the ship—it was probably another way the staff got to keep track of their charges while on a tour, or as people wandered around town looking for souvenirs—as well as on the outer decks of the ship. It was marketed as a freebie, a welcome gift if you like, but Jiro was sure it was included in the astronomical price tag of the cruise itself. And it was probably a great promotion tool as well. He'd chosen to stick to his Patagonia puffer he'd bought especially for the trip.

"Do you know what this other man looked like?" Jiro prompted, jumping in before Aurora could speak, and she shot him an irritated glance. "Or do you know whether my father left the hut with him?"

"Nah, I didn't get that far. Johan and his two sons from the neighboring property arrived, asking all sorts of questions, and so I needed to organize a search pattern. Tory could probably give you more details. She'll be back at work at nine tomorrow."

"This is great, thank you so much," Aurora said thoughtfully, her reply puzzling Jiro. Why wasn't she pressing the issue? They couldn't wait until tomorrow to talk to her; she might have been the last person who'd seen his father alive.

"We need to talk to this woman," Jiro said, leaning across the table to look Aurora directly in the eye. This wasn't good enough. Tory's observations of another man raised more questions than it answered, and they couldn't just leave it there. "She might remember something else about the guy." Jiro wanted to condemn Dávvet as well and ask him why he hadn't volunteered this information to the detective inspector earlier. But then he remembered how the cop had just waltzed in and taken over. Dávvet hadn't had the opportunity at first, and then Dalström had acted like such a know-it-all, the reindeer herder probably took offense and decided, fuck him.

"Hmm." Aurora made a noncommittal humming sound that could've meant anything.

"Do you have Tory's home address?" Jiro asked impatiently, his eyes not leaving the big man's face.

"Like I said, you can come back and talk to her tomorrow," Dávvet offered, pursing his lips, which made his beard bristle slightly.

"Thank you, we might do that," Aurora conceded, dipping her head to study her notebook. What? Why was she not pushing to find out this woman's last name? Her home address? It wasn't too late. They could speak to her tonight. But Aurora changed the topic, saying instead, "I also had a quick question about the fencing around your property. Do you have any?"

"Nope, not really," Dávvet replied. "Everyone around here knows where their boundary lines begin and end; there's no need for expensive fencing. And our reindeer are allowed to roam freely across all lands to forage for feed, so there's no need to keep them in. Or out. Why?"

"I was just wondering how easy it would be for someone to access your property if they didn't come in by the road." Jiro saw Dávvet's eyes narrow at Aurora's question. "Perhaps in a vehicle. Or maybe a snowmobile," she continued.

"You think someone took the old man? Why would they do that?" Dávvet cut straight to the chase.

"That's not what I'm saying." Aurora held up her hand, palm facing outward. "We simply need to follow all avenues; that's all."

"No car could gain entry to my property across country. Not even a 4WD, and not on any of my back access roads—the snow is too deep at the moment. If a snowmobile came close to any of my buildings, I'd know about it. My dogs would warn me if there were any strangers around." The big man sounded so confident, Jiro found it hard not to believe him. But how would his dogs know the difference between a busload of tourists and someone who wasn't meant to be here?

"How close would they have to come before your dogs sounded a warning?" Aurora asked, her tone implying that she believed his dogs could tell the difference.

"A good couple hundred meters," he replied, tilting his head slightly to one side as he considered the question.

"Okay, that helps a lot, thank you."

"I never considered the option that he might've been taken," Dávvet said quietly as if to himself. "Is there something going on in your father's life that would put him at risk? Dávvet was glaring at Jiro now, his direct question taking him by surprise.

"What? Of course not." He glared back at the reindeer herder. But this guy wasn't stupid, he caught on pretty quick to the implications of what Aurora had asked. And now Jiro considered the implications. If this were an abduction, it might mean there was more than one man involved. The insider, wearing the cruise jacket, and then an outsider, bringing in a snowmobile to transport his father away. Could one man have set this up and then carried it out himself? Jiro very much doubted it. His mind whirled with all the different permutations.

"Is my family in any danger?" Dávvet half-stood, looming over the table and over Jiro, his fist clenched at his side. "Is there something you're not telling me? Something I need to know."

"No, no, not at all," Aurora interjected. "Please sit down, Mr. Lindgren." She had remained seated, but Jiro could see her hand grasping the edge of the table, knuckles turning white as she readied herself for action if it were needed.

What the hell? This was getting out of hand very quickly. And this guy was scary. He wouldn't want to get on the wrong side of him.

"Like I said before, we just want to cover all bases. These are just normal questions that have to be asked. I am absolutely sure that you and your family are in no danger whatsoever."

Dávvet switched his intense gaze to Aurora, studying her face for many long seconds, before he finally re-took his seat. Jiro had to applaud her steely reserve; the woman had backbone. He also had to applaud her ability to lie through her teeth. Or perhaps it was just sheer optimism, hoping against hope that she was correct and this was nothing more than a simple man wandering off into the snow, and there was nothing more clandestine going on. But Jiro was starting to have his doubts.

His brother's phone message this morning had been playing on his mind all day. Was this what Taro's vague phone message had been about? A warning of some kind.

There was a niggling suspicion there. He needed to phone Taro and ask him exactly what he meant. Actually, he needed to phone Taro and fill him in on the day's events. He couldn't leave his brother in the dark now that his father was officially missing.

Jiro listened as Aurora placated the big man some more, reiterating that she would be in touch if they heard anything, anything at all. And thanking him profusely for his time. She was also a born diplomat, it seemed. He contributed nothing to the conversation, too busy turning everything that'd just been said over in his head, and seething over what hadn't been said. At last, she stood and offered her hand to Lindgren, and Jiro followed suit. But the man's candid lack of reserve from when he first invited them into his kitchen had evaporated, replaced with barely concealed wariness, and it seemed he couldn't get them out of the door quickly enough.

It was snowing hard now, and the cold hit him like a sledgehammer to the face—he'd forgotten for a few moments about the snowy night that waited for them right outside the door to the warm kitchen. Aurora didn't linger; she took off through the snow toward where the cruiser was parked a few hundred meters away under the trees, pulling on her hat and gloves as she did so.

"Wait." All his irritation came back as he stomped through the snow after her. There were so many things he wanted to say, he almost wasn't sure where to start. So he started with the thing that irritated him the most. "Why did you let him fob you off like that? Can't you force him to tell you that woman's address? Tell him he's obstructing an investigation? We need to see Tory. She could have vital information," he argued.

Aurora stopped in her tracks and turned around so sharply, he almost ran into her. "How I question a witness is not up for debate," she said, dark eyes turning flinty and hard. "You need to remember that."

His anger flared quick and hot. "Who are you trying to kid? You're just a rookie cop. You don't know what you're doing any more than I do."

"Don't I now?" she hissed. He could see the dark wisps of her hair escaping from beneath her beanie, blowing across her face in the light still seeping from the windows of the house. And he could see the furious set of her jaw. The way she stood up to her full height, chin lifted in defiance. But he could also see the hurt lurking in her gaze.

Shit. Perhaps he'd overstepped just a little.

She took a step toward him, and he could see the effort it cost her to rein in her temper. "You need to understand something. Things are different here in northern Sweden. Luleå is effectively a small country town. The locals here are tight-knit, and protective of each other. If you overstep the boundaries and force an issue, they might tell you what you need to know at the time. But then you will get nothing from there on in. Dávvet is wary of giving us an address for Tory for some reason. It could be something as simple as she has a prior conviction or misdemeanor and he doesn't want to get her in trouble. Or perhaps she's hiding out from an abusive ex; who knows? Whatever it is, we need to respect that. So, no, I was never going to force the issue tonight. And if you don't like it, you can find another way back to town." Her voice was as cold as the snow falling around them.

"Sorry," he apologized. "You're right, I don't know how things are up here. I just thought…" he lifted a shoulder in a part shrug. He'd gotten carried away. A small flame of hope had been ignited that maybe this Tory woman knew more than she was saying. And hope was a terrible thing. Rookie cop or not, Aurora didn't deserve his wrath. She was doing the best she could. And that was a whole damn lot better than what the detective inspector had done. He shouldn't be making her feel like she was lacking. It wasn't fair. She was the only one who was helping him, and now he felt like a right jackass. He knew she wouldn't really have left him here in the cold and that her threat was an empty one, but he was stupid to have forced the issue.

"Hmm." She spun on her heel, her reply doing nothing to convince him she'd accepted his apology, and they continued toward the car in silence.

Somewhere out in the dark night, a wolf howled. The long, mournful sound was drawn out and ethereal, floating over the treetops, tugging at his heartstrings. The sound was so reminiscent of the wolves he cared for back in San Diego, howling out their ancient songs. Both humans stopped to listen. He tipped his head back, letting the snowflakes fall on his face, land on his eyelashes and cheeks. It brought everything back into perspective. Reminded him that there were bigger things than just his petty worries out there in the world. He drew in a deep breath of freezing cold air, letting the last of his anger go on his exhale, listening to the answering howl of another wolf, this one farther away.

He didn't know much about the Swedish wolf population, but he did know it had come back from near-extinction in the early sixties. So he was probably extremely lucky to be hearing this small pack talk to each other in the night. And right then, he decided he needed to find out more.

"Aurora." He waited until she turned to face him. She was merely a shadow beneath the trees, and he couldn't make out her features. "I'm truly sorry I said that. I didn't mean it. You're doing a great job." He held his breath, needing her to believe he was sincere this time.

"Okay," she sighed, but when a woman sighed like that, he knew he wasn't really forgiven.

CHAPTER FIVE

Aurora sat heavily in her chair behind her desk and stared at Jiro. It was late, and the constables she shared the office with had all gone home for the night. They'd only been back at HQ for five minutes and she was already regretting asking Mårten to let her continue with this case. Why did she always get carried away with things? If she'd left work at the end of her shift instead of heading out to the reindeer farm, then she wouldn't have just offered Jiro her spare bedroom for the night. Stupid, stupid.

"Thank you, I really appreciate this," Jiro said, his ebony eyes shooting her a look of complete sincerity. "I'll just grab my bag from reception. I won't be long," he added, casting her an anxious glance as if she might leave without him.

Aurora rolled her eyes at his retreating back. God, she was such a sucker. Just because a good-looking guy needed a room for the night, she didn't need to be the one to extend the invitation. And yet she'd opened her mouth and let the words roll out anyway. Even after he'd been such a dick to her.

Jiro's words from earlier still stung. When he'd called her out as being just a rookie cop who had no idea what she was doing, her self-assurance had taken a hit. Probably because it was mostly true. She still had a lot to learn; a long way to go before she would make a decision without second-guessing herself. Yes, she still relied heavily on Mårten's guidance, but that was normal, wasn't it? She'd heard of young, green cops who'd been badly injured or even killed because they thought they knew it all and hadn't listened to a more mature partner. Experience was everything in this job. And she freely admitted she was severely lacking in experience. But she was glad she'd shown initiative tonight by asking to attend the case alone. She needed to step out of Mårten's shadow at some stage.

On the drive back to HQ, Jiro had phoned numerous hotels asking for a room for the night, but they all said there was some kind of conference going on in town, and no one had any spare. By the time they entered the police building, Jiro was checking Airbnb sites, but most of them seemed taken up as well, apart from the hugely expensive ones. He didn't say anything, but she could tell he was getting quietly desperate as she watched him tapping away at his phone.

She had a spare room. Kept mainly for when her sister came to visit, because she didn't have many other guests. It wasn't big, and she wracked her brain to make sure she'd put fresh linen on the bed. It made sense for her to offer him the spare bedroom. If new details emerged about his father, she could relay them to him immediately, and he could get a lift back to HQ with her in the morning so they could start the search again. Aurora tipped her head back to stare at the ceiling, biting her lip as she considered the pros and cons. Her father was the biggest con. But then she couldn't very well let Jiro sleep on the street. He was alone in a strange country, worried sick about his missing father, and something about his predicament tugged at her heartstrings. So she'd opened her mouth, and now she was stuck with him.

She'd already reported the basics of how the night had gone to Mårten—including Dalström's strange behavior, and excluding the fact she hadn't had his permission to talk to Dávvet—but now she sent another quick text to him, letting him know what she was doing. She didn't believe Jiro formed any sort of threat, but it never hurt to let someone else know what was going on. Just in case. Mårten surprised her by replying almost immediately.

Don't think that's a good idea.

She thought about it for a few seconds before she replied.

He's got nowhere else to go. All the hotels are full tonight.

There was almost a minute where the three dots kept scrolling before Mårten finally replied.

Okay. I trust you to be a good judge of character. I'll keep my phone on just in case you need me.

A balloon expanded in her chest. It felt good to know someone had faith in her. Mårten was giving her the benefit of the doubt, and that was why he was such a good mentor. He allowed her to make her own mistakes and learn from them. But he was also right there as backup if she needed it. He was such a good man. Summer was one lucky woman to have him.

But that balloon quickly deflated as she remembered that Jiro was about to meet her father. She wondered what kind of mood he would be in when they got home. He would probably say something rude or inappropriate when he saw she'd brought someone home with her. Especially because it was a man. Perhaps they should try one more time to find him a hotel room. Nope. She screwed up her courage. Her father was living in *her* cottage. She was taking care of *him*. She was doing *him* a favor. Not the other way around. She had every right to bring people home if she wanted to. He no longer had the authority to order her around like he had when she was a child.

Yeah, right. She just needed to keep telling herself that.

"I'm ready to go." Jiro reappeared in her office doorway,

his duffel bag slung over one shoulder. At least he seemed to travel light.

"Right." She stood wearily and led him toward the underground parking lot to retrieve her car.

It was only an eleven-minute drive to her house on the outskirts of town—Luleå was not very big, as she'd already iterated to Jiro. They drove in silence. Jiro had tried to start a conversation, but she was in no mood, fretting more than she would like to admit about how her father was going to take all this, and shoring up her reserve to deal with him.

It was only thanks to her mother that she'd been able to afford to buy a house in this northern town. Her mother had come from a well-to-do family and had set up a smallish trust fund for her and Astrid when they'd been very young to make sure they were taken care of if something ever happened to her. Which it had. Karin Karlsson had fallen through a patch of thin ice and drowned in the freezing water of a lake near their house eight years ago, almost to the day. If she hadn't set up the trust fund, neither of the girls would've seen a dime, as her father had squandered away everything else she'd left behind after she died. Which was the reason he was living with her now. Aurora could never figure out why her mother had married Karl; they were such complete opposites.

Her headlights lit up her house as she swung onto the driveway. The lights from the Christmas tree she'd set up in the front window twinkled playfully, as if welcoming her home, and for a second her heart lifted. Painted pale yellow, with white trim and a steeply sloped corrugated iron roof, the cottage was small and not in the best part of town, but at least it was hers. She pulled her car into the single garage, which was attached to the next-door neighbor's carport. You couldn't see it at the moment because it was dark, but the cottage backed onto a small body of water, Björsbyfjärden, where she could swim and lie on the little beaches that edged the inlet in summer. Well, she had done before her father had moved in, but now rarely found the time. In winter, the inlet was iced over, and could be dangerous to the unwary, as the ice often didn't get thick enough to walk on.

All the lights were blazing, which meant her father was still awake, and she clenched her teeth as she led Jiro up the ramp she'd installed last year to help her father gain wheelchair access to the front door. As she pulled out her keys, she stopped and swiveled to face him. He should probably be made aware of what he was in for.

"My father, Karl, lives with me, and has done so for the past year. He has early-onset Parkinson's, and I am his carer." She was straight to the point, but silently wondered if she was actually doing Jiro a disfavor by offering him a room. She gave a small shrug. At least Jiro could avoid Karl by staying in his room if he wanted; a luxury Aurora wasn't afforded.

"Oh, sorry, I didn't know. Are you sure it's okay for me to stay with you? I don't want to impose." He took a step back and had to grab the handrail to stop himself tumbling down the ramp. So much for it being safer than stairs.

"You're not imposing," she reassured him. "In fact, it'll probably do him good to have some company," she said with an ironic tilt of her head. More likely, it might make him hold his tongue for once. "I just need to warn you, the disease has made him… cantankerous. Don't mind what he says; he doesn't really mean it," she lied. She knew he meant every single word. And it wasn't the disease that'd made him cantankerous. He'd always had a mean streak. The disease was just an excuse to take his spitefulness up a few notches.

She took a deep breath and opened the door. "Fader, I'm home," she called as she ushered Jiro into the mudroom.

She heard him reply in Swedish, "It's about fucking time," but ignored his lack of a polite greeting and showed Jiro where to stash his shoes and jacket. The one silver lining to Jiro staying here was that he wouldn't understand most of what her father had to say because he'd never bothered to learn to speak much English. And she wouldn't be translating for him. He could catch the drift of most of what was said if people around him were speaking English, but he struggled to hold a two-way conversation.

Karl was talking as she entered the living room. "You sent that bloody woman around to feed me again. I told you I don't want her help. She's a witch and I—" He broke off suddenly when he saw Jiro. "Who's that?" he asked, instantly on guard.

"This is Jiro Nashimori. He's…a friend of mine. I met him when I was living in Gothenburg." At the last moment, she decided not to tell Karl the truth. She hoped Jiro followed her lead and wouldn't give too much away. "He's in town for one night and needs a place to stay, so I said he could have my spare bedroom."

"A friend of yours?" Karl queried, his eyes nearly disappearing into the folds of his skin as he squinted to see the man coming in behind her.

Karl hadn't taken a razor to his face for many weeks now, and his stubble was fast turning into a thick beard. It made him look even more haggard, more like a homeless man propped up in the single armchair—her chair that he had commandeered. The TV was blaring, and she went over to turn it down so that she could introduce Jiro properly.

Before Aurora could say anything more, however, Karl demanded, "I don't want no stranger staying here." As he spoke, his head twitched from side to side, and one of his feet began to jerk spasmodically, the heightened emotions bringing out the worst of his disease.

Aurora wanted to retort that this was her house, and he didn't get to say who stayed and who didn't, but instead, she said in English, "Jiro was on the cruise ship, Le Commandant Charcot. You know the one?" Her father was obsessed with cruise ships. He'd splashed out on a trip around the Caribbean right after her mother had died, and he still had some money left. The trip had been a highlight of his life, and he'd never stopped talking about it. Now he ordered every glossy brochure he could find, so that he could pore over the pictures, still dreaming of where he might go. In the summer months he would sometimes go down to the docks and watch the cruise ships come and go, lamenting the fact that this disease had now stripped of the opportunity to ever go on another journey. Aurora knew better; it wasn't just the disease stopping him now, it was his lack of finances combined with his lack of social graces. If Aurora were a better daughter, then perhaps she might offer to take him on one final cruise. But she wasn't a good daughter, and he wasn't a good father.

The luxury ice-breaking cruise ship was one of Karl's favorites. It had been the one ace up her sleeve when she'd invited Jiro to stay.

Karl levered himself up higher in the chair and switched to broken English. "You on boat?" He lifted a shaking hand and pointed at the couch next to him. "Come. Sit," he said imperiously, making it clear he wanted to hear about the cruise ship. Aurora hid a grimace as she noted her father's complete change of tune. *Now* he wanted to talk to the stranger.

"Let me show you around first; it won't take long," Aurora interceded. Her father could wait. "And you can dump your bag in your room."

"Great Christmas tree," Jiro commented, pointing to the bauble-covered tree in the window.

"Thank you," she said, slightly surprised that he'd even noticed it, but also a tad pleased. She'd spent the better half of a whole morning setting up the tree, trimming it, and then adding other traditional decorations and streamers around the house to give it a festive feel. Karl had grumbled at her the whole time, saying he disliked Christmas and she was just making the place look untidy. But she'd ignored him, deciding this was her house, and if she wanted to lift her spirits by making it look pretty, then she'd do just that. It was also a silent salute to her mother's memory. Karin had always made such an effort to make the house look and feel amazing for her two girls at Christmas, and Aurora had adopted that tradition as her own, feeling as if it brought her mother closer. It also helped her to remember the good times with her instead of being melancholy over her passing, the anniversary of which was coming soon after the new year. Almost unconsciously, Aurora touched a fingertip to one of the small, heart-shaped earrings she always wore. They'd been a present from her mother for her eighteenth birthday, and she rarely took them off.

Giving herself a mental shake, Aurora pushed the thoughts away and concentrated on showing Jiro around. "My bedroom is upstairs in the converted attic." She pointed at the stairs leading upward near the front door, but she's already decided he definitely didn't need to see up there. "The kitchen is through here," she continued, leading him through into the rear of the house.

This was probably her favorite room. Right before her father had moved in, she'd had the whole kitchen renovated. She'd done a lot of the work herself to keep the costs down. Ordered the flat pack cabinets from IKEA and put them together herself, then painted them a lovely duck-egg blue. The copper sink was one she found second-hand online, as was her pride and joy, a large barista-style coffee machine that sat in a corner of the countertop. She'd also found the old-fashioned timber window frames at a second-hand furniture joint and brought them back to life by sanding them and giving them a new paint job. Now she had a wonderful view out over her cute little garden and back patio. A friend of a friend knew a plumber who did the work for cash in hand, and the only thing she had to pay full price on was the electrical work. But it'd been worth it, because now the room was light and bright, and made her happy whenever she walked in. It was somewhere to escape from Fader as he rarely entered the kitchen; cooking was a woman's job.

"Nice." Jiro gave an appreciative nod. "Wow. You might be a woman after my own heart," he added as he spied the coffee machine. "Now that's impressive." He stepped up to the countertop and ran an admiring finger over the polished chrome. "I bet it makes bloody good coffee." He turned to face her, his eyes alight with sudden animation.

"It does," she agreed. As she watched him continue his appreciative study of the machine, she felt her shoulders begin to relax as some of her worry leached out of her muscles. At least they had one thing in common: a love of good coffee. Perhaps his stay here wouldn't be as bad as she was imagining.

"Your room is this way." She led him past the back door and down a long corridor that hugged the rear of the building. "There's the bathroom," she said, pushing open the first door on the right so he could look in as they went by, making a mental note to get him a clean towel. Her father needed help to shower, and so she knew the bathroom would be in fairly good condition, because she was always the one to clean up after him. "Sorry, it's not very big," she apologized, leading him along to the door at the end of the corridor. She poked her head in first to make sure it was all as she had left it last time she'd been in, grateful to see everything was still neat and tidy and in its place.

Her father slept in the bigger bedroom right next to the

bathroom, and she suddenly hoped that he wouldn't keep Jiro awake with his snoring. The walls were thin in this cottage. Aurora didn't hear it up in her attic room, but she should probably warn him to wear some earplugs.

"It's fine," Jiro assured her, dumping his duffel on the neatly made bed. "You know I'm grateful just to have a bed for the night," he added, flashing her a grin. It was the first time she'd seen him relax enough to actually smile. It was a very good smile. Showing straight, white teeth, and made his eyes crinkle up at the corners in a most endearing manner. It made her catch her breath as she realized just how good-looking he was.

Turning away, she tried to hide how flustered she was, by saying, "It's all good. Now, if you wouldn't mind keeping my father occupied for a few minutes, I'll make us a coffee." She knew she was dumping him in the deep end, but it was either that or he stay locked up in his room. "Or would you prefer something harder? Or softer," she added as an afterthought.

"Even though I'd love to taste a coffee from your amazing machine, I would very much like a beer right now, if you have one. It's been a kind of stressful day."

That was an understatement, she decided. And if he was going to spend any time talking to Karl, then he'd definitely need something more than just coffee. She didn't drink a lot of alcohol, and she rationed Karl's intake using the doctor's recommendations that drinking any alcohol would only bring on his symptoms quicker as her excuse. While in truth, it was because Karl became even more ornery when he drank. But she kept a secret stash in her small shed out in the backyard so he couldn't get to it for the odd occasion when she herself needed a drink. Perhaps tonight they could all do with a little loosening up.

"I'll get us all a beer," she replied. "I could use one too."

"Of course you could," he said, his features softening.

"Look, I was wrong to say those things earlier. I was angry, frustrated, stressed. And clearly I don't handle stress well." He touched her gently on the arm and gave a weak smile. "I'd hate to think that you took any of what I said to heart. And I'd hate to think I'd damaged our relationship."

"I know," she replied. "And you haven't." And this time she actually meant it, which surprised her a little. She had to force her gaze away from his. Those dark eyes had a compelling pull that she was finding hard to resist. It also surprised her he thought they had a *relationship*. Because they didn't; she'd only known him for a few hours. That wasn't long enough to form any sort of bond.

"Thank you." His voice remained soft, compassionate. Then he straightened his spine and said, "Right. Your father likes to hear about cruise ships, huh? Well, have I got some stories for him?" He gestured for her to precede him down the hallway, and she couldn't stop the small bubble of respect that rose from her gut; he was a man who took his duties seriously.

She led him back to the kitchen, where she opened the back door to go out to the shed to retrieve the beer, motioning for him to go back the way they'd come into the living room. The freezing air hit her as she put on a pair of Wellington boots she kept at the back door and ran through the snow to the small shed huddled in the back corner of her garden. At least she didn't need to keep the beer refrigerated in this weather.

Returning to the kitchen, she pulled down three containers —tall glasses for her and Jiro and a special no-spill cup for her father—from an overhead cupboard, and started to pour them all a beer, listening to the murmur of conversation coming from the living room. Jiro was talking, and for once her father seemed to be listening with rapt attention. Edging sideways, Aurora peered around the door frame, watching the two men as they talked. Jiro was waving his hands around in animation, his face in profile as he sat at the end of the couch nearest to Karl. Every now and then he would unconsciously push that wayward lock of hair up his forehead and away from his eyes. She could only see the back of Fader's head, but he was nodding enthusiastically as Jiro spoke. He probably understood half of what he was saying, but that didn't seem to matter.

Her father had ignored his early-onset Parkinson's symptoms for a very long time. She'd only found out after he moved in with her that they'd first started in his early forties, but it wasn't until almost five years ago that he'd finally admitted something was wrong. It would be his sixty-second birthday early in the new year, just after Christmas. Most men of that age were still considered just out of their prime, but Karl was on a steep downward spiral. It was his lack of money, however, that'd finally forced him to reach out to his daughters. The bank had foreclosed on the property he'd bought in Malmö with their mother's money because he hadn't honored any mortgage payments in nearly a year. The money was all gone, he said.

He'd gone to see Astrid first—who had remained living in Malmö—telling her his woeful tale of how he would soon need to get around in a wheelchair, peddling his usual truckload full of guilt and telling her it was her obligation as a daughter to look after him. His relationship with Astrid had remained sporadic at best, only visiting her once or twice in the past three years, even though they both lived in the same town. But Astrid lived in a small one-bedroom apartment, and it would've been hell on earth if she'd had to take her father. So she'd called Aurora, crying down the phone, almost hysterical as she relayed their father's plight.

What choice had Aurora had?

She hated that their father had practically ignored his two daughters ever since their mother had died, stating that it'd been Karin's choice to have kids, and now he was free of all burdens. But when it became obvious he could no longer cope on his own, he expected them to come running; it was their duty as good Swedish daughters. He was such a fucking hypocrite. Add to that, Aurora had moved to Gothenburg on the day she'd turned eighteen, three weeks after her mother had died, just to get away from him, and she wondered how he had the gall to even ask. But ask he had, and she couldn't let Astrid bear the burden. So she'd agreed. And now she found herself trapped in a cycle of never-ending regret, guilt and recriminations. She had no life of her own now; all her personal time was taken up caring for Karl.

But it was the guilt that ate at her the most. The doctor had warned her that Parkinson's wasn't just a disease that affected the physical body of a person. It had many mental implications as well. Top of the list being depression, because as the person became less able to do things for themselves, it could often lead to someone drowning in misery, turning on their carers as an outlet for their emotions. The doctor had warned that she would need to show more compassion and understanding as the disease progressed. But she found this part hard. Whenever her father wallowed in self-pity, bemoaning his life now trapped in a wheelchair, and perhaps soon losing the capacity to stand or even feed himself, all she could think about was the beatings he'd handed out when she was a child. Although his features had sagged and become sallow, she could still remember the look on his face as he hit her with his belt, the hard lines contorted with fury as he blustered about how ungrateful a child she was. And it was exactly the same now when he confronted her. His face was lined with indignant aggression, as if the world owed him something and he was going to take his pound of flesh out on her. She could find no sympathy in her heart for him. Which was when the guilt took over. He was her Fader, and he was sick and in need of help. She was his daughter. How could she still hate him so much? Time didn't seem to have healed any wounds.

Aurora finished pouring the beers——then plastered a smile on her face and took all three into the living room. Setting the cup down on the small table next to her father, she said, "A special treat because we have a guest." She couldn't very well exclude him, but she would make sure this was the only one he had. Handing Jiro his glass, she took a seat next to him.

"Thanks." Jiro clinked his glass against hers and then turned and waited patiently as Karl picked his up in a shaking hand and slowly brought it to meet theirs.

It was only then Aurora noticed that, for the first time in months, the habitual scowl had lifted from Karl's face. He was actually smiling, and Aurora was a little taken aback. She'd always known that Karl preferred the company of men. Whenever he'd been in a foul mood, he'd loudly reiterated to Aurora that he wished she'd been born a boy. It was one more of Aurora's disappointing flaws that she could do nothing about; not in his eyes anyway. One more reason she'd failed to live up to his expectations. But she hadn't realized how much Karl's personality changed in the company of another man. She'd been worried he might've been jealous she'd brought a boyfriend home. But as soon as she'd identified him as a *friend* only, Karl had jumped at the chance to talk to a real *man* for once.

Perhaps tonight would not be as unbearable as she'd first thought.

CHAPTER SIX

Jiro jerked awake, confusion clouding his mind for many moments before he finally worked out where he was. In Aurora's spare bedroom. She'd been kind enough to let him stay in her house. And he'd accepted her offer gladly. Until he'd found out she was caring for her sickly father, and then he was mortified that he'd encroached on her household. Shame flooded through him all over again at the thought that not only had he been mean to her when she was doing her best to help, but then he'd taken advantage of her kind nature and invaded the sanctity of her family matters. He peered out the tiny window, trying to figure out what time it was, but it was still pitch black outside, leaving him no clue as to whether it was the middle of the night or not.

He was just about to reach for his phone when it buzzed from the bedside table right next to his ear. The sound reminded him of what had awakened him in the first place. Someone was trying to get in touch. Sitting up, he groped around in the dark until he had his phone in his hand, but he had to squint his eyes a couple of times before he could make out who the caller was.

Taro.

Why was his brother ringing? He squinted even harder

until he could make out the time. It was actually ten past six in the morning, not midnight, as he had first thought. Which would make it around ten p.m. back in LA.

"Hello." His voice was croaky when he answered, and he cleared his throat a few times before he tried again, saying, "Hello, Taro, is that you? Thank God you finally called." He'd tried to phone Taro a few times last night, but had only managed to get his voicemail. Not wanting to break the news that their father was missing through a voicemail, he'd left a brief message requesting Taro call him back as soon as possible.

There was an extended silence on the other end of the phone, and Jiro was beginning to wonder if it was actually Taro on the other end of the line when his brother finally spoke. "I know that Papa is missing." Taro cut straight to the chase, his voice sounding flat and strange, completely unlike his normally confident, upbeat tone.

How could he already know? Jiro hadn't told anyone back in the US yet; he'd been hoping against hope that Papa would be found safe and well and he wouldn't have to be the bearer of bad tidings.

As Jiro struggled to keep up with the conversation, Taro continued, "You need to listen to me very carefully. I know where you can find Papa. You need to get to him as soon as you can. Do you have a car? Some sort of transport? I've got the coordinates. I can send them to you now."

For what felt like eons, Jiro's mind refused to process everything his brother had just told him. Finally, he said the first words that came into his mind. "What the hell, Taro?" he demanded. "What are you talking about? I haven't been able to get hold of you. I tried to call multiple times last night to let you know Papa was missing. And now you're telling me you knew all along? How? I don't understand."

"I know you don't understand, but I can't tell you the

details over the phone. You'll just have to trust me. I'm booked on the next flight to Sweden. I'll be there in twelve hours. I'll tell you all about it then."

"What the fuck is going on?" Jiro exploded, his voice rising in pitch so that he was nearly yelling.

"I know this is all hard to take in. But, Jiro, you need to stop asking questions and do as I tell you. Papa's life is at stake here."

Taro didn't need to remind him that their father's life could be in the balance; he knew all too well. He'd been the one out there in that freezing cold weather, worrying himself sick about how his father might survive. A ping sounded on his phone to alert him that a message had just arrived.

"I don't have time to argue with you. I've sent you the GPS coordinates of where Papa can be found. I believe it's not too far from the town where you're staying. You need to get out there now," Taro continued.

Jiro stared at his phone, his brain still slow to comprehend what Taro had sent him. He clicked on a link in the message, and it took him to a spot on Google Maps. Jiro zoomed out the map until he found the town of Luleå. The little red pin on the map showed a place on the outskirts of town in an isolated agricultural area. There seemed to be no houses or buildings in the area. Was it even in the same vicinity as the Luleå Adventures farm? Jiro couldn't tell; he needed more time to study the map.

None of this made any sense. How did his brother know where their father was? Had the old man somehow managed to send him the coordinates of where he was? It seemed highly unlikely. Both he sand the police had tried numerous times to contact Kenichi on his phone, but it was turned off, or out of range. And one of the first things Inspector Viskten had done even before they went back to the cruise ship last night, was to request a location find on Kenichi's phone, which had come back with his last known position at the barbecue hut on the reindeer farm. So it seemed the only alternative would be if someone else had sent Taro the coordinates. Jiro's mind jumped to the most obvious conclusion. "What are you saying? Was Papa kidnapped? Is he being held for ransom?" And if so, for what reason? Kenichi had no enemies as far as Jiro knew. But Taro, on the other hand, might have plenty.

"I, ah…" There was a long pause on the other end of the line.

Jiro had always had his suspicions about what Taro might be up to. He knew his business wasn't as legitimate as he made it out to be. Taro was making too much money. The antique and second-hand furniture business brought in a good income, but not nearly as much as Taro seemed to be spending. His lifestyle had spiraled out of control recently. He was living in a ten-million dollar mansion, and he and his wife were both driving high-end luxury cars. It was one of the things he and Papa argued about. Jiro was convinced Taro was living way beyond his means, either that or money was coming in from somewhere else. Somewhere like the black market. Or perhaps even underworld dealings. Papa wouldn't believe him, and so in the end Jiro had stopped trying and dropped the subject. Because Jiro lived in San Diego now, he saw his brother less often, and so it'd become harder for him to judge what was going on in his life.

"Aurora," a tremulous voice called out, echoing down the corridor. "Aurora, vad som händer?"

Shit, he'd forgotten about the old man asleep in the room next door. The last thing he wanted was to wake him up and cause him undue stress.

He bounded out of bed and began throwing clothes on, leaving his phone on speaker on the bed. He didn't know what was going on. Didn't know how Taro knew where to find Papa. But all those issues paled into insignificance with the single thought driving Jiro onward. He had to get to that GPS position right now. If his father was still alive—if he'd survived a night in these freezing temperatures—then he needed to get to him now.

"One more thing, Jiro." His brother's disembodied voice drifted from the phone. "No police. You can't involve the police, not under any circumstances. They made this very clear to me."

Jiro stalled with one leg half-way into his jeans. "Wait. Who made it clear?" Then, a second thought occurred to him. "Why no police? Should I be worried? Is this some sort of trap?" Was he in danger? By not involving the police, Taro was making a clear statement. There was something underhanded going on here. And what would happen if the police showed up? Would that forfeit his father's life?

"No. I promise you, it's no trap. This was a message meant for me. It's not about you. You just need to get going. Right now."

That just confirmed Jiro's fear—that this was something to do with Taro and his dodgy dealings. "Okay, okay," he breathed. He wasn't sure if he believed Taro, but he knew he would go to that spot on the map anyway, danger or no danger. But there was one thing he hadn't yet told Taro; it was a little too late for not getting the police involved.

He was just about to open his mouth and tell Taro he'd already been to the police station and that he was currently sleeping in one of the constable's houses, when two things happened. Taro abruptly ended the call, and Aurora opened the door to his room without knocking, the look on her face saying she had heard at least some of that phone call.

"I'm coming with you, whether you like it or not," she said firmly. She'd obviously come straight downstairs when she heard her father cry out, and was dressed in pretty pink and white striped pajamas, the flannelette kind. Her hair hung long and was tousled from sleep, with one side of her bangs sticking out at an odd angle. She didn't look dangerous, not at all like the tough cop she usually presented to the world. She looked very young and naïve, her eyes wide and unguarded. In that moment, he felt something tighten in his chest. It was a feeling he couldn't put his finger on, but it made him want to demand that she stay here, where she could look after the needs of her father, where it was safe. And not come out into the frozen wilderness with him, where danger might lurk. Which was ridiculous. She was a cop; it was her job to protect other people. She wasn't the one who needed protection. Why then did he suddenly, desperately, not want to get her involved in this any more than she already was?

He still had one leg halfway into his jeans, and now he had to hop around to keep his balance. "Shit." He managed to sit on the bed before he fell, finally being able to pull up his pants. "No, you can't," he said, avoiding looking directly at her as he grabbed his phone from the bed and sweater and thermal top from where they lay on top of his duffel bag. All the rest of his clothes—beanie, gloves, shoes and jacket—were in the mudroom. He needed to get them on and get out of here as quickly as possible. Away from here so she couldn't follow him. Maybe he could call an Uber. He wasn't game enough to ask if he could use her car; he already knew the answer to that one.

"Stop right there." Her small palm landed squarely in the middle of his bare chest, and he pulled up short. He was much bigger than she was, taller and stronger. He could've pushed past her if he'd wanted to. But that one little touch had him pinned to the spot. Her hand on his skin was warm, and a trickle of awareness ran through him as he glanced down to look at her fine-boned fingers as they curved around his pec. "Who was that on the phone?" she demanded, dragging his focus back to her face.

He stared down into her deep-brown eyes, trying to ignore the feeling of her skin on his. "My brother." He could see no harm in telling her who it was. It would make no difference whether she came with him. She wasn't coming, and that was final.

"Okay." She digested that news thoughtfully, and he wondered what she made of it. As a cop, she would probably know better than most that families could hide many secrets, and so maybe she wasn't as surprised as she should be to hear his brother was involved. "And how do you even plan on getting to your father without a car?"

"I was going to call an Uber."

Aurora snorted, the sound loud in the quiet house. "Go right ahead." Her fingertips flexed against his chest as she pushed a little harder. "Go on." She pointed to the phone he now held in his hand. "I guarantee that if you actually get one to come out here this early in the morning, it will be at least an hour before it arrives. Do you really want to wait that long?"

"What?" Jiro glanced at his phone, tempted to open the Uber app. She could be bluffing.

"This isn't New York or LA. You're in a small Swedish northern town. So you see, you need my car, which means you need me."

"Aurora." Karl's plaintive cry echoed down the hallway.

She said something in Swedish, which she assumed meant she would be there in a minute, but she didn't take her gaze away from Jiro's face.

"What if they see your uniform and... do something bad to Papa?" He couldn't bring himself to say *kill him*. But then he had no idea what would be waiting for them where the little red pin sat amongst the forest on the map.

"I won't wear my uniform if that's what you want. I'll go undercover."

Shit, he couldn't believe he was actually even thinking about this. Not only was he taking along a police officer against Taro's strict instructions, but he was also putting a person he was fast coming to like in possible danger.

"I will find this place much quicker than you could," she added. Which was true. Even if he asked Google Maps to take him to where the pin dropped on his phone, he could easily get lost. And he was unaccustomed to driving in these snowy conditions in the dark. She'd told him last night she hadn't been born in Luleå, but had moved here a year ago to complete her six months field placement and then had been offered a permanent position. So her knowledge wouldn't be exhaustive, but she was a native Swede and would definitely have a better grasp on the countryside than he did.

He sighed deeply, causing her palm to rasp against the hairs on his chest. "You can't let anyone else know. You can't even tell Viskten," he said at last. Jiro knew it was a big ask. She was a rookie cop, so her first instinct would be to report to her supervisor, to call in the people she could trust, people who would have her back.

Aurora screwed up her nose, clearly hoping to do just that. He watched as various emotions flickered across her face before she finally came to a conclusion.

"All right then. We'll do it your way. But Mårten won't be pleased." The last part was said almost under her breath.

"Aurora." Her father's call was louder this time, less plaintive and more demanding. He must be fully awake now and wondering what was going on.

Her hand was still plastered to the middle of his chest.

"Are you going to let me past?"

"What?" She was looking up into his face, dark eyes unfocused, her mind obviously racing with the details of what to do next. But it was as if she realized for the first time he was standing there half naked and she had her hand pressed against his bare chest as she stared up into his face. She pulled back quickly. "Oh, yes. Sorry." A red flush spread up her neck as she turned away. It was cute. "Sorry," she mumbled again, but he wasn't sure what she was apologizing for. He hadn't minded her holding him back with her hand; in fact, he'd quite liked the sensation. Had quite liked her taking charge, not afraid of him, not flinching away from him. But there was no time to analyze any of this. They had to get going.

"I need five minutes to sort out my father," she said.

Oh, shit, of course she did. His mind was screaming that they needed to get going now, but she couldn't very well leave her disabled father in bed alone.

"I can help," he said.

She looked at him with a critical eye as she wavered. "Normally, I would ask Millie to come and help, but it's so early. She's my next-door neighbor," she added as an afterthought. "But Fader hates it when I ask her to come in. He hates accepting help from anyone. She's the most caring, most compassionate person I know, but Karl has taken it upon himself to dislike her intensely. Probably because she's seen him at his worst, weak and incapacitated, and he can't get over that."

Jiro didn't really care about the intricacies of her father's character flaws right now; all he wanted to do was get moving.

"Right." Aurora seemed to have come to a decision. "I'll get him up and dressed if you could prepare breakfast for him. I'll be as quick as I can, I promise." She continued to give him directions as to what to prepare for the morning meal as she ducked into her father's room and he hurried down the hallway. Impatience roiled in his stomach; the last thing he needed to do right now was prepare a breakfast. But he couldn't do this without Aurora. And she couldn't do this without caring for her father first.

He busied himself in the kitchen, hurriedly dragging out two slices of the dark rye bread Aurora had said he liked for breakfast and then finding the cheese and cold cuts in the fridge. Aurora's complicated coffee maker was beyond him at the moment, but he found one of the old-fashioned percolators in a cupboard and set that up on the stove instead. The sound of conversation drifted down the hallway, and even though he couldn't understand what was being said, it was clear that Karl was not happy with being forced out of bed this early in the morning. Three minutes later, the old man was still grumbling as Aurora pushed him in his wheelchair into the kitchen.

Karl said something to Aurora, a clear whining edge to his voice, and she answered him in English for Jiro's sake in an exasperated tone that suggested she was only barely controlling her frustration. "I know it's early for breakfast, but you can keep it in the fridge for later if you don't want to eat now. It's either that, or I ask Millie to come in."

The look of distaste that flashed across Karl's haggard face said it all. It also gave him an insight into the man's true nature. He'd caught flashes of it last night, especially in the way he treated Aurora. While he'd been perfectly amiable when he spoke to Jiro, his tone changed when he talked to Aurora. Most of what he said to her was in Swedish, which of course he didn't understand, but he got the gist of the old man's intent from his body language. Karl had a temper, and it seemed he was perpetually unhappy with her. With everything she did and everything she said. Jiro had watched Aurora bite her tongue on more than one occasion and plaster on a friendly smile for his benefit.

Perhaps this was more like the true Karl that he was seeing

this morning. The old man's ungrateful attitude didn't seem that much out of the ordinary for Aurora, and a flash of sympathy for her cramped his guts. She'd taken over the duty of being his carer, but it felt to Jiro as if Karl wasn't the least bit appreciative of her help and compassion. Which must be hard for her. He knew what it was like to deal with a difficult father. But at least he lived in a separate city and was capable of looking after himself. Jiro didn't know if he would be able to take on the task that she had committed to. It must certainly affect her life. Which was probably why she didn't have anyone special in her life at the moment.

He found out that little gem of information last night when they'd been chatting. He'd casually dropped into the conversation the question of whether anyone else lived in the cottage with them, a sibling, or someone else who helped with Karl's care. Technically, he'd been trying to find out if she had any sisters or brothers to help bear the burden, but there was also a small part of him that wanted to know if there was someone else. A boyfriend. Or girlfriend—he was pretty sure she wasn't gay, but you could never rule anything out. It was actually Karl who had said with a snort of derision that his other daughter, Astrid, was too busy with her career down in Malmö to even come and visit, but Aurora was more than capable, and the last thing she needed was anyone else to help her, certainly not a boyfriend to distract her.

Aurora had merely shrugged, raising an expressive eyebrow as if to say *What was she to do?* Then she had agreed with her father, saying, "Karl definitely keeps me busy. Much too busy to have any sort of social life, that's for sure." And Jiro read between the lines, understanding that a boyfriend would be too hard to juggle at the moment. Which was a little sad, because she was a beautiful woman, who seemed to have a lot to give, and for her not to have someone who loved her was a tragedy. She was one fascinating lady, who seemed to be doing it hard right now, and part of him wanted to find out more about her, wanted to help her in someway, although he didn't exactly know how.

"I just need to get dressed," Aurora said, talking over the top of whatever else Karl was complaining about. "If you could set him up at the table with his meal, I'll be down in two minutes."

"Sure," Jiro answered, already taking charge of the wheelchair and shooing her towards the stairs. As he wheeled Karl to his spot at the table, however, Jiro's gaze followed Aurora's figure as she headed up to her room, not quiet able to stop himself from staring at her curvy shape and pert backside as she bounded up the stairs. Even wearing pink flannel pajamas, there was something about her he couldn't deny.

But the last thing he needed at the moment was an entanglement with a woman, no matter how appealing she was to his senses. He had other priorities on his mind; top most was finding his father. Second was confronting Taro about what was going on. There was no room for a dalliance here, and he needed to stop thinking with his dick and start thinking with his head.

He brought the plate of food and the coffee over to where Karl sat, knowing that the old man would probably complain bitterly about the percolated coffee if Aurora was around, but he'd just have to suck it up, because that was all Jiro was capable of. Just as he'd thought, Karl sneered at the food as he placed it on the table, but Jiro ignored the disrespect. He wondered what the old man did all day, left here on his own. Surely he didn't sit inside and watch television for the whole time? It must be hard to become so diminished as a man who clearly had strong opinions, and it made him wonder what Karl had done for a living in his early days. A sliver of sympathy trickled into Jiro's heart. The man was a grumpy old bugger, but maybe he had a few reasons to be so. He still didn't like the way Karl treated his daughter, but there were plenty of men out there with egos the size of a house who would probably act the same way if they were in his shoes. His own father being one of them.

Thinking of his father reminded him they needed to get a hurry on. He left Karl sitting at the table, with a promise they would be back as soon as possible, and went to find his outer clothing. Once he was fully dressed, he stood waiting impatiently in the mudroom for Aurora to appear, which she did half a minute later. Dressed casually in thick black leggings and a dark hoodie, he almost didn't recognize her as the same woman he'd admired in her police uniform yesterday. Back then, she'd caught his eye and made him wonder why he'd never noticed a woman in uniform before. But now, fresh-faced, she looked even more alluring somehow. Less sexy, yet authoritative, and more girl next-door gorgeous. Wow, if he didn't have so much else on his mind, he might be in trouble here.

CHAPTER SEVEN

Aurora reversed the car out of her driveway and put her foot down on the gas as much as she dared while she negotiated the icy road. It was still dark, but at least it had stopped snowing. Silently, she hoped they hadn't had too much snowfall outside the town limits. Even if the graders were out already, they might not have made it to the outer country roads. If the snow had got too deep, they wouldn't be going far, even with the winter tires on her car. She didn't tell Jiro this, however, as he was already overly anxious, his knee juddering up and down with impatience, even as he read the directions from the map app to her.

The pin on the map was fairly close to the reindeer farm where they'd been yesterday, only a little further out in a more isolated spot that looked to be surrounded by forest. An area they hadn't searched yet. She couldn't tell if it was private land or not, but they would navigate that problem when they got there. Although she'd agreed not to wear her uniform, she was still carrying her gun tucked up in her shoulder holster underneath her hoodie, as well as her police badge in her jeans pocket. Which would help to identify her if the need arose. And she really hoped it didn't, because that would mean things had got out of hand.

God, she hoped Mr. Nashimori was still alive. She had serious doubts about his welfare. If he had been abducted—which seemed more likely now—had he been hurt or tortured in the interim? And even if he hadn't, could he have survived the freezing overnight temperatures? Especially without any shelter?

Aurora had debated constantly with herself as she got dressed whether she should let Mårten know what was going on. A big part of her knew it was stupid to go in blindly without backup, without proper intel, and without her supervisor's express permission. She could get into a lot of trouble for doing this. But something about Jiro's pleading expression had made her agree. Mårten would lecture her long and loudly, but hopefully he believed in her enough not to throw her to the wolves in the end. But would his backing be enough? She didn't want to lose her job, not this early in her career. Hopefully, they found Jiro's father with no fuss, alive and well, and she would be able to report a good outcome before Mårten even got out of bed. Then he wouldn't be able to fault her. But she knew she was taking a big risk here.

"I want you to know that if anything goes wrong, and I mean anything, or if I feel we are in danger, I am going to call Inspector Viskten," she said, not looking at Jiro as she uttered her ultimatum. When he made no answer, she took it as his consent. Although he couldn't really argue. If he did, she would just turn right around and head back home. They continued to drive in silence, and Aurora found her mind drifting backward in time.

The first image that appeared was that of her palm resting on Jiro's very naked chest. She hadn't realized at first what she'd been doing; she'd been so focused on stopping him from leaving. But when he'd finally made her aware of her skin on his, there'd been a surge of heat through her fingertips so intense, she'd practically flinched away from him. But even though she'd removed the physical contact, she hadn't been able to drag her eyes away from all that stunning olive skin. Tracing the dark curls scattered across his pecs, down to his washboard stomach and then the trail that disappeared into his waistband with her gaze. The initial surge of heat had turned into a fiery hot flush that'd raced through her body and erupted up her neck, and she'd had to turn away, embarrassed. Nothing like that had ever happened before. Certainly not with a victim of crime who was currently under her protection.

Sending her thoughts skittering away from that embarrassing episode, she trained her thoughts on their interaction last night instead, and how he had made her feel so at ease. They'd settled in with their glasses of beer, and she'd listened to Jiro explain in exquisite detail how life on the ice-breaking cruise ship worked. Karl had lapped up his every word. The man was outgoing and demonstrative with an air of confidence that she'd picked up almost the first moment he walked into the police headquarters. She'd put it down to a very American trait; it was the way they were brought up, to believe they were good at everything they did. And at the time she'd shied away from such an overt show of ego. But now she considered that perhaps it wasn't such a bad way to live after all. Very different from the conservative, often reticent personalities of most Swedish people.

She'd watched him charm her father, and then began to slip under his spell herself, as he turned to include her in the conversation. Noticeably, he kept any mention of his missing father out of the discussion. She liked he was perceptive enough to know it would upset her father greatly. One thing Jiro wasn't perceptive enough to know, however, was the exact reason why it would upset him; because Karl was a narcissist and disliked talk of anything else besides himself or anything that directly interested him. It must've taken great effort on Jiro's part, because if she'd been in his shoes, her missing father would've been the only thing she would've thought about.

She found it effortless to talk to him, and he was the first man she'd had an almost normal conversation with in quite a while. If their talk could be called normal, with her father sitting there like a ghoulish old man listening to everything detail. They talked about such mundane things as what it was like to live here in this northern snowy wilderness and did she enjoy her job? Jiro revealed he worked at a wildlife park dedicated to the conservation of wolves in California, which was incredibly interesting. Even if Karl hadn't understood everything that was said, he certainly butted in whenever he could, and it had made Aurora wish for a few moments alone with Jiro. A few moments of peace to talk to a good-looking man. Now wouldn't that be blissful? Not that she even wanted the conversation to go anywhere, she just wanted to feel like a grown woman talking to a grown man—okay, yes, one that she was attracted to, but what was wrong with a little flirting?—for ten minutes. That wasn't much to ask, was it?

Perhaps that was part of the reason why she'd offered to let Jiro stay at her house. Not just that he was good-looking, but it was a chance to pretend for a little while. Pretend that her life wasn't ruled by her father's demands. Her work gave her some reprieve, but at the end of the day she always returned to Karl. She couldn't really see a way out of this endless loop of work and care. The doctor had said that with early-onset Parkinson's, patients usually lived longer as symptoms progressed more slowly than those who were affected in later life. Karl had already lived with Parkinson's for at least sixteen years, and even though the symptoms had increased at a rapid rate more recently, he could live for at least ten or fifteen more years. And with all the leaps and bounds medicine was taking in neurological diseases, perhaps that time frame could even be extended, the doctor had gone on to confirm with an encouraging smile. Aurora had to hide her shudder of fear when the doctor had spoken these words; he thought he was offering her hope as any loving daughter would surely want. But the idea of spending the next fifteen years as a prisoner in her own house didn't even bear thinking about, and so now she forced her mind to think of something else.

"Can you zoom in and see if there are any buildings in the area of the pin," she requested, breaking the silence in the car. Jiro bent his head closer to the screen, and she could see in her peripheral vision the blue light illuminating his high cheekbones within the dark interior of the car.

"Nope. Nothing showing up, not even when I use the satellite image. All I can see is lots of trees. The nearest building looks to be at least a couple of kilometers away."

That didn't bode well for Mr. Nashimori. If there were no shelter, he most likely wouldn't have survived the night. Would the abductor really be spiteful enough to send them to retrieve a dead body? Or was there something else altogether waiting for them at the designated spot? Without any information on who, what, or why, she couldn't answer that question.

"What about roads? How close can we get to the spot before we have to get out and walk?" Aurora had taken a quick look at the map before they'd left the house, so she had a pretty good idea where they were headed, following the main road west out of town that would take them further inland, then they'd turn off onto a secondary road heading more north on which the reindeer farm was situated. But in her quick perusal, she could see no roads or even tracks leading directly into the thickly forested area where the pin had been dropped.

"There is some sort of minor road that turns off soon after Luleå Adventures," he replied. "But after that, nothing. We might have to walk in. Perhaps even a couple of kilometers," he ended thoughtfully.

"Hmm." That didn't sound good. They weren't really dressed appropriately for a hike into the wilderness. Jiro's shoes didn't even look to be waterproof, which could be a big problem. But at least the roads were fairly clear, even if they were icy, which meant there hadn't been too much snow overnight, and so perhaps they might not have to slog their way through waist-deep snowdrifts. One small miracle.

Even though Jiro's knee kept jiggling up and down, she had to hand it to him; he didn't ask her to drive any faster; at least he appreciated how treacherous the roads were after a night of subzero temperatures. Perhaps now might be a good time to learn more about his backstory. Every little detail counted in cases like these, and conversation would help to distract him from whatever was coming.

"Are going to tell me what your brother has to do with this?" she asked into the ensuing silence.

"I know as much as you do," he snapped back, then drew a deep breath. "Sorry," he apologized. "Taro's involvement came as much of a shock to me as it probably did to you." He glanced over at her, and she risked taking her eyes off the road to shoot him a quick look. From the expression on his face, he was telling the truth. Or was he? Was there something else he was keeping back? Was this what Mårten had been trying to warn her about?

"But then again, perhaps it didn't come as much of a shock to you as it did to me," he qualified. "I bet you see all kinds of corrupt dealings when family members betray each other. I'm sure it happens all the time. Just not in our family. Or so I thought," he added, his mouth twisting with scorn.

"You're not wrong," she replied at last. It happened way more often than people liked to imagine. Whenever a crime occurred, the first suspects were always close family or friends. Greed, lust, and power were strong driving forces. She wanted to know more about the family dynamics; maybe there was a clue she might gain from something he revealed. Jiro hadn't spoken much about his family last night, probably because he didn't want to bring up anything to do with his father in front of Karl. So now seemed the opportune time.

"Tell me more about your brother. Is he your only sibling? Older or younger? Do you get along with him? That kind of thing," she prompted.

"I'm not sure how—"

"Just humor me," she broke in.

"Okay." Jiro settled back into the seat. "Taro is two years older. We look quite similar; people often comment that we could even be twins," he said, raising an ironic eyebrow. "But believe me, that is where the similarity stops." His leg had ceased jiggling, but now she noticed his hand was clenched so tightly around his phone that his knuckles were turning white. "Even though we were brought up with the same morals and standards, we are as different as chalk and cheese in personality. Taro is…let's just say he's more ambitious than I am. He runs a successful business in LA, which my father helped him to start. He's married with two young kids, and lives a lavish lifestyle. Whereas, I live in San Diego and get by on the relatively small wage from my wildlife job." He stopped talking and turned to stare at her. "Is any of this helping?" he asked.

"I don't know. But keep talking anyway. Tell me about your parents." She was starting to sketch an outline of the family order, and one thing was clear: Jiro didn't approve of everything his brother did.

"My father immigrated to Grand Rapids, Minnesota, from

Kobe in Japan, with his family when he was only fifteen. He married my mother, Deborah, who is American, when he was twenty-five." Was it her imagination, or did his voice just hitch on the mention of his mother? "So, both my brother and I were born in America. But my father still had the Japanese culture in his heart, and we adhered to many of the strict traditions. He moved our family from Minnesota to LA when I was fourteen and Taro was sixteen to set up his second-hand furniture business. He must've hit the market at just the right time and filled a niche where cashed-up celebrities were looking for authentic Japanese furniture to kit out their houses, because business boomed."

"Okay," Aurora mused. All of that sounded fairly normal, no red flags so far. Then, a sudden thought occurred to her. "And your mother, where is she from?"

"She was born in Grand Rapids. But she passed away eight years ago, nearly to the day. So now it's only me, Taro and Papa."

A sudden chill ran down Aurora's spine. Her own mother had died exactly eight years ago as well. She wasn't sure if that was an omen or not, but it was definitely something they had in common. She decided to ignore it for now. At least it explained the hitch in his voice earlier. He was obviously very close to his mother.

"I'm sorry," she said, softening her tone. "That must've been hard to lose your mother." If he were the same age as her, then he would've been eighteen when she died, just like her. An impressionable age, where a girl needed her mother. But in someways it'd been serendipitous, because Aurora had officially become an adult and so she'd taken the opportunity to flee the only home she'd known up till then.

"Yeah, I guess." He kept his voice devoid of any emotion, which only helped her to understand how much genuine feeling he was holding back. "She was ten years younger than

Papa. Sometimes I don't know why she married him." The last part was said almost to himself, and so she didn't pry.

Aurora slowed the car as they came to turn off, taking the right-hand turn slowly so as not to send the car into a skid. This was the way toward the reindeer farm, and Jiro sat straighter in his seat, eyes focused intently on the road ahead.

"You'll need to tell me when to turn next," she said. This was as far as her recollection of where the pin was dropped went. It was up to Jiro now to find his father. They drove past the entrance to Luleå Adventures, and both of them stared at the closed gate as they sailed past. Everything was dark and locked up tight; no one was stirring yet. It was almost as if the gathering of all the locals and the search effort last night had never happened. As if everyone had forgotten a man was missing in the snow.

Jiro went back to focusing on his phone. "Slow down," he said after five minutes. "The turn will be coming up soon, but it doesn't seem to be signposted." They would be well past the boundaries of Dávvet's property by now. As soon as she had the thought, row upon row of tall, straight pine trees appeared on each side of the road. Sweden had millions of hectares planted with pine trees for the forestry industry. The problem was, some of it was state-owned land, some of it was privately owned, and some of it was owned by large industrial forestry companies. It was impossible to know which category this land fell into unless they saw a sign, or she rang HQ and asked them to research it for her. And she wasn't about to do the latter.

"It should be here somewhere." Jiro indicated the roadside to the right, and she slowed the car to a crawl, flicking her headlights up to high beam. "There. Is that it?" He pointed to a small gap between the rows of trees. It looked to be some kind of access road for whatever forestry company owned this land. It was dirt and completely ungraded. She wasn't sure how far her old Subaru would take them. It was a good solid vehicle, but it wasn't a four-wheel-drive, and if the road got any worse, they'd definitely have to get out and walk. Just as she turned onto the road, she noticed tire tracks in the snow disappearing up the dark track. They'd been made after most of the snow had fallen early last night, as they were only covered by a light dusting of snow. Which meant the car had probably driven up here sometime after midnight.

"Someone has been here before us." Jiro said the exact thing she was thinking.

But now she was in a quandary, because if she drove over the top of the tracks, she might ruin any evidence that might help them find out who and what this was all about. Making a quick decision, she stopped the car on the road verge and hopped out. The cold hit her with an icy slap to the face, and she zipped up her jacket.

"What are you doing?" Jiro said, opening his door and standing on the empty road.

"I just need a few photographs," she replied, waving him back into the car. Using the flash, she took some close-up photos of the tire tracks, hoping that it would be enough to help them find the vehicle that'd made them if need be. Then she hopped back into the car and drove slowly up the incline, following the trail as it led them deeper into the slate-dark woods. Thankfully, the access road remained remarkably drivable. Which meant this plantation was probably owned by private industry, as they tended to keep everything well-maintained.

"Wait, stop. Look over there," Jiro said. She'd been concentrating so hard on staying on the track and within the two tire tracks, she almost missed a tiny cut-out in the trail up ahead. But the tire tracks told the story; the vehicle must've pulled in and stopped next to a locked gate. "This looks about right," Jiro announced, opening his door before she'd even come to a full stop. "The map shows the pin is a couple hundred meters away, in that direction." He stood in the glare of her headlights, and she followed where his arm was pointing directly into the plantation. She turned off the ignition and got out of the car, leaving her headlights on so she could survey the area.

Two sets of footprints could be seen leading away through the snow on the other side of the gate. Did one of these sets belong to Kenichi? Or did this confirm they were following two culprits? Should they just follow the footprints? Could it really be this easy? It seemed as if a trail had been left for them to follow. Including intentionally making the tire tracks after the snow had stopped falling, to make it easier to see them. But what was waiting for them at the other end? Were the owners of those footprints waiting for them? Perhaps hiding in the forest with a gun aimed at their heads.

"Come on, then," Jiro said impatiently, taking a few steps toward the gate.

"Wait." She held up a hand. She really needed more time to process this. Her brain went immediately to asking what Mårten would do in this situation. Her fingers hovered over the pocket in which her phone sat as she equivocated. But her partner wasn't here, and it was up to her now to make the decision. She'd come this far; she needed to see this through. This was her first real test as a police officer acting on her own.

She shut off the headlights and closed the car door. They stood beside the car, letting their eyes adjust to the darkness. It was pitch black and as silent as a morgue, except for the icy breeze that whistled in the branches above. It was eerie, and the hair on the back of her neck rose up. She suddenly felt very vulnerable. Protocol dictated she didn't remove her gun from its holster unless she intended to use it. But these were mitigating circumstances, and she definitely intended to use it if the need transpired. So she unzipped her jacket and withdrew her weapon from the shoulder holster, holding it with the muzzle facing toward the ground.

"Stay behind me at all times," she whispered, although why she was whispering was anyone's guess. If there were someone waiting in the trees to shoot them, they would've already made it blindingly obvious of their position with the bright headlights of her car. And if there was no one waiting, then there was no need to be quiet. Jiro used the flashlight app on his phone to show them the way. She was tempted to tell him to turn it off, but there was no point in them stumbling around in complete blackness, so she left it. She climbed over the gate a little awkwardly because she was holding the gun in one hand, but she wasn't about to relinquish it. Then she waited for Jiro to do the same. Beyond the gate was a walking trail, made by whom, she had no idea. But it'd clearly been used and kept clear of any underbrush. The only sounds were the crunch of their boots as they made their way carefully up the walking trail, and her breathing rasping quietly in and out.

After a surprisingly short distance, they emerged from beneath the branches of the plantation into a more open area of natural forest. Aurora's heart rate ramped up even more until she could feel the pulse pounding in her neck. Where the hell were they going? She disliked this situation more and more with every step they took. Jiro's impatient presence at her back was the only thing that pushed her onward. He was counting on her. And so was his father.

The trail continued into the woodland, and so she followed it slowly and warily, her eyes darting in every direction. Not that she would see an ambush coming, someone could be standing ten feet away in the dark and she wouldn't know it. They reached the edge of a clearing, the unobstructed sky above a blessed relief, but she didn't advance into the open area just yet, as they would become sitting ducks if someone was waiting to pick them off, remaining instead hidden just inside the line of trees. A carpet of soft snow blanketed the clearing, the ice crystals glinting in the reflection from the torch. The footprints led straight across the clearing toward an indistinct, large shape that loomed at the opposite edge of the clearing. An old hunting cabin, perhaps. This might explain the existence of the trail through the plantation, to allow the traditional owners access to their hut. She studied the blocky shape minutely, looking for any movement or shaft of light that might give away someone's presence.

Jiro touched her shoulder. "This could be it," he whispered. Yes, she was well aware of that fact. But she wasn't going to advance until she was as sure as she could be this wasn't a trap.

"Let's circle around through the forest," she whispered back. "Use the trees for cover. And turn off your torch." The last thing they needed was to wave a red flag to anyone who might be watching. He merely nodded his agreement, turning to his left, trying to find a path through the underbrush, but she pulled him back. Had he forgotten already? He was an unarmed citizen, so it was her job to lead the way. He grimaced as she shot him a look, but stepped aside to let her through. Aurora took a few steps, letting her eyes adjust to the dim light, while trying to stay as quiet as possible. There was a pale strip of indigo on the horizon, heralding the rising sun. It would be many hours yet before it was fully light, but dawn was definitely on the way.

Jiro did a surprisingly good job of staying quiet as they worked their way through the undergrowth. Almost better than her own effort. He had told her he worked in conservation, and so he was probably used to making his little sound as possible while stalking through the wilderness to track down a wolf pack. It didn't take long for them to work their way closer to the hut. Now she could see it was a rustic building, probably a traditional hunting cabin, perhaps even built hundreds of years ago. She stopped behind a tree about twenty meters from the hut, surveying the area.

Everything looked deserted. Nothing moved. Not even the rustle of a leaf in the wind or the hoot of an owl broke the silence.

"Is he in there?" Jiro hissed from behind her. There was probably only one way to find out, but Aurora wanted to be one-hundred percent sure this wasn't some kind of ambush or trap.

All of a sudden, Jiro rushed past her. "Wait. Stop," she shouted, but to no avail. Jiro had already wrenched the door open and turned on his flashlight. She ran forward, gun at the ready. "Fuck, fuck, fuck." She shouldn't have let him get past her. He could be in—

"He's here," Jiro shouted, dropping to his knees on the earthen floor beside the prostrate body just as she breached the doorway. Her breath left her lungs in a rush of relief as she saw there was no one else inside the hut. But that didn't mean they were out of danger. She turned and scanned the exterior, keeping her back to Jiro and gun pointed out at the forest, half expecting someone to charge out of the dark at them. Her breath pounded in her lungs, large puffs of steam on every exhalation filling the air around her. But nothing moved. Everything remained quiet and still.

"Is he alive?" It was a question she dreaded the answer to, but it had to be asked.

There was silence, and Aurora risked a glance over her shoulder. Jiro was crouched low over his father, almost nose to nose with him, fingers feeling at his neck for a pulse. As he did so, he pulled back a thick, woolen blanket; someone had tried to keep him warm. Which meant they intended for him to live through the night. The old man looked to be dressed in the same clothing he would've been wearing at the reindeer farm; waterproof pants, boots, and the large cruise-issued jacket that swamped his frail body. Was that and the blanket enough to have kept him warm overnight? Even inside the shelter of the cabin, Aurora wasn't sure; it was probably the same temperature outside as it was in. Aurora had noticed no other blankets, or sign of a fire in the hut.

"Yes!" Jiro's jubilant cry sent her heart juddering.

Oh, thank God. She wanted to sink to her knees also, the adrenaline rush starting to leave her body. But this was only part of the rescue. They still had to find out what condition he was in, get him back to the car and to the hospital as soon as possible. He was most likely suffering from severe hypothermia, but hopefully that's all it was. Perhaps it was time to call in the cavalry now. The only thing stopping her was Taro's warning not to involve the cops. But how would the people who had put Mr. Nashimori here know the cops were involved? Unless they were watching.

That thought sent a shiver of premonition through her. This might not have been a trap, but there was definitely someone watching them. Waiting to see if they retrieved the old man. But to what end? And now they had him, what was the next step? Was this all part of someone else's complicated plan? Would they be requiring more from Jiro and his family? Even if the old man was safe, did that mean this ordeal was over? Or was it just beginning?

CHAPTER EIGHT

Jiro sat with his head in his hands. It was nearly midnight. Eighteen hours since they rescued Papa and there was still no sign of him waking up. He lay just as still and unmoving in his hospital bed as he had when they first brought him in. Non-responsive, the doctors had said. But that didn't tell Jiro anything. He needed to know whether his father was going to wake up. Kenichi had been suffering from severe hypothermia, and had been very close to death. When they first arrived at the hospital, Kenichi had suffered a cardiac arrest. Thank God the doctors had been right there to resuscitate him. And now they were doing their best to warm him up slowly; had even put him on a blood-warming machine for a short time. Now, there were tubes and machines all around the bed monitoring his vitals. But his age was a limiting factor, and at the moment the doctors would not give him any proper prognosis. It was just *wait-and-see,* especially after the cardiac arrest.

A small sound from the direction of the window brought him back to the present, and he remembered Aurora was still here. "You should go home." He lifted his head to look at her. "There's no point in your staying." He couldn't remember exactly when she had arrived—probably around eight, when her shift finished—but she had come bearing a chicken burrito, for which he was eternally grateful, remembering he hadn't actually eaten all day.

She looked from Jiro, who was sitting in a visitor's chair in the corner, to his father lying in the bed, and back again. He could tell something was bothering her, but he couldn't figure out what.

Aurora had been his pillar of support today. Without her, he didn't think he would've made it through. He certainly wouldn't have been able to get his comatose father out of the cabin and back to the car on his own. Between the two of them, they'd managed to carry Kenichi back down the trail, he holding his shoulders, and she his legs. Getting him over the locked gate was an awkward act of juggling and trying not to drop him. But once they had him in the backseat of the car, Jiro cradled his head in his lap, willing him to continue breathing, while Aurora drove as fast as she dared on the icy roads, Aurora calling head to the hospital to let them know they were coming in—an ambulance would've taken too long to reach them she'd told him.

When they had found Papa in the cabin, she'd wanted to call her partner in to help, but Jiro had argued that if any police were glimpsed at the scene, it might turn out badly for them. Or for his brother. So she'd relented, but only after getting him to agree that as soon as they arrived at the hospital, she could call Viskten. They would keep it on the down low; he could enter discreetly through a side door and keep the police presence to a minimum. But they needed to at least let the authorities know Kenichi had been found and to call off the search. Jiro eventually agreed; they couldn't keep this from the police forever. But he asked that they keep his brother out of it for now. Tell her supervisors he'd received an anonymous tip-off. She'd only agreed because an anonymous tip-off was a better excuse for her not to have informed the inspector straight away. She thought it was probably going to be a dead end, and therefore decided not to involve the whole police force, which would've wasted everyone's time following false leads, instead going to check it out alone first. It was a good story, and so far it seemed to be holding up.

As soon as they'd entered the emergency department, Aurora had left Jiro to stay by his father's side, while she went off to face Viskten. An hour later, she'd returned to find him in the room they allocated to his father, her face drawn and pale, but her shoulders straight and filled with purpose.

"I need to go into the office for a while," she'd said. "But I will be back, I promise. Send me a message if there's any improvement." Then she did something completely unexpected. She stepped in and gave him a quick hug. He wasn't sure why she had done it. She hadn't offered him this kind of comfort at all yesterday or last night, so what was the difference today? Perhaps there was something in his face that was telling of his utter distress. Or was she somehow more invested in his story now? After all, she cared for her sick father and would understand a little of the trauma he was going through. Jiro had felt a short period of relief when he'd found his father's pulse at his neck, but that had quickly turned to anguish when the doctors could give him no real hope of whether he would survive or not. And now his anguish and lack of sleep were turning into a deep-seated trepidation as he worried about what the future might hold for him, his father, and even his brother. Aurora must've sensed some of this panic and dread and reached out to him. Which he was very grateful for. He had let her go with some regret—she'd felt good in his arms and under different circumstances he would've relished the closeness of her body against his.

Aurora had been true to her word and had returned just after lunchtime to check on them both. This time she'd been wearing her uniform and had Inspector Viskten by her side. The inspector had interviewed Jiro earlier in the morning, but Jiro had stuck to his story that it'd been an anonymous tip that'd sent them out into the snow. But when the inspector had requested to see his cell phone, Jiro had resisted, shaking his head in apology, saying that he had accidentally deleted the message—when really he had gone back and purposefully deleted the incriminating text message from his brother. It was clear Viskten didn't believe him, but he couldn't argue when Aurora backed him up. Jiro only hoped that Aurora would keep his secret; he could tell she was struggling not to reveal the truth to her police partner. Perhaps it was even the first time she had told a bald-faced lie to him. Add that guilt on top of the guilt he was feeling over watching his father lie in a hospital bed, and he felt like he might drown. Aurora had left again soon after, but then returned later in the night bearing the much-needed burrito, and had remained by his side, both of them listening to his father's heartbeat through the monitor attached to his finger. She'd let him wallow in his silence, for which he was grateful, her presence a balm for his soul.

"I don't want to leave you alone," Aurora replied now, taking a step toward him.

It was sweet that she cared about him enough to sit by his side all night, but it was about time he stopped using her as a crutch. "It's okay. You need to get some sleep." She would be expected to turn up to work tomorrow and would need to catch some rest if she was going to function properly. "My brother should be here soon anyway."

"Are you sure?" She looked uncertain, but the glare of the fluorescent lighting above the hospital bed did nothing to hide the dark circles under her eyes, and he could see how tired she really was.

"Yes," he replied gently. "You should go."

Jiro stood and made his way over to her until they were only a few inches apart. He stared down into her face, getting lost for a second in her dark-brown eyes, warm as chocolate. They might be lined with fatigue but he still found them fascinating. She was a very interesting woman. Caring. Compassionate. But clearly, with a backbone of steel. The glint of silver from her stud earrings caught his eye again. He suddenly wondered what'd made her want to join the police force. There was an inscrutability in her gaze that seemed to hint at a history of past adversity. But he knew she wasn't the type to offer up her secrets easily. As he stared deep into her eyes, he suddenly wanted to know some of those secrets, to delve a little deeper into the dark recesses of her life story. Find out more about the woman behind the enigmatic stare.

She moved as if to step away, breaking his reverie, but before she could retreat out of his reach this time, it was he who initiated contact, wrapping his arms around her to give her a quick hug. "Thank you for everything you've done for me and my father. You're a rockstar in a police uniform."

She laughed at that and withdrew from his embrace, but he kept hold of her hands, not wanting to let her go entirely. He hadn't forgotten about his father lying there in the bed next to them, but Aurora's touch felt good, distracted him for just a second from the here and now, and he didn't want to lose that. They stood in silence for a few moments, and his eyes drifted down to her mouth almost of their own accord. She had full lips, and when she smiled, her mouth was wide and expressive. But now, as she regarded him pensively, he noted how her front teeth protruded just slightly. Some people might say she had buck teeth, but that wouldn't be fair; it was more like cute bunny teeth that he found incredibly sexy. In fact, he'd like to kiss those lips, swipe his tongue into her mouth and explore those amazing teeth. He dipped his head.

All of a sudden, the door swung open, and Jiro reared

back. Shit, he'd been about to kiss her.

When he turned to see who it was, relief flared in his chest. Taro had arrived. He would know what to do; he'd always been the one to take charge in times of trouble. But his relief was quickly replaced by misgiving when Taro's glare fixed on the woman standing at Jiro's side, his face twisting in a grimace.

"I thought I told you, no cops," he growled.

Jiro had forgotten he was still holding Aurora's hands, but she was the one to quickly withdraw toward the window, taking up a protective stance, arms crossed and legs akimbo as she faced Taro. Jiro suddenly understood how this might look to his brother, who'd expressly forbidden him to involve the police. He opened his mouth to tell him everything was okay, that she was one of them, when Taro spoke again.

"What the fuck is she doing here?" He pointed menacingly at Aurora, lowering his head, almost like a bull getting ready to charge. She uncrossed her arms, and one hand went to rest on the holster hanging low on her hip.

Shit. How had this situation turned so suddenly? Jiro had been just about to kiss Aurora, and now she was sizing up Taro, getting ready to use force to control him if need be. He needed to prevent his brother from escalating this even further before he did something they both regretted. Jiro moved between his brother and Aurora, getting in his line of sight and forcing Taro's gaze back onto him. But where was he to start with his story? What would Taro believe?

"Aurora is a friend. I wouldn't have been able to get to Papa without her." That was the truth, but it didn't begin to explain the complicated relationship that was forming between himself and the rookie cop. Fleetingly he wondered if Aurora considered herself *his* friend, but left that question for another time.

"I don't give a shit. You've put us all in danger by

involving her," Taro exploded. "Get out of here now," he demanded, staring angrily over Jiro's shoulder at Aurora. All of Jiro's relief at seeing his older brother walk through that door now washed away as reality hit. Taro might not be here to save the day as he'd hoped; he might be bringing more complications. One thing was for certain, however, he certainly didn't get to talk to either of them that way.

"She's not going anywhere. Not until you tell me why you don't want the cops involved." Now it was Jiro's turn to go on the attack. He took a step forward and got up into his brother's face; he had two inches on Taro and he intended to use every bit of that height advantage. Jiro could count on one hand the number of times he'd confronted Taro like this; he wasn't normally one for conflict, which was why Taro often won their arguments. But not this time. "You haven't told me jack shit about anything that's going on. You don't know what I've been through in the past forty-eight hours. You can't just fly in here and start dropping orders as if you're in charge." He kept his voice low and in control, but he saw Taro's eyes widen ever so slightly in surprise. He could feel Aurora's gaze boring into his back, and he hoped she didn't still have her hand on her gun holster, because that wouldn't solve anything.

Taro was the first to take a step back. He glared at Jiro for many long seconds before his gaze finally flittered away to look at the body lying unmoving on the hospital bed.

"Tell me about his condition," Taro demanded, his about-face in their conversation making Jiro's head spin. Taro strode over to the bed to stare down at his father, now completely ignoring Aurora, who moved a few more steps into the corner to give them space. Jiro noted that her hands were now by her sides, but her wary focus never left his brother. What must she think of his family now? Probably even more fucked up than she had imagined.

"Still non-responsive," Jiro replied through gritted teeth, going around to the other side of the bed, ostensibly so he could look directly at his brother, but also getting closer to Aurora. "The doctors can give us no prognosis at the moment. They surmise he was probably in that freezing cold cabin for at least six hours." Which might be the only thing that would save him. For some reason, it seemed as if the kidnappers had kept Kenichi somewhere else when they'd first taken him, then transferred him to the cabin around midnight, after the snow had stopped falling. Almost as if they were leaving a trail for Jiro to follow. "He'd been drugged so that he wouldn't escape," Jiro continued. "He's suffering severe hypothermia, and he went into cardiac arrest just as we got him into the hospital. Luckily, they were able to resuscitate him, but they're not sure if there's any brain damage."

"Fuuuuck." Taro breathed the word on a long exhale. "I'm so sorry, Papa," he whispered, leaning over the bed. Then, as if his knees might buckle, Taro groped for the chair beside the bed, sitting down heavily. All his bluster and bluff seemed to drain right out of him. "This is all my fault." Taro put his head in his hands, much like Jiro had done moments earlier.

"What's going on?" Jiro hunkered down next to his brother, his voice soft, pleading. "I need to know."

"I know you do," Taro relented, lifting his head, features now pale and drawn. Jiro didn't think he'd ever seen his brother look more defeated. "But you have to get rid of her first."

Jiro hesitated. He wanted to hear what Taro had to say, but Aurora had been through everything so far with him, and part of him wanted to demand that she stay. And depending on what Taro told them, she might even be able to help. But he could tell by the grim set of Taro's mouth that he wouldn't speak unless Aurora left the room. If he sent Aurora away, she might never trust him again. But he wasn't sure he had a choice.

Aurora made the choice for him. "It's okay, I was just leaving anyway." She made for the door, but as her fingers reached for the handle, she turned and said, "I hope you're not getting in too deep here." Her words were meant for Jiro alone, and he knew it. Flicking her gaze toward Taro, she narrowed her eyes, but said nothing more as she slipped through the doorway.

Jiro had to stop himself from going after her. Had to remind himself that this was his family, his mess to sort out, and the last thing he needed was to be airing his dirty laundry in front of a Swedish police officer. But he knew she was more than just a police officer. She'd risked his life for him and for his father. Risked her career as well, most likely. And he still wondered why she'd done that. It was hard for him to disentangle all the emotions that floated around them like a tangled spiderweb. He liked her. A lot. Yet if Taro was to be believed, he needed to have nothing to do with her. And what was the point in liking a woman who lived so far away from where he'd settled his home and carer? It made no sense.

"Have you finished ogling that copper's backside yet?" Taro's voice broke into his musings. He chose not to react to his brother's jibe. He did agree on one thing, however, it was a very shapely backside, made even more shapely by the tight, dark-blue uniform.

Refocusing his energy, he turned around and fixed his brother with a steely stare. "Right, let's get into it." He leaned a hip against the hospital bed, choosing to stand so that he had a height advantage over his brother. "Tell me everything."

Taro grimaced and shot a quick look at their father. "Are you sure Papa can't hear us?

Jiro just nodded. He had no idea whether Kenichi could hear what was being said, and even if he could, would he remember it? But that wasn't going to stop him from asking the questions. It was time everything came out into the open.

"Why was Papa kidnapped? I'm assuming that's what happened, because there is no way he drove himself to that cabin, drugged himself so that he passed out, and then nearly died of hypothermia. And how did you know where to find him? What the fuck is going on, Taro?"

"It's complicated," his brother replied, but Jiro merely leveled a hard stare at him until he shrugged and said, "You have to believe me. I was trying to get out. I told them I'd had enough. But they didn't agree." Taro hung his head again.

"Who are *they*?" Jiro prompted.

Taro sighed again and rubbed his lips together. "You have to understand how difficult this is for me."

"I'm trying to understand, but all this talking in circles is doing my head in. Just start at the beginning, Taro." Jiro hoped he'd moderated his tone so that his frustration didn't show, but he wasn't sure it was working. Drawing in a couple of deep breaths, Jiro tried to calm himself. They were going to get nowhere if this descended into a shouting match, so he pursed his lips and waited for his brother to speak.

As he waited, he took his first really good look at Taro, and what he saw shocked him. Taro was still wearing the casual clothes he'd traveled in, which were rumpled and creased. That was highly unusual, as his brother was usually immaculately dressed; some might even call him vain. Even when he traveled, he always made sure he looked perfect, not a hair out of place when he arrived at his destination. He was also sporting a five o'clock shadow. His luxurious hair, normally slicked back and styled flawlessly, was wildly tousled as if he'd been running his hands through it all night. Jiro knew the trip would've been taxing—it was a twelve-hour flight to Stockholm, and then another two-hour hop by plane up to Luleå, with at least a couple of hours' layover at the airport.

But the long hours of traveling weren't the only thing showing on Taro's face. Jiro had never seen his older brother look so haggard, so stressed. He was always so sure of himself. Always larger than life. Nothing seemed to faze Taro; no problem was too hard or too big to overcome. He was always animated and full of energy. He also had a quick temper, which'd caused more than a few problems between the two brothers. But none of those attributes were apparent right now.

"At the beginning, huh?" Taro finally said, furrowing his brow. He sat a little straighter in the chair, shaking his arms out as if lifting an invisible blanket from his shoulders. "I guess I may as well tell you everything if you're going to help me protect Papa. Protect us all." That sounded a little ominous, but Jiro kept his mouth shut and listened. "Okay." Taro paused as if still unsure how to start. "As you probably know, Japan has some of the strictest gun control laws in the world."

"Yep." This was a very random place to start a conversation, but his guts began to roil at the mention of guns.

"And the rigorous government rules are an attempt to try and control the deadly Yakuza gangs, I'm sure you've heard of all that too," Taro continued.

Of course he had. While he and his brother had never lived in Japan, both of them being born in America, they'd heard snippets and rumors from their father and other Japanese relatives about certain underground illegal activities, as well as what they saw in the media. Contrary to popular belief, the Yakuza was not one large entity, but rather a conglomeration of smaller criminal gangs, each with their own agenda and principles, coming together under the umbrella of the Yakuza, much like the American Mafia, who operated within different families.

"What does that have to do with anything?" Jiro asked, but he had a sneaking suspicion he knew. He'd suspected Taro was up to something illegal all along. But the Yakuza… well, that was just a different league altogether.

"A man named Hiroshi Kiyota approached me one night about four years ago while I was sitting at my local bar enjoying a quiet drink. He said he knew I'd started up a new business, and he was impressed with how quickly I'd turned it into a profitable enterprise. He said he knew a way in which I could increase my profit, double or triple it with no extra work on my part. At first, I told him to take a hike. I wanted to have nothing to do with him, because what he was saying was obviously too good to be true. But he kept talking, and he was very persuasive." Taro looked up at Jiro, meeting his gaze for the first time since he'd started speaking, his gaze pleading for understanding. Jiro knew it'd been the money that'd been the persuasive factor, because Taro had always been driven by money. Always needing more, always wanting better, bigger, having to keep up with the Joneses.

Was that flaw in Taro's character in part their father's fault? He'd definitely instilled in both of them a drive to succeed, to excel. Status was important to Kenichi, and in his mind, the best way to achieve status was by increasing his wealth. If you were rich, you were important. Kenichi's second-hand furniture business had always done very well, and their family had never wanted for anything. A lot of people would've considered them rich. But in the end, Jiro had rejected that way of life as being too shallow. He valued intrinsic things more, wanting to help save the planet, not destroy it with greed and avarice. But Taro had followed his father's teachings, deciding that money was definitely the key to happiness. But had his quest for endless happiness in fact been the harbinger of his downfall?

"The long and the short of it is that Hiroshi had ties to a group called the Kyodo-kai. I later found out that this is a splinter Yakuza group situated in Hiroshima. They are warring with the Yamaguchi Federation, one of the bigger groups, and so needed guns to help fight their war. Which is where I came in."

"So you're smuggling guns into Japan for a Yakuza group?" Jiro could barely believe the words that came out of his mouth.

Taro had the grace to hang his head. "In a nutshell, I guess so. At first, it was good, exactly as Hiroshi explained. One small crate of handguns stashed in the back of an empty sea container now and then—I usually send them empty over to Japan and bring them back full. It wasn't every shipment, and I had nothing to do with any of the illegal parts. Hiroshi carried out all the dirty work. They paid extremely well. It was like taking candy from a baby." He lifted his head and stared out the window, his knee beginning to jiggle up and down in agitation. "Soon it was two crates, this time guns and ammunition. Then it became four." Taro shrugged. "You can guess how it went from there. After a couple of years, they were asking for more and more. Now, every shipment I made contained something illegal. I think recently they were also shipping drugs, but I can't confirm that."

Jiro was almost speechless. When he finally found his voice, he asked, "Weren't you ever worried you were going to get caught by the police?" He was flabbergasted at how easy it all seemed. And perhaps that was why Taro had become complacent about the whole thing.

"At first, yes. But Hiroshi made it sound so commonplace, as if I were doing nothing wrong. I was shipping empty containers to Japan so I could fill them with antiques and bring them back to my stores here in America. What was the problem if one or two of those containers had a bit of extra cargo in them? It was no skin off my nose. I never touched one of the guns, never even saw them. Hiroshi saw to everything, including paying off the dock security to make sure nothing untoward was ever found."

"Wow," Jiro breathed, finding this extremely hard to process. Maybe it was a good thing Aurora hadn't been here to listen to all this. What would she have done with the information? Would she have been duty-bound to report it? The criminal activity was taking place in a foreign country and well out of her jurisdiction. But he guessed the Swedish police force would communicate this kind of information back to their American counterparts, especially something this big.

"Yeah, wow," Taro repeated. He stood and paced over to the window, staring out at the dark landscape below but without really seeing it. "About a year ago I started to have severe misgivings about the whole thing. Thalia was pregnant with Ren, and she had really bad preeclampsia. She was admitted to the hospital, and the doctor said it was serious; she could even lose the baby if she didn't take care."

"Shit, sorry, bro, I didn't know." Jiro felt a rush of shame that it'd got to the stage where he and his brother led such completely separate lives that Taro wouldn't even confide in him about something as intimate as this. Ren was Taro's second child, a boy born in June this year. Jiro had gone to visit about a month after the birth, to see his new nephew, and reacquaint himself with Taro's first born, Hana. She was three years old now, and cute as a button. And he'd only been to see her three times over her lifetime. Another source of guilt as he thought about what a bad uncle he had been.

"We didn't tell many people, so don't beat yourself up too much." Taro lifted a wry eyebrow in Jiro's direction. "She spent about a week in hospital, then was allowed to come home, but had to be on bed rest most of the time." Taro waved a hand as if to dismiss any more discussion. "The point is, it made me think a lot about her and my kids. I was really stressed at work, and also by Hiroshi's increasing demands, and I knew I was taking that stress out on Thalia. We were fighting all the time, and I was worried that perhaps I was the cause of her high blood pressure. The fact that we could lose our little baby was a huge shock. It made me take stock of myself and my entire life."

Again, Jiro was hit with a new rush of guilt. His brother might be a greedy asshole sometimes, but he was still human, with very human emotions and feelings, and he was also Jiro's flesh and blood. He should have been more understanding, perhaps tried to talk to Taro instead of always assuming that his brother was fine. Taro's hard outer shell was a façade, a face he showed to everyone that made him seem invincible. But Jiro should know better; he wasn't indestructible.

"The other reason I was stressed was the Kyodo-kai had just put forward another business proposition to me. They had a really big shipment, one that could make me millions of dollars. This was different from the normal weapons we were running. Hiroshi wouldn't tell me exactly what it was, but I have my suspicions." Taro leaned his forehead against the windowpane, and Jiro held his breath as he waited for the explanation. "I think it might have been some sort of nuclear material. Hiroshi said there would need to be extra safety precautions."

"What the…?" Jiro couldn't believe what he was hearing.

Taro held up his hand. "I don't think it was a nuclear bomb, so don't go all Ninja Turtle on me. But it could have been weapons-grade plutonium; I'm not sure."

"Holy fuck," Jiro breathed. "That's big shit, bro."

"Don't I know it. And it would also increase the risk of being found out. I'm pretty sure American law-enforcement agencies would be keeping a strict eye open for things like that, don't you?"

"Ya think?" Jiro was so astonished he could barely speak.

"I asked for some time to think about it, and then I arranged another face-to-face meeting with Hiroshi. I told him I wasn't happy with the big shipment, and didn't agree to it. I also wanted to scale back on the other shipments."

"What was his reply?" Jiro asked the question even though he already knew the answer.

"He was very polite, very matter of fact. He said that unfortunately at the moment, my services were too valuable to be reduced or let go."

"He didn't make any threats? Demand that you keep their agreement, or else?"

"No, he just didn't give me an option. And it doesn't take a genius to work out that when the Yakuza says no, it means no."

"Jesus Christ, Taro." Jiro was the one who felt the need to sit down now. His mind was spinning; this was too much to take in all at once. Even though he had suspected something like this, he'd never dreamed it would be this huge. Coming back to practicalities for the moment, he asked, "So is that why Papa was kidnapped? As a message to you? To make sure you kept up your end of the bargain?"

"I guess so. They were showing me how easy it is to get to my family," Taro nodded glumly. "But they possibly also found out I was secretly investigating other avenues. A way to find some leverage on them so I could get out."

"Oh." His older brother suddenly went up in Jiro's estimation. At least he was trying to fight back, trying to right one of the many wrongs he had committed. "Did you find anything?"

"I have a contact in the LA police department. I asked him to pass the information up to the FBI, and I was waiting for a meeting with confirmation from my police guy. I was hoping to cut a deal, give them information that would help catch the big honchos and break up the smuggling ring, in exchange for my testimony. I'm just a small fry in the scheme of things, really."

"That's risky. You could still end up in jail, you know." Jiro had no idea Taro was dealing with all this. No wonder the poor guy was looking stressed and disheveled. Even if he managed to find a way out of being an unwilling partner with the Yakuza, he could still spend time in a maximum security prison.

"I know. But right now, that seems a better option than constantly watching my back. Constantly being worried about my family's welfare. I sent Thalia and the kids away to try to keep them safe. Thalia wasn't happy, but I eventually told her the truth, and she's going to stay with our uncle in Grand Rapids."

"Shit, that's intense." Up until this point, Jiro hadn't even considered his wife and kids. What a complete fuck-up. "But you didn't think to warn me and Papa?"

Taro sighed heavily, and a look of pure remorse crossed his face. "I was going to," he admitted. "But I thought you were probably safe all the way down in San Diego. And I guess I stupidly assumed they wouldn't mess with an old man. I thought Hiroshi had more respect than that. I also hoped that this cruise would keep you out of harm's way while I made the deal and that it would all be over by the time you returned. I was due to meet with this FBI contact tomorrow. But Hiroshi must've got wind of it somehow." Taro's face screwed up, and for a second Jiro was afraid he was going to cry. His brother had not cried in front of him since they were both very little. And for a few seconds, Jiro stood frozen, unsure whether to comfort his brother or pretend everything was fine. Tarot hated any show of weakness and would hate that Jiro had seen his moment of vulnerability. In the end, his brother collected himself, clenching his fists at his side, his face going hard as stone.

"So you see, I need your help. I need a plan to get away from this fucking Yakuza group. And I need to do it before they carry through on more of their threats."

Jiro didn't know what to say. How the hell were they going to come up with an idea that would free his older brother from a criminal group who were renowned for exacting revenge on people who double-crossed them? And who was he to even be thinking he could do such a thing?

CHAPTER NINE

Aurora sat at her kitchen table still in her pajamas. Karl was seated next to her, but neither of them spoke. This was their normal morning routine. She got him out of bed as he grumbled and complained all the while about the fact his socks were too tight, or his sweater too itchy. Then she fixed breakfast, and they both sat and ate before she got ready for work. He could no longer eat the Frukost breakfast crackers he loved so much, as he had difficulty chewing and swallowing them now, and so she'd had to swap it out for a softer rye bread, but he still protested about not being allowed to eat what he wanted every morning. Now his grumbling had finally come to an end, and they were sitting in blessed silence as she listened to him chew. Today, her shift didn't start until midday, so she had a few errands she wanted to get done this morning.

Even though it was still dark outside—the sun yet to rise although it was after seven-thirty a.m.—she could see snow was beginning to drift lightly down from the indigo sky. Bugger, she'd been hoping there'd be no snow today; she hadn't managed to clear the driveway and the front path from yesterday's fall. It would mean Karl wouldn't get out today either. She didn't like his being cooped up in the house all day, but there were few other options for him, especially in freezing weather such as this. Last time she'd taken him to see the doctor, just as she was leaving, he'd handed Aurora a couple of pamphlets to do with support for carers and respite care. Aurora already knew the Luleå Municipality offered various options for day trips or tours run for people with disabilities, and sometimes she thought she might organize one for her father. To get him out of the house, as well as give her some breathing space. But then she realized he would hate it, socializing with all those other people, and most likely be rude and unhelpful to any of the well-meaning staff. He was his own worst enemy. And she didn't have the spare time to take him out much. Sometimes she would wheel him down to the lakeshore, or on a day off, take him into town to look at the cruise ships. But more often than not he was an ungrateful grump, and they always returned from these trips with her feeling frustrated and miserable.

As she stared out the window, her mind drifted inevitably to Jiro. She'd texted him a few times last night before she went to bed but had no reply and so decided to leave it for this morning. Her phone was on charge next to her bed, and if he had any news he wanted to relay then he'd get in touch. A tiny part of her had hoped he'd contact her anyway, even if there was no more news about his father, but she'd quickly brushed that silly thought away. Their relationship was purely platonic. Purely professional. And she shouldn't hope for any more.

But… had he been about to kiss her last night before his brother walked in and ruined everything? Her heart told her he had. And her body told her too; the physical reaction to his closeness had been extreme. First, he'd surprised her when he'd pulled her in close for a hug, which had set off all her internal proximity alarm bells ringing—in a good way. God, he'd smelled like a pine forest and fresh snow, all woodsy and masculine somehow. And without that bulky puffer jacket, she could feel the definition of all those flexed muscles as she wrapped her hands across his back. And he'd called her a rock star of all things, which had filled her with a surge of foolish pride. Then, instead of letting her step away, he'd held onto her hands, gazing down into her face. They both had similar colored eyes, his perhaps a little darker than hers, making them almost black, and she liked getting lost in their depths for those few precious moments. As they stood together, his gaze had drifted to her mouth, and she'd had to stop herself from standing on tiptoes to reach for his lips.

How long had it been since she'd kissed a man? Aurora tipped her head to the side to contemplate the answer. There'd been no one special since she'd moved to Luleå two years ago, and certainly not since her father had moved in with her. Sure, she'd had a crush on her new partner Mårten when she'd first started working with him, but who wouldn't under the same circumstances? It was probably more of a reaction to her loneliness than anything else. Erik, the IT guy, was the only one who seemed remotely keen on her at the moment. And before Jiro had walked through the reception door yesterday, she might've even considered going out with him. But not anymore; her taste for geeky guys seemed to have evaporated all of a sudden. Now, her mind was occupied with tall, athletic men who had dark eyes and a mop of curly black hair.

A sudden loud knock at the door pulled her out of her daydream.

"Who is that? It's too early in the morning," her father snapped, lifting his head from his cold cuts of meat and cheese to squint his eyes in the direction of the front door.

"I don't know. I'll go and see, shall I?" she replied in a sarcastic tone, which she immediately regretted. She needed to stop snapping at her father. She should be the bigger person and try not to stoop to his level all the time.

"You didn't ask that witch to come around again to look after me, did you?" His rheumy eyes turned brittle.

She rolled her eyes, but didn't deign to answer this time. Let him sweat over it a little. This was why it was so hard to hold her temper with him; he never had a nice word to say. But as she approached the front door, she wondered who it could be, before suddenly realizing she was still wearing her pajamas. Shit, she hoped it wasn't Mårten coming round to have another private *chat* with her about her antics yesterday. He'd already spoken to her back at HQ and made his feelings about her going out alone perfectly clear, very loudly. He also made it clear that he wasn't angry because he doubted her abilities; he was angry because no one, not even a seasoned officer, could control a situation if they were taken by surprise and they had no backup. She was not to do it again under any circumstances, and she'd agreed she wouldn't as she stood with shoulders back, chin in the air. It was the first time Mårten had really reamed her out about anything. Probably because it was the first time she'd ever really stepped out of line.

Knowing Mårten, he would probably regret his outburst— his unusual yelling the reason she knew she'd scared the shit out of him, and he was more worried about her than actually angry—so he might want to drop by to see if she was okay, which would be his form of an apology. Perhaps he might've brought her a takeaway coffee. Even though she'd already had her first morning brew from her wonderful espresso machine, she would never turn down another one.

But it wasn't Mårten standing on her doorstep, shivering; it was Jiro.

"I need your help," he said, without as much as a hello or how do you do.

She couldn't stop the slow somersault in her stomach at the

sight of him. There'd been a distinct possibility she might not see him again, but now here he was standing on her front step looking all delicious. Then, her cop brain kicked in, and she noticed the haggard look on his face. Oh shit, had his father died during the night? And she was leaving him standing outside on her doorstep ogling him, while he was freezing and desperate.

"Come in, come in." She beckoned him into the warmth. She was almost shivering herself by the time she shut the door on the icy wind that was whipping up the snow outside. Jiro's teeth were chattering as if he'd been out in the cold for a long time.

"Who's there?" her father called from the kitchen.

But she didn't answer, instead saying, "Let me help you." She was unable to watch him fumble with his zipper any longer with his numb fingers. "Where are your gloves? And your beanie? Why would you go out in this weather without them?" She didn't wait for him to reply, instead pulling down his zipper and helping him out of his jacket. Then, without asking, she bent down and unlaced his boots, assisting him to step out of those as well. "Your socks are soaking. You need better boots than these." She'd noted the same fact yesterday when they'd gone out to rescue Kenichi, but had no time to lecture him about it then. If he were going to stay any longer in northern Sweden, he'd need to do something about his inadequate clothes.

"I know," he replied, teeth chattering. "Living in San Diego doesn't really prepare you for these types of temperatures." He tried to smile, but it turned into a grimace as he rubbed his hands together to try and warm them.

Then something occurred to her. "Wait, how did you get here?"

He wouldn't quite meet her eye. "I didn't know your proper address, and the Uber driver got mad when I kept giving him vague answers, so I ended up walking." His teeth were still chattering as he blew on his hands to warm them.

"You what? Not all the way from the hospital?" Aurora was aghast. The hospital was on the outskirts of town and at least fifteen kilometers from her place, so it would've taken him hours to walk that far in these conditions and in the dark. Instinctively, she took his hands between her own. They were like ice blocks. She began to rub them gently, trying to impart some of her warmth into his frozen digits. Even ice-cold, there was something about having his hands in hers. The touch was electric, and even though she tried to ignore the sensation, it reminded her of their hands entwined last night, and threatened to bring back those thoughts of wanting to kiss him. She suddenly became acutely aware that she was only wearing her worn cotton pajamas. This was the second time in two days he'd encountered her in her fluffy pink nightclothes, and she mentally kicked herself. Why couldn't she have been wearing something a little sexier? Like that cute little pair of silk pajamas she'd bought on a whim last year. But no, he had to see her in her most frumpy outfit. She avoided his gaze, not wanting him to see how embarrassed she was.

His voice brought her back to the present problem at hand. "No, only from the main road that skirts your suburb. I got that much right at least. But then the Uber driver got confused, and then mad at me because I asked him to drive up and down all the streets, so we both agreed he would drop me at that big roundabout out on the main road."

"You mean Bensbyvägen?" That was the large arterial road that serviced her suburb, leading back out to the main highway. Even if he'd known exactly where to come, the walk would've taken him twenty minutes or so, but it sounded like he was out there walking up and down the streets for perhaps an hour or more.

"Probably. That sounds about right. I didn't think it would take me quite so long to find your place, I must admit. This place is like a maze…" His voice trailed off, and she looked up to find his gaze fixed on her. "That feels nice," he acknowledged, his fingers tightening around hers. Was that a flash of desire she saw in his eyes? That wasn't what she been aiming for when she took up his hands to warm them, but now… She couldn't believe she was actually thinking this, but if her father hadn't been in the next room, she might've even leaned in to try to taste him. It really wasn't the time or the place, but try telling her hormones that. Her body was suddenly alight with craving. Craving to take his mouth in hers, find out if those lips were as delectable as they looked. Find out if he too felt this overwhelming desire like she did. He would be a great kisser, she just knew it.

"Tell me who is there." Karl demanded from the kitchen, his voice breaking into their intimate interlude, hitting her like a slap in the face.

"Bloody hell," Aurora whispered. But knowing she needed to answer him, she said more loudly, "It's my friend Jiro, from the other night. We'll be in in a second." Time to stop her daydreaming and get on with reality. Dropping her voice to a whisper again, she asked, "Why didn't you message me? I would've come and got you."

"I've been trying to text you for the past hour," he replied, raising both eyebrows so they disappeared beneath his lock of unruly hair.

Aurora stopped chafing his hands between hers. "What? But my phone is… Oh, God, I'm sorry, it's next to my bed. I leave it on silent so it doesn't annoy my father first thing in the morning. And I just haven't checked it since I got up."

"It's not your fault," he assured her. "I left the hospital in a rush, which is why I forgot my gloves and beanie." He glanced down at where their hands were still joined. "But I might leave my gloves behind more often if this is the treatment I get."

Aurora smiled at that. "Come on, let me make you a hot coffee and get you something hot to eat." Reluctantly, she let go of his hands and turned to go into the kitchen.

"I don't have time to eat," Jiro countered as he reached into the front pocket of his pants and pulled out his phone. "I wasn't joking when I said I needed your help. I can't find Taro. I left the hospital room to get something to eat this morning. I was only gone for half an hour, but when I came back, Taro was nowhere to be found."

"Okay." Aurora wasn't sure why that was such an emergency.

"I tried to call him and message him, but his phone must be turned off. It's weird. Taro had nowhere to go and no one to see. We were both waiting for Papa to wake up. Why would he just leave?"

That did sound a little weird. But she hadn't been privy to their conversation last night. What had Taro told him about their father's potential kidnapping? Before she'd left the hospital room, Taro had said something about it being his fault. She didn't know exactly what he meant by that, but he clearly knew more than he was letting on to the cops. Which didn't bode well for anyone in that family, including Jiro.

"Did he say something last night that might make you think he could be in trouble too?" she asked, her cop brain taking over as she studied him with narrowed eyes.

"Look…" he paused and gritted his teeth. "Yes, he did. But I'm not sure what I can reveal. Yet." He hesitated again, his face screwing up in aggravation as he rubbed the back of his neck. "He's trying to find a way out of this without anyone else getting hurt. But…"

"But what?" she queried. "It doesn't sound like his plan is working if he's gone missing. Has he been kidnapped too?"

This was beginning to sound surreal all over again. First Kenichi, and now the older brother. There was something going on in his family.

"It's possible." Jiro's handsome face paled as he made the admission. "I got this text as soon as I walked into the hospital room." He held out his phone so she could read the words.

If you want to see your brother alive, you need to do exactly as I say. Follow the clues I send you, and they will lead you to him. Taro has been a very naughty boy, but he is learning his lesson. And so will you. The same rules apply as before, no police. If you do go to the cops, Taro will not survive. Apart from one exception. Make sure to take your pig girlfriend with you. If you don't, there may be a terrible and very tragic accident at work for her in the future. Delete this message as soon as you have read it.

"What the actual fuck?" She was assuming by *pig girlfriend*, this person meant her; she'd heard the term *pig* used on American television as a derogatory term for a police officer. And what exactly did they mean by a tragic accident? Were they threatening her? Because if they were, that was unacceptable. Now she understood the pained expression on Jiro's face. This had become very personal for her. Whoever this was, they were playing dirty. But he'd already admitted he knew more than he was telling her. So, she needed him to answer her questions. "Who is this person? And why do they want me to go with you?"

"I'd be guessing." Jiro raised his palms upward in supplication when she gave an exasperated snort, and said, "Look, I have my suspicions from what Taro told me last night, and it possibly has something to do with a link to the Yakuza, but any more than that I can't say. And as to why you have to go, I've been thinking about that on my way over here. Perhaps he—whoever he is—thinks you know too much?" Jiro looked as if he was going to be sick. "God,

Aurora, I'm so sorry. I didn't mean to get you involved. But now I don't know what to do."

The Yakuza? Aurora was completely thrown by that statement. She knew very little about the criminal groups that made up the larger entity, but according to her police knowledge, small as that may be, they didn't have much Yakuza activity here in northern Sweden. So it seemed perhaps the Nashimori family had brought their trouble along with them.

One thing she knew for sure; she shouldn't go with Jiro. She'd already promised Mårten she wouldn't get involved in anything else outside the strict line of her duties. Going off alone with Jiro would break all the rules yet again and break all trust with Mårten. She didn't want to do that. There was a lot she needed to dissect in the message that Jiro had just delivered. Too much to digest in only a few moments; she would need to gather as much information as she could first.

She asked the next logical question that came to mind. "Have you had any more messages since that one?"

"No," he shook his head with a rueful grimace.

So what was this guy waiting for? How would he know when to send the first clue? Was he tracking Jiro? Did he know that he was now at Aurora's house recruiting her to the cause? Waiting to send the next message until he knew she'd agreed to the terms. The thought made her sick to her stomach. Because it meant that now she wasn't the only one in danger. If they knew where she lived, Karl could be next on their hit list. Fuck that. She might struggle to love her father, but she certainly wasn't going to leave him to the mercies of some thug.

"I'm so sorry, Aurora," Jiro said again. She wasn't sure what to do with the apology. She understood that Jiro was exceedingly troubled about the whole thing, and really didn't want her mixed up in it, but it didn't make the circumstances any less dire. Or get her out of this sticky situation.

"I need time to think about this," she said. "You'll have to come into the kitchen and talk to my father for a few minutes. I need to grab my phone. This is not as simple as my just leaving the house with you, you know?" The look on his face showed that was what he'd been hoping for, but this was too big and she needed more information before she came to any conclusion. The likelihood was, she was going to have to make another hard decision. One that she didn't think Mårten was going to like.

All of her earlier agreeable emotions, all the attraction she'd felt for this man only moments ago, now disappeared in a puff of smoke. Why was her love life so doomed? Why couldn't she have a simple relationship? If she'd met Jiro in a bar some night in town, they could've gone home together, had wild, orgasmic sex, then she could've seen him off on the cruise, happy, satisfied and just a little bit in love. No harm done, and no long-term commitment made. But now, it all became terribly complicated, and there was no hope for either of them.

Pulling her features into some sort of composure, she led Jiro into the kitchen. "Fader, you remember Jiro?" she asked cordially.

"What's he doing here so early in the morning? Is this going to be a common occurrence with you two now?" he replied in Swedish. Karl had not been happy that she and Jiro had decamped so early yesterday morning, leaving him in the care of Millie. It seemed like his initial liking for Jiro had evaporated as quickly as it had formed.

Not capable of dealing with her father's sharp tongue, she said to Jiro, "I'm just gonna get my phone and get dressed. I won't be long." She pivoted toward the stairs up to her room, then turned back again, deciding to give him a warning. "I'm sorry. He's not in a good mood." It was a weak explanation, but Jiro was a grown man; he'd just have to deal with Karl's spitefulness the best way he knew how.

Five minutes later, she descended the stairs dressed in civilian clothes to find both men sitting at the table, chatting away much as they had done the other night. Jiro had obviously worked his magic again. Jiro looked up and then stood as he heard her footsteps. "I helped myself to a coffee," he said, holding up a mug. "I hope you don't mind."

Before she could answer, her phone jangled in her hand with an incoming call. Checking the caller ID, she swore softly under her breath. "I have to take this. It's Mårten."

Jiro stiffened at the mention of his name, probably wondering what she was going to say to her police partner. And she was wondering pretty much the same thing. But she couldn't avoid this call. He might have something important about the case to tell her. If they'd caught the guys who kidnapped Kenichi, then all this clandestine stuff might already have been resolved. She went back upstairs to her bedroom and shut the door to take the call privately.

"Hej, Mårten, god morgon," she said, making her tone bright and breezy.

"God morgon, Aurora." Mårten's voice was deep, familiar and completely normal, which was good news from her point of view. "Sorry to call you at home like this; I know you don't start work until midday."

She had to keep reminding herself that he knew nothing of what it transpired at her house this morning, and she just had to keep it together not to give any of it away. "Not a problem, Mårten. What's up?"

"Chief Rydberg has requested I go down to Malmö to help out with a gang-related bombing. Two people died in the attack. It's getting out of hand down there. I am leaving this morning, so I wanted to let you know in person. Hopefully, I will only be gone a few days."

"Oh. Okay." Aurora tried to pretend she wasn't taken aback. This kind of thing happened all the time. Inspectors got assigned, constables got moved to different cases, staff were allocated where they were needed most, and cases with high priority got more action. And the bombings in Malmö were becoming more and more of an issue, as second and third-generation immigrants who'd been brought in as refugees transferred their gang culture and violent crimes to their new country. It seemed as if the officers down there were stretched to the limits, and now they were reporting two or three bombings a day, often with the use of hand grenades, which was a relatively new development. The government had started cracking down by trying to address the issues in the poorer areas, but everyone in the force silently agreed rampant crime was still out of control.

"What about our kidnapping case?" she asked. It was stretching the truth to say it was *their* case. Just because she and Mårten had been the first to speak to Jiro, and she'd been instrumental in recovering his father from the cabin in the woods didn't mean it was *their* case. Aurora's jaw ached with the effort not to say the words on the tip of her tongue. "I'd like to stay on that if—"

Mårten cut her off. "I'm really sorry, but Chief Rydberg has handed the Nashimori case over to Inspector Dalström. That's another reason I called. I wanted to tell you myself. Dalström has said he doesn't require your assistance. Which I find a little… unexpected," he said. Mårten would never come out and directly criticize a fellow inspector; in fact, he had told her more than once that Dalström was a solid guy— which she was now finding very hard to believe. But she could hear the puzzlement in his voice as he wondered why she was being excluded from the case. But Mårten wasn't prepared to argue with the chief. Not at the moment.

"They hope to interview the old man when he comes out of

his coma." His unspoken words hovered between them. It wasn't *when* the old man woke up, but *if*. "Rydberg still needs convincing that this was actually a kidnapping case. I know you have your theories on it," he continued quickly, not letting her get a word in. "But without Kenichi's testimony, I think they feel this is pretty much a dead end."

"What?" She could barely believe what she was hearing. Any thoughts she might have had about revealing to Mårten what Jiro had just told her this morning fled. She certainly wasn't going to take this to Dalström. If she did and he fucked it up like he had done with the search the other night, then Taro could end up dead. Potentially, Jiro could even end up dead. And she wasn't prepared to take that risk.

"But there are all kinds of leads we need to pursue. What about the footprints around the cabin?" They couldn't just ignore that, could they? There was definitely someone else out there. "And what about the woman, Tory, who said she saw him talking to someone in the barbecue hut right before he disappeared? She might've seen the guy who was instrumental in his going missing. I was going to talk to her today." Aurora was kicking herself that she hadn't done it earlier. But with all the chaos surrounding finding the old man and taking him to the hospital, then getting reamed out by everybody for doing it without permission, Aurora hadn't really had time. But Tory was still one of the best leads they had. Someone had abducted the old man, and this guy who'd been talking to him in the barbecue hut might well be top of the suspect list. He could also be the person responsible for sending the text to Jiro, but she wasn't about to tell Mårten that. "Is Dalström going to follow up with her?"

"I'm really sorry, Aurora." She could hear the empathy in his voice; he understood that this case meant a lot to her, even if he didn't know all the details of why. He would know how hard it was to be removed from a case that you were invested in. "But there is plenty to keep you occupied while I'm gone," he continued, and began to reel off a list of the current cases they were investigating. Of course there was always the obligatory paperwork to be done, some research on a cold case they'd reopened into the death of a child ten years ago when fresh evidence had to come to light, and follow-up interviews with witnesses to a mugging and assault the other day down at the train station. She also knew that in Mårten's absence she would probably be allocated front desk duty most days on her shift anyway. Her heart sank, and her thoughts drifted so that she almost didn't notice when Mårten stopped talking. "Are you okay with all of that, Aurora?"

"Yes, yes, that's fine." She allowed the flat tone in her voice to leak through. It would do him no harm to know she was disappointed. But if he thought she was otherwise occupied, it would also throw him off the trail of what he was really up to. Because in that moment she decided she was going to help Jiro. "Let me know how it goes down in Malmö. Stay safe," she added before she rang off.

She didn't trust Dalström to follow up on anything after the way he'd handled the search the other night. She'd mentioned her misgivings to Mårten yesterday, and while he'd been puzzled, he also reiterated that Dalström was a genuine cop with a good record. Perhaps there'd been something else going on the other night, he'd suggested. Some other pressures from work, or even from his personal life. But Aurora had a suspicion that Dalström might come up with some half-assed theory that the old man had got lost and wandered off to the cabin because that was the easiest assumption. Although how he might explain away the second set of footprints, plus the drugs in the old man's system, was anyone's guess. Perhaps if Kenichi woke up and was cognizant enough to reveal what it happened, then

Dalström might order a proper investigation, but it also might be too late by then.

She knew she'd made up her mind. But they still needed a plan of action. She took the stairs two at a time back down to the kitchen to let Jiro know she was in.

CHAPTER TEN

Jiro waited by the front door, listening to Aurora talk in rapid Swedish as she explained something to her father. He could barely believe his luck. Aurora had agreed to go with him. He wasn't sure what had made up her mind. When she'd taken that call from Viskten, he was sure she was going to tell him everything about Taro's disappearance and the blackmailing attempt, then the police would barge in and take over. Viskten, or even worse, that ineffectual detective inspector from the other night, would take charge and Jiro would lose all control. If that happened, he was terrified he would never see Taro again. Jiro knew that giving in to a blackmailer's demands was the last thing you should do, but right now he was running out of options. This way, at least he controlled everything that happened in the next few hours. If Taro died now, it would be on his head, but it was a burden he was prepared to carry if it meant he could keep his family failings out of police hands for now, and perhaps protect Taro and his reputation. It was a matter of family pride.

Jiro wasn't stupid. If Taro survived and made it back to America in one piece, he might well end up in jail for his criminal activities. But surely that was preferable to Jiro never seeing his brother again; for him not to have to be the one to break it to his wife and children that their husband and provider was dead; for Taro's unborn child to never know his father. Taro had a lot of reasons to keep on living. One of the most important—to Jiro's mind at least—was Kenichi's health. If he woke up from his coma to find out that not only was his eldest son a gun-smuggling criminal, but he'd been killed by a bloodthirsty Yakuza gang, Kenichi might not survive that double blow. And Jiro needed his father to get through this. They might be at loggerheads sometimes, but he would never wish his father ill.

While he waited, Jiro had already donned a jacket, gloves, beanie and boots, all borrowed, courtesy of Karl. His boots were still wet, and he had to admit they'd been inadequate, and while Karl's boots might be half a size too big, they were waterproof with ankle protection, and built-in studs on the sole to handle the ice and snow. Karl's thick, waterproof jacket came almost to Jiro's knees, which felt a little awkward and bulky, but Aurora assured him it would keep him much warmer than the blue puffer he'd been wearing. That hadn't even been waterproof, which was one of the reasons he'd been so cold walking to find Aurora's house this morning, as the melting snow had seeped through the fabric.

The other small win he had today was convincing Aurora not to change into her police uniform. Although the blackmailer/ kidnapper/ whatever they were, had decreed she should be included as the exception on this macabre treasure hunt, they'd also stated no police. So he figured they probably didn't want her wearing her uniform, which might attract undue attention. She was still carrying her gum, however, underneath her jacket, the same as she had yesterday.

"Right, let's go." Aurora appeared beside him, the corners of her mouth turned down, in a sign he was fast becoming to recognize as her trying to rein in her emotions. It seemed Karl wasn't happy with being left on his own again, and he briefly wondered how she coped leaving him to go to work every day. She clearly had her own struggles with Karl, and he felt suddenly like his problems with his own father were petty in comparison. Jiro opened the front door, but before he could walk through it, Aurora handed him something that looked like a pair of plastic soles for the bottom of some giant's shoes.

"Snowshoes," she explained, tucking another pair under her arm. I have no idea where we're going to end up on this wild goose chase, but with the amount of snow we've had in the past few days, we may need them.

Jiro said nothing as he threw them in the rear of her car and got into the passenger seat. She got in beside him, and then turned and said, "Now where to?"

"I don't know. Perhaps just start driving. Maybe head toward the hospital. They might be waiting back there for us." He wasn't sure how this all worked, and maybe he didn't really want to.

"Or they might be tracking you already," she replied darkly, backing slowly out of the driveway.

But they got their answer sooner than they expected. The second she took off down her road, a ping sounded on Jiro's phone, and he looked down to read the text.

"Jesus Christ. How did they know where we are?"

"What does it say?" she cut in. "The *how* isn't really as important as the *what* right now," she clarified, and he guessed she was probably right, although this whole tracking thing was freaking him out.

"Go back to the cabin in the clearing. That's all it says," Jiro huffed. Then he looked up and locked eyes with her. "I guess it can mean only one thing."

She nodded her acknowledgement. There was only one cabin they had both been to in the past few days; the one they had found Kenichi comatose inside. She drove in silence for a few moments, both of them digesting this new clue. He wondered what might be waiting for them when they got there. Would it be the same as yesterday? Would they find Taro drugged and nearly frozen to death inside? At least the sun had risen above the horizon, and the snow had stopped falling since he'd been inside Aurora's house, so the roads wouldn't be inundated again. These dark mornings were hard to take.

Aurora broke the silence. "I really want to talk to Tory. You know the staff member who saw your dad talking to someone in the hut right before he disappeared?" she added when he gave her a puzzled frown. "That stranger could be the clue to this. He could even be the person behind these texts."

"Okay." That made sense now that he thought about it. After they'd found his father, their little chat with Dävvet had completely left his mind. "But I'm worried that someone is watching us. Perhaps even tracking your phone? And if we go to Tory's house, they will know," she continued.

Jiro stared down at his cell in his hand as it became blindingly clear that this was the reason the blackmailer knew where they were. "Should I ditch it?" he asked, already winding down the window and getting ready to throw it out of the moving car.

"No," she nearly shouted. "Without your phone, we have no way of contacting this person."

"Fuck." He threw it on the floor between his feet, not wanting to touch the horrid thing.

But he knew it meant they were stuck between a rock and a hard place. He couldn't get rid of the phone, but that would mean whoever was watching them would know every minute detail of where they went and when. Which ruled out a stop at Tory's house.

"I'll put in a request with a colleague of mine, Senior Constable Andreas Tuckburg, to see if he will do some under-the-radar work for us. He should be able to contact Tory and find out what she knows without letting on he's doing it for me. I've been taken off the case," she admitted. He turned to look at her, the first time since they got into the car. Her dark hair was tucked beneath a light-gray beanie, but a few wisps escaped to frame her face. Aurora seemed to struggle to tame her hair; it was always getting loose from her low bun, and she was constantly tucking it behind her ear. But he liked the way her untidy hair seemed to be a constant source of frustration for her. It gave her a slightly vulnerable look, softening the severe edge of the professional cop persona. Made her seem more human. More approachable.

"Shit. I'm sorry, I didn't know."

"Because I didn't tell you," she snapped in reply.

"What does that mean, you've been taken off the case?" This could have all sorts of bad connotations. Perhaps they wouldn't have access to vital information when it became available. She might be excluded from everything the—

"It means I'm really going rogue on this. So you better bloody hope we find your brother," she said, cutting into his thoughts.

"Oh, God." He hadn't realized how much of a bad position he'd also put her in. And now he could read the fear hovering at the back of her eyes. Fear she might stuff this up. Fear of the repercussions she might face later on. Fear that she might lose her job over this.

"I'm so sorry, Aurora." And he meant it. Perhaps they should forget all about this. Perhaps he should take this to the police after all; maybe they were both in over their heads.

"I know," she replied with a sigh. Then, as if sensing his doubts, she added, "But I think we made the right decision. Inspector Viskten has been called away to another job, and so they put Dalström as lead, and while I should trust my superior officers, after his erratic behavior the other night…" she didn't need to finish her sentence. Jiro had as little faith in the detective inspector as she seemed to. So that was it; they were going down this path, for now at least. He closed his eyes briefly. This had all gone to shit so quickly. He really, really wished he hadn't involved her, but she was in it now and seemed intent on following this through, so he should respect her decision. They were a team now.

He hadn't wanted to mention this earlier, but now they were heading out to God knew where, it'd become urgent. "I'm worried about my father," he said, focussing on the icy road in front of the windshield. They were following the exact route they'd taken yesterday morning, a bit of déjà vu. "Should he have some sort of protection? A police guard maybe? Could he still be in danger?"

"I've thought about this too," she replied. "The problem is, every time I contact another officer, or ask about something to do with this case, I run the risk of letting the cat out of the bag. I can ask Tuckburg if he can put one of the junior constables on the door," she said, uncertainty clear in her voice. "But if I do that and questions get asked as to why he's gone behind Dalström's back…" She lifted one shoulder in a slight shrug. "I'm also worried about my father," she admitted. "He's now home alone, and whoever is on the end of those texts probably knows it. I hope I'm just being paranoid, because now both of us have something to lose; a father who might be under threat."

Jiro stared at her as he digested her words. Then he leaned forward and put his head in his hands. "This is getting more fucked up by the second. Is it worth it?" he asked. "My father is in danger because of my brother's stupidity," he finally said when she continued to stare out the windshield. "But you didn't sign up for this. I shouldn't be making you do this." He sat up straight, preparing to tell her to turn around.

"I didn't tell you that to make you feel guilty," she said. "I told you that, so you know what is at stake. It's a risk I'm prepared to take. At the moment," she clarified. "Even though you won't give me actual details, I don't believe that hurting my father will achieve them anything—whoever they are. Do you?"

"No," he answered slowly. "I'm guessing the only reason you've been included is because they think I have some kind of connection with you." He hesitated slightly over the word connection. They certainly did have a connection, but he wasn't sure how deep it went. She owed him nothing; technically, she was a cop doing her job. But he owed her everything. She'd stood by him, believed him when nobody else had. Given him a place to sleep last night. Without her input, he may not have found his father yesterday morning. Was that why he felt this extraordinary attraction? Because he was indebted to her? Or was it more profound than that? Even now with everything else going on, sitting this close to her in the car, he was acutely aware of her presence. Couldn't help wanting to reach out and touch the side of her long, slender neck.

"I'm guessing so too. Plus, I'm a cop, so I could cause them more trouble than you on your own. I think they might be trying to get me out of the way."

"Oh. You think?" This was a new idea that hadn't occurred to him.

"Could Taro be the one sending these messages?" she asked suddenly.

"What? Why? That would be ridiculous," he scoffed.

"Well, you're not telling me why you think your father was kidnapped, even though you clearly know. So what else am I supposed to think? I heard Taro say this was his fault," she accused. "So you can see why I might think he has something to do with it."

"Well, he doesn't, so you'll have to trust me on that." God, this was so hard keeping it all from her. But he'd promised Taro. Promised to let him try to sort it out his way first. But how long did he let that go on until it became obvious Taro's plan wasn't working? Last night the two brothers had schemed and brainstormed and thrown ideas around, most of them ridiculous, to see what they could come up with. Taro still thought his contact at the FBI might be able to help, but he would need to be back in America to make that connection. Which meant they somehow needed to stall, to make the Kyodo-kai group believe he was now intimidated enough to do whatever they asked. It wouldn't be hard to pretend that he was distraught and terrified over how they'd targeted his family while on holiday, and that he'd learned a valuable lesson. Taro was going to try and get in touch with Hiroshi, to see if he could pass the message on to call off whoever had attacked their father here in Sweden. Ask for them to wait for him to get back to America, and then he would agree to all of their demands. Hopefully, this would give them a few days to work secretly on getting the FBI onside. And hopefully Papa would wake up, so that Taro could return to the States with his mind at ease, able to focus completely on saving their family from this complicated criminal game he'd entangled them all in. They never discussed the other option; what if Papa didn't wake up?

When he first found Taro missing this morning, he'd thought perhaps his brother had gone somewhere quiet to make his phone calls. But when the text had come in, he'd been blindsided, not knowing which way to turn. He didn't even know if Taro had had enough time to get in touch with Hiroshi. His first thought had been to take this to Aurora. His justification had been, because if he did what he was told, then perhaps they could recover Taro in one piece. But wasn't it also really just another chance to see her again? And did that make him a pathetic human being?

"Please, Aurora, can you trust me on this?" he asked again, more gently this time.

"I guess so," she said at last, but the lines around her eyes hardened. "But because you believe Taro is not involved, and if there is definitely a malicious threat out there, then I will ask Tuckburg to put a guard on your father's room, as well as have a unit drive past my house as often as they can be spared."

"Good idea." He was on board with that, and if it meant that at some stage in the near future this Tuckburg would have to reveal where his request came from, then they'd deal with it at the time.

"If I were still officially on the case, I would put a trace on the phone number that is texting you," she muttered, almost to herself. "But it's a high possibility that it's a burner, so that might be a dead end anyway, so I'll leave it for now." Jiro guessed there were only so many things she could ask of this Tuckburg guy. He wondered if things might be different if Viskten were still in town. She might be able to call him and plead her case to get his help. Or the opposite might occur, and he might forbid her to be involved, taking charge himself and burning all the bridges. He didn't know the man well enough to decide which way he would go.

He listened while Aurora made the call on her hands-free directly to Andreas Tuckburg's private line, knowing that he probably shouldn't be privy to this call, but they had no option. Tuckburg was more than a little surprised to hear from her and also nonplussed to hear that she wanted her requests to be kept out of Dalström's ear. But he agreed in the end, perhaps because he didn't know she'd been removed from the case yet; and she didn't tell him. He'd probably find out sooner or later, but hopefully by then he'd carried out her bidding.

After she ended the call, they drove in silence until they reached the same turn onto the dirt track leading to the abandoned cabin.

"I never found out who owned this land," she said quietly. "Maybe I should've researched it straight away. It might be important. There could be a connection to the kidnapper here somewhere. There were lots of things I should've done yesterday that I didn't do. After we rescued your father, I thought we had time. How wrong was I?" She parked the car and turned off the engine.

"Don't beat yourself up," he said with a smile, placing his hand over hers. He was beginning to learn that Aurora was nothing if not a perfectionist. She had very high standards, both for herself and for everyone around her. She'd been busy yesterday, fielding all sorts of interrogation from her supervisors, then spending every other available moment with him in the hospital room waiting for his Papa to wake up, so she had plenty of excuses not to have done everything. "You did an incredible job yesterday. We found my father, and he's still alive; that's the most important thing."

She turned to stare at him, dark eyes wide with something akin to confusion. "Thanks," she said at last. "I guess you're right. Sometimes I get bogged down in the small details and forget to look at the big picture." Her gaze dropped to where his hand still rested over hers on the middle console, and when she looked back up at him, the confusion had been replaced by something close to regret. Slowly, she removed her hand. "We might as well get going." Was he imagining it, or had she been reluctant to withdraw her hand? Had her fingers lingered for just a second on his? Or was it just wishful thinking?

Exiting the car, they climbed over the gate to access the walking trail. The police had trampled all over the area yesterday as they'd checked out the site after Kenichi had been rescued. But now it was abandoned and completely quiet once more. It was immediately obvious that no one had been this way this morning, as all of their footprints from yesterday were now covered with a light dusting of snow and there were no fresh ones that he could see. Aurora conveyed the fact that she noticed this as well with a raised eyebrow, but neither of them spoke as they moved quickly through the forest. As the sun continued to rise, the clouds had begun to clear above, turning wispy and washed-out, revealing a pale-blue sky. For the first time, he noticed how hushed the forest was. How flawless the unbroken snow looked as they paced quietly along the trail, the blanket of white muffling every sound. He tipped his head back to look up at the branches above; the needles covered with a thick layer of frosting looked like they'd just been plucked from a glossy magazine showing the picture-perfect winter wonderland.

It was incredibly beautiful. Of course he knew it would be like this, and he'd appreciated the beauty on the day they had gone out to the reindeer farm, but this was different somehow. Just him and Aurora walking through the wilderness. He stopped and stood to listen, a strange kind of peace washing over him. Strange, because the last thing he should be feeling was peaceful. They were on their way to a hunting cabin to find God knew what. He should be anxious, alert, wary, fearful. But he was none of those things. It was almost as if he felt at home here.

Aurora turned, sensing he'd stopped, her mouth quirked up at one side as if to say, *what the hell*?

"Sorry, I'm coming," he said, hurrying to catch up with her. He wouldn't be able to explain exactly how he was feeling, and even if he did, she probably wouldn't understand; her thoughts would be fixed firmly on getting to the cabin, as his should be. They were nearly at the clearing now, but only half of his mind was focused on where they were going and what they would find when they got there. The other half was focused on the strange feeling flowing through him. The only other time he felt like this was when he was camping out in the wilderness, or on one of the field trips to track the wolves they were studying during his work at the center.

He'd remembered hearing the wolves howling the other night when they'd been at the reindeer farm. It'd been soulful and fierce—there was nothing quite like the sound of untamed wolves howling in unison. At the time, he'd made a promise to himself to find out more about the Nordic wolf population. Sadly, he'd been preoccupied with other things and hadn't done so. Yet.

He knew some of the Nordic wolf's traits would probably be much the same as its Californian brothers. Such as the fact that all wolf pups had blue eyes when they were first born, with their eyes turning yellow usually before the end of their first year. The wolves that he studied could travel long distances, up to forty or fifty kilometers a day if their territory allowed for it. He wondered if the Nordic wolves traveled even further because they had large corridors of unbroken wilderness in which to roam.

Aurora slowed her pace in front of him, and he realized he'd been daydreaming. Shaking his head, he refocused. They were close to the edge of the clearing now, but this time she didn't stop to survey the surroundings, instead turning left and following the trail they'd made yesterday when they'd come to rescue his father. He was grateful for the use of Karl's snow gear as they waded through knee-deep drifts. His feet were still dry and toasty warm, unlike when he'd been wearing his own boots yesterday. And although it was probably still ten below zero, he was almost too warm in the thick jacket and waterproof gloves. Now he understood what Aurora had been trying to tell him. He'd spent a lot of time in the wilderness, hiking, camping, tracking his wolves, even during winter in the snowcapped mountains of Montana. So he'd thought he was prepared, but he'd been wrong.

Jiro caught glimpses of the cabin as they threaded through the trees; it looked exactly the same as it had when they were last here. Why had the kidnappers chosen this particular hut? Was Aurora correct when she theorized that whoever owned this land might be connected somehow? It didn't really matter now anyway. What mattered was getting inside.

Jiro's heart rate picked up even as Aurora waved her hand at him behind her back to warn him to be quiet. They hunkered down and edged more slowly around the clearing until they were close to where the cabin nestled in a small copes of birch trees. Aurora drew her weapon, but kept it pointed at the ground. Jiro had to stop himself from shouting out Taro's name as he kneeled in the snow. Was his brother in there? And was he alive?

They finally got into a position where they could see directly into the single entrance. Unlike yesterday, the door now gaped open, exactly the way they'd left it when they carried Papa out. The mess of footprints they and the other police had left behind was still visible in the snow outside. But it was clear that no one had been near this place since they'd left yesterday morning.

"This is a dead end," he said, standing up to his full height. "Taro isn't here."

Aurora also stood, replacing her gun in her holster. "It seems that way," she agreed. "We should check it out anyway."

He let her go first, knowing that he would just get a lecture if he tried to push past her. But when they both peered around the edge of the door, he found exactly what he was expecting. Nothing. It was completely empty. Now what? Was this a dead end? Would the kidnapper send him another message? He had to resist the urge to ram his fist into the wall. They were wasting time. They needed to find Taro.

CHAPTER ELEVEN

Aurora stood staring out into the clearing, not really seeing what was in front of her. She wanted to scream out her frustration. Although she'd half-expected this, it was still gut-wrenching not to have found Taro. Jiro's face looked like thunder, and she knew he was close to losing it, even though he was trying to hide it behind his ferocious frown. The urgent need to go up and take him in her arms nearly drowned out all other emotions. It was as if his palpable fear and anguish were leaching into her, obscuring all her logical thoughts. She'd never wanted to comfort anyone quite so desperately as she wanted to soothe Jiro. But she couldn't let her personal feelings overtake her professional mind. Although she wasn't here in an official capacity, she was still the one with the badge, the one with the training who needed to stay calm and keep control, to stop him from becoming desperate and doing something stupid.

What would Mårten do in this situation? Think this through logically, that's what. So she closed her eyes, blocking out the image of Jiro's forlorn face and concentrated. Of course, how stupid could she be? If the kidnapper was indeed playing games with them—and most likely watching them from afar—then he would send them another clue, wouldn't he? So why hadn't the next clue come in?

"Have you got reception on your phone?" she asked.

Startled, he looked around from where he'd been glowering at the side of the hut as if he could burn holes through it with the intensity of his gaze. "What?" But he seemed to grasp what she was saying even as he spoke, and pulled his phone out from the side pocket of his jacket, studying it for many moments. "No." His shoulders collapsed with disappointment. "Wait… Maybe." He took a few steps into the clearing, holding the cell up above his head. After what felt like an eon, as he danced around in the snow waving his phone in the air, there was a loud *ping*, indicating an incoming message.

"Is it from him? What does it say?" She hustled over to where he stood, leaning against his shoulder so she could read the text.

Did you really expect I would reveal his whereabouts so quickly? That was foolish of you. But you need to stay the course if you want to save his life. Look out beyond the lake and walk toward the Torrberget. Head directly north. Taro is out there, you just have to find him. Remember, no cops, or Taro will die.

"What is the Torrberget?" Jiro asked before she'd finished reading.

"It's a mountain. Out that way." Aurora swiveled and pointed out beyond the clearing in the exact direction opposite to where they'd left the car. Her stomach dropped as she scrutinized the vista beyond.

"Oh, shit." Jiro followed where she pointed with his gaze. She knew he would be seeing the same as her; a never-ending forest with a hazy blue mountain rising above it all in the distance. This wasn't good. She didn't know the area well— she'd only lived in the region for two years—but she had driven and hiked through this section once or twice, as it was fairly close to the outskirts of town. It was just open forest out there. At least until they got to the lake, which they would have to cross if they were to continue in a direct line toward the mountain. But how far the lake was and how long it would take them to get there, she would be guessing. "Do you think he wants us to hike out there?" Jiro asked, still frowning in the direction of the lonely mountain.

"Can't see any other option." There was no point in hiding it from him. "You can drive to Torrberget, and there is a hiking trail that takes you to the peak. But if we do that, we may well miss something that this guy wants us to see. A hut or a dwelling." Hell, they could have even dumped Taro by the side of the lake and left him there to freeze to death. Then a darker voice in her head said quietly, *or in the lake*. She didn't mention this to Jiro, however.

"We'll need the snowshoes if we're going to attempt that," she decided. If they were going to hike cross country, the amount of snow that'd fallen over the past few days would make the going almost impossible without them. She was very glad she'd sent off a message to Millie this morning, asking if she could check in on her father, because who knew what time they would get back from this mission. Millie hadn't replied straight away, which was a little unusual, but Aurora was sure she would get the message soon.

"But that means going back to the car to get them. It's wasting time and energy," he argued, turning to stare down at her. "We need to go now."

"We'll waste more time getting bogged down in snowdrifts if we don't," she countered, her frustration building at his lack of understanding, as well as their lack of success in finding Taro so far. She knew she was probably overreacting, but her emotions weren't listening. They were standing nose to nose now, as the conversation became heated; she wasn't about to let him win this one. So she stepped in and got right up in his face. "I know what I'm doing, Jiro. I want to find your brother as much as you do. You asked me to trust you before. Now I'm asking you for the same thing in return. I can get us where we need to go, but only with the right equipment." And that was probably an understatement. If they were going to hike out into the middle of nowhere, they should have backpacks full of food and water, a first aid kit and all kinds of other essential gear to keep them alive if they got stuck out there. As it was, she had a couple of bottles of water in the car, a stash of chocolate bars, and a small emergency survival kit that she'd never had to use. Up till now.

Her words seemed to get through to him, as the fire in his eyes began to die. But that emotion was quickly replaced with something else. Something equally hot and passionate. "I do trust you, Aurora. How could I not? But…?"

As she waited for him to finish, she realized how near they were to each other, and how she could see little flecks of gold buried deep within the richness of his irises. How the surrounding air seemed to go completely still, encasing them in a bubble of awareness that was just the two of them. How she wanted to reach out and run her fingers over the stubble on his cheek, to find out if it was soft or scratchy. This was no good. She needed to curtail her runaway emotional state right now, but it was as if he were creating a veil of attraction that she was finding harder and harder to push aside. Drawing in a deep breath, she went to turn away from him, to break the spell.

"Wait. This is crazy." Jiro pulled her back around to face him, trapping her gloved hands within his, and bringing her back into his circle of influence. For a second, she thought he was referring to the unspoken desire pulsing between them. "What if we get lost? If there is little to no reception here, what's it going to be like out there?" he asked. It was a valid question, but her body was on a completely different trajectory, and she found it hard to pull herself back to the matter at hand.

She pursed her lips but said nothing. The probability of them getting lost was higher than he might think. Like most Swedes, she'd spent a lot of her recreation time outdoors. So she knew how to navigate well, how to find a path through the wilderness. But that was all when she'd lived in the south. Northern Sweden was a whole other kettle of fish.

"I'm serious, Aurora, I've already put you in enough danger. I think we might have to draw the line here." He leaned down so his mouth was mere inches from hers. Part of her understood that he was being chivalrous, giving her a way out of this whole mess, and she should take him up on his offer. But the other part responded with a *hell no*, because his delicious mouth was there for the taking, and the last thing she wanted was for this to end.

The previous time they'd stood this close together, he had nearly kissed her. There were so many reasons he shouldn't kiss her. So many reasons she shouldn't kiss him. But she couldn't bring one to mind right now. She didn't want him to give her a way out; she wanted to see this through. And she also desperately wanted to taste his full, masculine lips.

So she did.

Perhaps she *was* crazy. Instead of taking a step back and agreeing with him, she stood on tiptoe, reached up and took his mouth, and placed her lips on his. Softly, an exploration, but leaving him in no doubt that she wanted more if he would give it. The searing sensation was immediate, swift and devastating, filling her with heat and blinding light so overwhelming she could only think of one thing. More. She wanted more.

And his response was exactly what she'd hoped for. Dropping her hands, he wrapped his arms around her waist and pulled her up so he could meet her lips fully with his.

His tongue flicked over her lips, asking permission to be allowed entry. And so she opened her mouth, letting delicious sensations flow over her as their lips locked and he delved deep, desperate to taste her.

They kissed for moments untold as she lost track of time and was set adrift by him, and she savored every taste, every pull, every suck of his mouth. Until he jerked back, leaving her bereft. But it was only so he could unzip the top of her jacket, finding the soft skin of her neck beneath, leaning in and nipping with his teeth and sending heat flooding straight to her core. She almost melted in his arms right there. Then, he lifted his head to stare into her eyes. That look. No one had ever looked at her quite like that. It was haunting, as if he understood something about her that no one else did.

Removing one of his gloves, he traced gentle fingers down the side of her cheek. The touch was electric. Their thick snow jackets hampered their movements, and she wanted to rip hers off and throw it down in the snow so she could have more access to his body. So he could have more access to her body. God, she wanted to feel his hands on her hips, on her stomach, on her thighs. Wanted him to stoke the fire raging within her.

If only they weren't standing in the middle of a clearing right now, they could... The thought brought her back to reality with a thump.

They were standing in the middle of a clearing because they had a job to do. Giving in to this attraction wouldn't solve anything, and it certainly wouldn't help Taro.

Slowly, she pulled away. Both of their breathing was labored. His eyes locked with hers, and she saw deep regret swimming in their depths. "Not the right time or place, huh?" he said softly, but his hand remained resting against the side of her face.

"No," she replied.

"Can I just say that I've wanted to do that for a while now? And I would like to do it again. Soon."

"Okay." His response buoyed her, but she wasn't going to admit to feeling the same. She couldn't see how or why they would have another chance.

He was the one who finally broke their embrace. She looked away, readjusting her hair beneath her beanie and closing the zipper on her jacket. She opened her mouth to apologize; that kiss had been her fault after all. But then decided against it, because she wasn't sorry, and it seemed as if he wasn't either. One thing Mårten had taught her was that she needed to stand by her convictions. He probably hadn't been referring to kissing a witness connected with an ongoing case, but it was still a valid point.

"I'll go back to the car and get the snowshoes," she said determinedly. While he looked fit and strong, she was more used to working in these conditions. It would be better if he stayed here and rested, then they could start the arduous hike as soon as she returned.

Shockingly, he didn't argue, and for a second, she thought she'd won.

"You can wait in the cabin if you like," she said, already turning to start the ten-minute trek back to the car. But of course she'd only taken a few steps when he fell in beside her.

"What did I just—"

"I'm not letting you go anywhere alone. I don't think either of us should be alone out here." There was sense in his statement; this time, it was her turn not to argue.

"Fine." She made a show of stomping through the snow; her way of letting him know that even though he might be right, she didn't have to be happy with it. They may as well cut across the clearing now rather than take the longer route around the edge. While they walked, she told him the strategy in mind. "When I get back to the car, I'm going to send an email to Mårten... Inspector Viskten," she said, looking back over her shoulder at him. "I'll schedule it to send in twelve hours' time, telling him what our plan is. If we're not back by then, we're going to need help," she added. She really hoped that she was back in time to stop that email from going out. But they needed a backup plan, and she knew Mårten would act first and ask questions later.

"Good idea," he replied. Finally, something they both agreed on.

Back at her car, she grabbed the snowshoes and handed them to him, then dug around in her trunk to find the spare water, candy bars, and the survival kit. Most people who lived in the frozen north carried one, usually in the car, or in a backpack, if they were partaking in outdoor winter activities. It was the size of a large lunchbox but contained essential items such as a lightweight Mylar blanket, bandages and other first aid equipment, storm matches, as well as a flint and striker, a torch, a large multi-tool with a knife edge and a saw, a length of rope, a compass, and even fishing line and hooks. And last of all, but definitely not least, a flare that could be set off to show their location. The black bag was attached to a single strap so she could wear it slung across her shoulder and it wouldn't get in the way. They would have to carry the water and food inside their jackets to keep it from freezing. She removed the compass and put it in her pocket. They would need that if they were to stay walking due north. She'd learned to navigate by the sun, but if the clouds returned and obscured it, then she wasn't going to take the chance of getting lost.

"Take a drink now," she commanded. "We can fill them with snow, and it will melt as we walk.

"Cool." He seemed pleased with the idea, but his gaze was focused back the way they had come, clearly itching to get going.

She sent the email to Mårten while he restocked their water bottles. Curiously, there was still no reply from Millie, but there was nothing Aurora could do about it now. She'd made a quick lunch for Karl and left it in the fridge for him. He shouldn't need anyone until dinnertime, and hopefully by then Millie would have got the message.

It took them less than ten minutes to get back to the cabin on the now-familiar trail. She stopped, pulled out the compass to get her bearings, and then glanced at Jiro. "Are we ready?"

"As we'll ever be," he replied with a genuine smile that went straight to her heart. He was so handsome, and she really, really wanted to kiss him again. If only they could be two normal people out on a winter's day expedition. But life was never going to be that easy. She'd learned that the hard way.

It was hard going, threading their way through the tall birches and spruce pines. The snow wasn't of an even depth throughout because there was no trail or road to follow and often drifted into deeper piles where there were no overhanging branches. There were traps for the unwary as well, even with the snowshoes on. Hidden beneath clumps of fresh snow there were hollows formed by leafy undergrowth, and more than once she or Jiro fell in up to their waist, or even deeper. If someone had brought Taro this way, she could see no sign of anyone else going in this direction, either on foot, or more likely, riding a snowmobile. They could be following a slightly different route. Or they could be on a wild-goose chase.

If Aurora had the time or energy, she might have admired the sheer beauty and tranquility of the area. With the sun riding low on the horizon, glowing rays of sunlight slanted through the tree trunks, turning the snowy vista into a magical, perfect forest.

They stopped every fifteen minutes or so, ostensibly to take a drink and a breather, but Aurora was keeping a close eye on Jiro. Watching for signs of things like hypothermia or fatigue. Jiro had already mentioned he spent time outdoors—even if it was mostly in the warmer climes of California. And she'd noted his athletic physique—more than once—so his fitness was standing him in good stead as he barely seemed to be out of breath. She also checked in with herself; the last thing either of them needed was for their guide to become incapacitated. And she also made sure they weren't being followed. Or watched. There was no sign of anything out of the ordinary, however. But that didn't mean a lot. Someone could be hiding behind a tree thirty paces away, aiming a gun at their hearts, and they probably wouldn't even know.

She examined the compass to make sure they were headed in the correct direction, and on they went. And on. And on. For an hour, the forest just kept going, and the mountain didn't seem to get any closer. Aurora started to think about what might happen if they had to spend the night out here. She had the backup of her email to Mårten, but that wouldn't help them until the following morning. Her mind wandered back to the problem of how this kidnapper was tracking them. Because neither of them had any reception now; they were too deep into the forest. So even if he had been tracking them through Jiro's phone earlier, surely he was no longer doing that.

Perhaps it didn't matter anymore. Perhaps they needed no more clues, and it was up to them to find Taro now. Which might mean they were close. Or never going to find him. But Aurora had a growing suspicion that there was something else at play here. Whoever was on the other end of the phone wanted her and Jiro out of the way. But to what end? Was he holding Taro somewhere back in town instead? Interrogating him? Or forcing him to do something he didn't want to do.

Jiro's reluctance to let Aurora know what Taro was involved with was becoming increasingly frustrating. If they didn't find his older brother soon, Aurora might just refuse to go on until he told her everything. It was like she was walking around in the dark with only a torch to guide her, so she could only see what was directly in front, when really she needed to turn on the overhead lights and illuminate the whole scene.

Hopefully, Tuckburg had done as she'd asked and both her father and Kenichi were safe. Had he caught up with Tory yet? Perhaps even now he had a description of the man in the barbecue hut. Would Tuckburg follow up on the information if he got it? He would probably know by now that she was off the case, but he'd been a cop for a long time now, hopefully he had enough experience and wisdom to see beneath the surface and wonder why she was asking this of him; perhaps figure out that Dalström wasn't covering this case as fully as he should.

"The trees are thinning out." Jiro's comment from behind startled her back to the present. It was true, the trunks were becoming less crowded, and she got a glimpse of a large flat area ahead. This must be the lake. They would sit down and take a break when they reached the edge, so she could assess their next movements. While the lake would be frozen over, it was still early in the season, and so the thickness of the ice could be variable. It might not be possible to walk directly across. Which would mean a complicated and time-consuming detour around. But Aurora was hesitant to walk straight across. She had an innate wariness about frozen lakes, and if there was another option, she usually took it.

"Let's stop here," she said, finding a fallen log close to the edge and brushing the snow away so they could sit. She could tell he wanted to keep going by the stubborn tightening of his jaw, but he helped her brush the snow away, and sat next to her as stiff as a board.

"Here." She handed him one of the candy bars and opened the wrapper on another. "You didn't have any breakfast, did you?"

"No," he replied with a guilty smile. "Thanks for this," he added, his shoulders dropping as he took first one, and then another large bite. "You're right, I needed food," he muttered through his mouthful. "Maybe I was getting a bit hangry."

She looked at him askance.

"It means angry because I'm hungry," he replied with a laugh.

He finished his chocolate bar before her, and she debated internally whether to give him another one, but decided to save it for later; who knew what they were about to encounter. As she chewed, she contemplated the frozen lake. Trying to put aside her reservations, she studied it impassively. It was covered with a uniform layer of thick, fresh snow. Mostly pristine, but there were signs of animals in the area, deer tracks as well as a few smaller footprints, possibly fox, as well as rabbits and stoat. The deer tracks were made by at least half a dozen animals, and led straight across the lake, which was a good sign. If they thought it was safe to cross, then it probably was, as an individual deer weighs more than most humans.

There was no sign of any human activity around this edge of the lake. She scanned to the left and to the right of them, but there was nothing obvious to be seen. If the kidnapper had left Taro out here, would he have made him easy for them to find? Perhaps staking an orange flag or wrapping him in a brightly colored tarp. There were no signs of habitation on this side of the lake, but she thought she could make out one or two red specks nestled between the trees on the other side, which could be hunting cabins. Most lakes in Sweden, be they big or small, were usually ringed by at least one or two cabins, handed down through ancestral families, and used as summer getaways, or winter hunting huts. Could Taro be in one of those?

At the thought of walking out onto all that ice, she broke out in a cold sweat. But as she followed the edge of the lake with her gaze, and saw that it curved off to the left, until the tree line disappeared around the bend. That end of the lake ran at least two kilometers to the east before she could see the boundary re-emerging in the distance. It was the same to the west; the lake was long and thin, the circumference must be a good ten kilometers. Either way would add a couple of hours at least to their journey. The shortest distance would be to go straight across. But that was not the way she wanted to go. Aurora gritted her teeth, not wanting Jiro to suspect her internal struggle.

She couldn't let her own personal demons get in the way of finding a victim. She had walked across sheets of ice before in the past eight years, so she could do it again. Having made her decision, she stood up. "We're going to follow the deer tracks," she announced. It would be much quicker this way. "But I want you to stay behind me. I will be checking the ice with every step." This was usually done with a long thin pole, but she didn't have the luxury of one of those, so she would just have to use her eyes, ears, and the feeling beneath her boots to tell if the ice was thinning or cracking below them.

"Will do," Jiro stated, but when she cast him a look from beneath lowered brows, wondering why he was suddenly so compliant, he took a step closer. "I took that to heart, what you said back at the cabin. This is your country, and I trust you to get us through it." Leaning down, he placed a chaste kiss on her lips, almost as if sealing the deal. Or perhaps it was a taste of things to come. A hint of something in the future. She licked her lips and turned away. But the kiss had done the trick; she no longer felt such trepidation. His trust had replaced her fear with a sense of… hope.

"Good" was all she said in reply.

They started out onto the ice, her testing every step before she took it. The deer had made a pathway through the snow, revealing the ice beneath, which made it easier to see what was going on. If they made it past the first ten or twenty meters, they should be safe, as ice was always thinner around the edges of a body of water. As they progressed, she didn't let her guard down, however. Plenty of people had died by becoming complacent while out in the middle of a frozen lake.

Her mother had been one of those people.

Aurora shied away from the thought. Now was not the time to be thinking about her mother falling through the ice of the lake near where they'd lived, and Karl dragging her drowned body out, heaving with the exertion. Or, of the way Aurora fell to her knees as she watched the scene unfold.

Nope. She shook her head to rid it of the memories.

Keep putting one foot in front of the other; that was how she would get across this barrier; both mental and physical.

It took them only five minutes or so to reach the middle of the lake. "Can we stop for a second?" Jiro asked. "It's just so beautiful here." He did a slow twirl, taking in the entirety of the body of frozen water, and the snow-fringed trees that lined the boundary. She stopped to look as well. It was spectacular, and she was suddenly so glad she lived in this amazing country.

Tipping his head to the sky, Jiro let out a sigh of pleasure. "I know we're looking for my brother, but sometimes you just have to stop and smell the roses."

She couldn't agree more. She bent down to pick up a handful of snow, intent on making a snowball to throw at his face.

A sound rang out from somewhere in the trees behind them, and something whizzed overhead. She straightened and turned to look back the way they had come. It took a few seconds for her brain to compute. That was a gunshot. Someone was shooting at them. And they had just missed her when she bent down to pick up the snow. A figure emerged from behind a large tree trunk, rifle raised to their shoulder, aimed directly at her and Jiro.

"What was that?" Jiro said as Aurora yelled, "Get down," at exactly the same time. She tried to pull him down into the snow with her, but he resisted, staring back at the man on the edge of the lake. Until another loud crack echoed in the silence. "He's shooting at us." Jiro sounded almost surprised. "Fuck, we have to get out of here."

"No, wait." Aurora knew they were marooned out here. If they ran, they would be sitting ducks, and the man could pick them off at his leisure. Or they could dive into the snow, where they would no longer be a target, and wait for him to advance on them. But she had her gun, so she could defend them. Perhaps if she got a chance, she might even kill the guy before he killed them.

But Jiro wasn't listening. "Come on." He grabbed the back of her jacket, tugging her along behind him as he ran further out onto the lake. She resisted, finally dragging herself free, and landing with a thump in the snow.

"Jiro, wait," she screamed. "Get down. Use the snow for cover."

But he kept running. Hampered by his snowshoes, his retreat was slow and ungainly. And he wasn't following the deer trail; he was heading toward the closest edge of the lake. Another shot rang out, and Aurora turned on instinct. Struggling to release her weapon from underneath her jacket, she hunkered down in the snow until she had the Glock in her hand. Then, lying prostrate, she lined up the sniper and took a carefully aimed shot at him. He ducked behind the tree; she had missed. But at least the guy now knew she was armed. Perhaps that would make him think twice. Not daring to lift her head too far above the snow, she took a quick glance back at Jiro.

Just in time to see him vanish out of sight with a slight cry of surprise.

What?

Then it hit her like a ton of bricks. Jiro had fallen through the ice.

He would die within minutes if he couldn't get out; if she didn't get to him in time.

But the man with the gun was still standing at the lake edge, waiting for her to make one wrong move. If she ran out onto the ice, he could pick her off easily, but if she stayed where she was and continued to defend her position, Jiro could die. She was between a rock and a hard place. And there was only one decision to make.

CHATPER TWELVE

The freezing water was excruciating, the cold cutting into him like a thousand knives. He gasped for breath, the frigid water squeezing the muscles around his lungs so that it was almost impossible to drag in air. Grappling for the edge of the broken ice, he managed to grasp on and keep his head above water. Fully clothed, with the snowshoes dragging his feet down, he knew he would never be able to swim if he let go of that ice. But the gloves were making it difficult to grip, and while he wanted to rip them off, he dared not let go now he had a hold.

One minute he'd been running for his life; the next minute the ice had disappeared beneath him. Fuck, he was so stupid. He hadn't listened to Aurora, instead running away against her command. But he'd never been shot at before; never had someone try to kill him. He was going purely on instinct. When she hadn't followed, part of him thought he was doing her a favor by running—he could draw the sniper's focus away from her and onto him, as he zigzagged across the ice to avoid being hit, so she could shoot back. But the other part of him had just been running like a frightened rabbit. Those thoughts were all fleeting, however, as the need to survive pushed everything else out of his head. He tried to remember what you were supposed to do if you fell through the ice. Things such as *stay calm*, and *try to float parallel to the surface to make it easier to get onto the ice*, drifted through his head. But both of these things seemed impossible to do right now.

Somewhere in the corner of his mind, he could hear gunshots echoing across the frozen landscape. That must be Aurora firing back. Did she know he had fallen in? Because without her help, he wasn't sure he was going to get out. The freezing water was sapping his energy quickly, as well as his ability to think.

He had to do something now. Even though the snowshoes were weighing him down, he kicked hard with his legs in an attempt to bring his body to the surface, while also scrambling at the edge of the ice. He managed to get one elbow up onto the slippery surface, but was gasping for air like a stranded fish and he slipped back in. Thank God he hadn't been wearing a backpack, because he was pretty sure he would've sunk like a stone if he had been.

Fuck, fuck, fuck. How long could someone survive in zero-degree water? Not long, he suspected. So he tried again to heave himself up onto the ice. This time he succeeded in getting both elbows out of the water, but then he had to stop so that he could suck in enough air to keep going. But he could feel himself sliding backwards, the cold dragging him down and under again.

No, no, no. This wasn't how it was supposed to end. He was supposed to be helping Taro, not drowning in a frozen lake.

There was a sudden flurry of movement, and something crashed into the snow nearby. "Jiro, I'm here," Aurora called. "Hang on, I'm going to crawl on my belly across the ice to get to you."

Within seconds, her face appeared as she shoveled her way through the thick blanket of snow, using her elbows and knees to commando crawl across the ice. "Grab my hand," she ordered. "Quickly," she said when he was slow to obey. Didn't she know he was doing the best he could? His body was numb and lethargic, and he knew he was moving slowly, but every tiny movement was a momentous effort now. Using the last of his energy, with a mighty heave, he lunged up and out, fumbling at her hand and almost missing. If she hadn't snagged his wrist at the last moment, he might have fallen back into the water, and kept going down, down, down.

She pulled with all her might as he kicked feebly until he finally rolled out of the water like a beached walrus and lay on his back, dragging in great gulps of air.

"Keep moving," she prompted. "We need to get further away from the hole. The ice is still thin here."

He wasn't sure he could move, but he rolled over with a groan, his wet clothing hampering his progress. "Follow me. Do it like this." She was commando crawling back the way she had come. He wasn't sure how he did it, but he followed her. His teeth were chattering now. Clashing together so hard, he thought he might break a tooth. He'd never been so cold in his entire life. He needed to get warm really soon or hypothermia was going to set in. They only crawled a couple of meters, but it felt like a couple of miles when she stopped, and whispered fiercely, "Keep your head down." They were in a little hollow, where the snow had been pushed aside to make a sort of trench. Glancing at her for the first time, he could see she was wet, too. Not soaked through like he was, but the water had welled up over the ice as she pulled him out, and the front half of her torso was wet. It wasn't until much later that he realized how much danger Aurora had put herself in rescuing him. She could have easily fallen in as well.

"Fuck, where's he gone?" Aurora popped her head above the snow three or four times, like a meerkat bobbing up and down. What was she doing? Then it hit him. For the few blissful seconds as he'd lain on the ice panting, Jiro had forgotten the reason he had fallen through the ice in the first place. Forgotten that a sniper had been trying to kill them.

Now he remembered, Aurora had been shooting at him, so she must've made the decision to take her eyes off him to come and rescue Jiro instead. The guy had been a good couple of hundred meters away, and Jiro was sure he couldn't have run that distance in the short time it took Aurora to pull him to safety.

"Could he still be hiding in the trees?" he asked through teeth chattering so hard now he wasn't sure she would understand his words.

"Probably," she replied tightly. "Either that, or he's run out onto the ice and now he's hiding in a snowdrift just like we are. Waiting for us to pop up so he can pick us off." She'd turned to look at him as she spoke, and her face fell as she took him in. "Shit, your lips are blue. You need to get your wet clothes off."

"What?" That seemed counterintuitive. The air around them was below zero, surely if he removed his clothes, he would still freeze to death. But he slipped off his wet gloves, rubbing his hands together to get some circulation going.

"I'll give you my jacket, and I've got a Mylar blanket in my pack," she replied, tearing her gaze away from him so she could continue her surveillance of the surroundings. "But you need to get your wet clothing away from your skin, otherwise they will continue to draw heat away from your body."

"Okay." He wasn't going to make the mistake of not trusting her this time. Although with a gunman stalking them across the ice, it seemed like the last thing he should be doing was getting naked. What if they needed to run?

Without taking her eyes away from scanning the edge of

the lake, she began to remove her jacket.

"No, you'll freeze," he argued. "Not as quickly as you will," she snapped. "Put the fucking thing on." Her glare was like a thousand hot knives slicing into him.

"Okay," he replied meekly.

"I think I saw him over there." Aurora pointed toward a spot further around the lake from where Jiro had first seen the shooter. He must be creeping around the perimeter, using the trees as cover, trying to get closer to where he and Aurora were hunkered down. And the shooter wasn't wrong, because as Jiro raised his head above the snow, he could see a finger of land jutting out into the lake, and if the gunman made it round there, the distance as the crow flies he would have to cover to get to them would be almost halved.

"I'm going after him. You stay here." Aurora crouched on the ice, gathering herself to leap forward.

Jiro wanted to argue, but the way his teeth were chattering, and his numb fingers were fumbling just to undo the zipper on his jacket, he knew he would be of no help to her; probably more of a hindrance.

He watched the profile of her face as it became resolute. More wisps of hair had now floated free of her beanie and were whipping about her face as she stared across the snow. She was so beautiful. Fierce and strong and beautiful. She wasn't afraid to walk toward danger. Wasn't afraid to confront this crazy killer head on. He suddenly knew he couldn't bear to lose her. Couldn't bear it if she were injured, or worse.

"Aurora, wait." His voice came out feeble, like an old man. How could he put what he was feeling into words? She'd come to mean a lot to him over the past forty-eight hours. He liked her. Really liked her. Cared for her deeply, even.

She turned just her head to look at him, dark eyes deep and bewitching, most of her focus still on the criminal who was trying to hunt them down. Then her face softened, almost as if she understood what his words couldn't say. "I know," she said. "I'll be careful, I promise. I won't leave you out here alone." Then, she was gone.

After she disappeared through the snow, Jiro spent many moments contemplating his fate. She was going out to save his life yet again, and all he could do was lie here and shiver. The least he could do was try to survive long enough to thank her. So he slowly and painfully got to his knees, pulled his beanie off and his wet fleece and then the thermal shirt over his head. The icy breeze sliced into his bare skin, and he could barely move his arms to pull on Aurora's jacket. It was too tight, but even though the front section was damp inside, her body warmth remained in the fabric, and it was the most euphoric feeling he'd ever had. He hugged her jacket tightly around him, sucking in every bit of heat he could, and drawing in the smell of Aurora, her essence. She'd told him to take off all his clothes, but his numb fingers were incapable of undoing his pants or bootlaces. So he left both of them on for now. Remembering what Aurora had told him, he lay back down on the ice, and rolled himself into the Mylar blanket, like a caterpillar in a cocoon. It didn't stop his teeth chattering, however. And he knew his thought processes had slowed right down; it was like he was thinking in slow motion. If Aurora came and told him he had to run for his life right now, he wasn't sure he would be able. But he left his legs free of his cocoon just in case.

All he really wanted to do was close his eyes. Sleep was calling to him. But he knew that was dangerous, probably a sign of hypothermia. So he rubbed his arms inside his cocoon, even though it seemed to make no difference; he didn't feel like he was getting any warmer.

It was quiet. Too quiet. He hadn't heard any more gunshots, but wasn't sure if that was a good thing. He needed to know what was going on. With a groan, he hauled himself up to sitting, then wriggled forward until he could peep over the top of the snowy layer. Nothing moved out in the sea of white. Where was Aurora? He couldn't see her anywhere, and he tried to follow the trail she'd left as she crawled through the snow, but it soon blurred and disappeared into the whiteness. She could be anywhere between him and the lake edge.

Suddenly, a figure emerged from behind a tree right out on the end of the land jutting into the lake. He raised his gun to his shoulder, and Jiro ducked just as a bullet whistled overhead. Fuck, the guy had spotted him. Aurora had been right to tell him to keep his head down.

He lay down again, teeth still chattering, praying that the man had gone back behind the tree. It was deathly quiet, only the sighing sound of a rising breeze shifting the snow like they were grains of sand broke the silence. The quiet stretched on and on until it all became too much. He needed to take one more look. This time he would be more careful. As cautious as a church mouse, he inched his head up until his eye was just above the snow, and then he quickly popped down again. Shit. The man was making a beeline straight for him across the ice. Stupidly, he'd given away his position by wanting to know what was going on.

But where was Aurora? Should he call out to her? No, because if she answered it would give away her position too and alert the man to the fact they were no longer together—if he didn't already know. What should he do? He got awkwardly to his knees, the Mylar blanket rustling around him. Would the guy be able to hear that? Perhaps he should drop the blanket. Make a run for it like he had before. But no, that'd ended in disaster, he had to stay here and trust that Aurora would handle this.

He popped his head up again and saw that the guy was

closer now. Another bullet buzzed into the snow nearby as he dived for cover. This guy was deadly serious. He was out to murder them both.

All of a sudden, three gunshots rang out in succession. Taking a chance, Jiro peeked over again in time to see the man take two stumbling steps, then turn toward the direction the bullets had come. Aurora stood about fifty meters away from him, closer to the shoreline. She had her arms raised, gun pointed in his direction. She must've been hiding there all along, jumping up and taking him my surprise from behind.

Had she hit the guy? Jiro wasn't sure, because if she had it didn't seem to stop him. He began to run toward her, raising his rifle as he did so. Aurora didn't flinch, however, firing off two more shots from her weapon. Jiro wasn't sure what happened first; the man seemed to falter, but then suddenly he just disappeared.

As if he had fallen through the ice.

Which was exactly what'd happened.

Jiro got to his knees, preparing to stand up, but Aurora sent him a look that made him stay where he was. Without lowering the gun, she stalked slowly toward where the man had disappeared, lifting her knees high to get through the virgin snow, testing every step before she took it. He couldn't take his eyes off her, off the scene unfolding in front of him. At last she reached the spot where the man had fallen in. He watched as she leaned down, weapon still held in one hand, but he couldn't see what she was doing with the layer of snow blocking his view. Finally, she straightened and tucked the gun into her shoulder holster. He took that as a sign it was safe and stood up.

Aurora made her way toward him.

"Is he dead?" Jiro asked. She merely nodded in reply, her face grim. As she got closer, he could see she was nearly as cold as he was. Her teeth were chattering, and she wrapped her arms around her body. She'd been lying in the snow on the ice with only a sweater to keep out the biting cold. It seemed they were both in danger of suffering hypothermia now.

Before he could open his mouth and ask how the man had died—was it by gunshot or drowning—she said, "We're going to head toward that cabin over there." She lifted her hand and pointed behind his right shoulder. "Our priority now is to get warm, and we can't stay out here. Can you walk?" Stopping in front of him, she studied his face. He studied her in return. Dark eyes were wide and alert, her mouth was a grim line in her pale features. She'd just shot a man—probably killed him—and her main priority even now was to keep him alive.

"Of course I can," he replied, lifting his chin. He wanted to stop her and ask the same thing; she was shaking like a leaf. But it was perhaps as much a reaction to the adrenaline as to the cold, so he didn't question her. They would be warmer if they could both wrap themselves in the blanket, but that would make walking across the thigh-deep snow almost impossible. And he knew without asking that she wouldn't accept the blanket if he offered it to her, so he gritted his teeth and kept quiet.

"Where is your phone?" she asked suddenly, the question taking him by surprise.

"Umm, it was in the front pocket of my jacket." He pointed to the pile of clothing lying on the ice. He wondered if it would still be working after being dunked in the freezing water. She rummaged around until she found it.

"I'm turning it off," she announced. "I don't want to give that bastard any more chances to track us." It was a good idea, and he wished he'd thought of it. They might not have reception out here right now, but you never knew.

"We need to make it back to the deer tracks, that will be the safest route," she said, gathering up his wet clothes, and barely stopping to tuck them under her arm, before she took off in the direction of the opposite side of the lake. They were about midway, perhaps a little closer to the other side, but to Jiro, it looked like they were going to walk to the ends of the Earth.

But he was going to make it to that cabin if it killed him.

It took them fifteen excruciating minutes to get to the other side. By that time, his teeth had stopped chattering. Perhaps the exertion had warmed him up a bit, even though he still felt frozen through, the Mylar blanket flapping around him as he walked. All the while he had kept his gaze focused on the red dot partially hidden by the trees. He was eternally grateful for the Swedish tradition of painting their houses and cabins a very particular red color. Instead of blending into the environment, they stood out, which was a blessing for them today.

Aurora led them carefully across the danger zone near the edge of the lake, where the ice was often thinner, and then they trudged up the slight incline and into the trees. "Do you know who owns this place?" he asked, but realized even as he phrased the question how silly it was.

"No. But whoever they are, I'm sure they won't mind if we use it to save our lives," she replied with a grim smile.

Jiro was totally shocked when Aurora stomped up the two stairs to the little front entrance and calmly swung the door open. "It's not locked?" He'd been expecting her to have to break in.

"You're in Sweden now," she shot back over her shoulder. "We're a very trusting crowd, especially up here in the north. And what would be the point of locking it? If someone was intent on breaking in, they would." She shrugged and gestured him to come inside. It was dark, and it took a few moments for his eyes to adjust. The place was small and dank, clearly not used very often. The hut contained the basics, only a little better than the one they had rescued Kenichi from the other day. A fireplace, a rustic bench running along one wall—probably used as a bed—a small wooden table and two rickety chairs. The worn material hanging over the windows did little to block out any light. That was it. Not the homey, comforting cabin he'd been hoping for, but it was shelter nonetheless.

"At least they've kept the place stocked with wood," Aurora commented, draping his now frozen-stiff clothes over the back of a chair, and dumping her little black bag on the table. "I'll light the fire, you get your wet pants and boots off," she said, sending him a look that said she would brook no argument. He watched as she removed her gloves and fumbled with the zip on her bag; her fingers clearly as cold and useless as his.

Even though he kept his hands wrapped tightly inside the blanket, they were still numb and barely working. But he did as he was told, dropping the silver covering onto the bench and sitting down so he could attack his shoelaces. He felt like he was a hundred years old; he could hardly work the knot free, and he swore more than once out loud at the bothersome thing. He did finally get them both undone, but then he struggled to get the wet, heavy boots off his feet. He looked up to see Aurora crouched by the fireplace, coaxing a small flame into life.

"I can't…" He wasn't sure how to phrase it, didn't want to tell her that he was as helpless as a child.

"I'm coming," she said, glancing back over her shoulder. She helped him tug off his boots, which made a loud sucking noise as they suddenly released, almost sending her onto her backside. She pulled off his soaking wet socks as well, and his feet felt like blocks of ice, and now that they were outside the support of the boots, they began to throb with cold. Without comment, she pulled him up to standing, and helped him undo the buttons of his pants, then pushed him back to sitting so she could tug each leg free. Should he be embarrassed that she was helping him undress like he was a three-year-old? He was now sitting in his boxer briefs, her too-tight jacket wrapped around his torso, but couldn't raise the energy to feel anything but relief. Her fingers had been like ice where they touched his bare skin.

"You're just as cold as I am," he commented.

"Nearly," she agreed. "Which is why we both need to get warm." Sitting down beside him, she began to undo her own boots. He watched as she removed her socks and then pants as well, leaving her standing in the tiny room with only her brief panties on. The purely male part of him took note of the fact they were black lace. As well as her nicely shaped legs and athletic calves. But the rest of him was still wondering how he was going to get warm without any dry clothes to put on.

"I'm going to stoke up the fire, really get it blazing," she said without preamble, as if standing half naked in a rundown cabin in the middle of a Swedish wilderness was an everyday occurrence. "Can you spread out the blanket so that we can lie on it on the bench? But leave enough room to wrap around both of us."

"Both of us?" he asked stupidly.

"Shared body heat is the best way to get warm," she added matter-of-factly.

Aha, the plan was beginning to dawn on him. He did as she had asked, making a little bed for the two of them on the bench. It wasn't very wide, but they both should be able to fit side-by-side. "What now?" he asked.

"Take the jacket off, we'll use it as an extra cover over both of us. Then you lie down and get comfy. I'll be with you in a second." He lay down, the silver material icy to the touch and watched as she finished her task of hanging up his wet clothing as best she could near the now-raging fire to try and get them dry. He wished she would hurry up, because he was beginning to shiver again. At last she walked over and stood beside the bench, staring down at him. Was that hesitation he saw in her eyes? Whatever it was, she drew in a deep breath as if reaching a decision, then lifted her own sweater and thermal shirt over her head, revealing a matching lacy bra. The all-male part of him woke up a little more at the sight. She was bloody gorgeous. Better even than he'd imagined. But he didn't have long to take in all that glorious skin, as she crawled in beside him, draping her jacket over the top of their bodies, then wrapping the silver blanket around them both, tucking it in over their feet, and pulling it up over the heads as she lay down, so they were cocooned together. Her skin was icy to the touch, much the same as his. But her breath was warm on his cheek as she settled her head against his shoulder.

Well now, this was much better. He had to say he was almost enjoying himself. He wasn't any warmer yet, but there was something special about having her body draped against his. Something intimate, and deeply satisfying.

CHAPTER THIRTEEN

Aurora was exquisitely aware of each and every spot along her body that was touching his. They were like two frozen icicles swathed together, but that didn't stop her nerves jangling. She wasn't even sure this body-heat thing was going to work because she'd never been in a situation exactly like this before. But it was part of her police training; survival in extreme conditions. And this was what they'd told her to do. The only thing they hadn't mentioned was that being skin to skin with someone—especially someone you were highly attracted—to could be an excruciating experience. Even though his skin was cold, she remained acutely aware of his lithe body, of the muscles in his arm as he wrapped it around her waist, of the firmness of his pecs where her cheek rested, the curling hairs tickling her cheek.

He'd been shaking like a leaf when she'd first nestled in next to him, but now the shaking had almost ceased, and he'd gone as still as a statue, almost as if he was holding himself completely motionless. Was that for her sake? Or had he just lapsed into a hypothermic coma?

"You okay?" she asked, suddenly worried.

"Yep, never better," he replied. But his words were clipped, as if he were keeping them tightly controlled.

"Are you getting any warmer?"

"Nope. What about you?"

"Not really," she admitted. She was beginning to doubt the wisdom of her training, but before she could say anything more, he seemed to lose some of his stiffness.

"Maybe we need to get closer then," he said, wrapping his arms tighter around her middle and snuggling right in against her. And she did the same, until they were almost melded together, and she couldn't tell where she ended and he started anymore. "How about now?" he asked once they were settled, but she could barely form a reply. His chin was resting on top of her head, as she nestled into the hollow next to his collarbone.

"Umm, better, I think," she said at last. And that was an understatement. She wasn't sure her insides were any warmer, but her skin was certainly tingling from the feeling of him against her, sending shots of heat up and down her limbs. They lay in awkward silence, Aurora suddenly unsure what to say, or even whether to speak, worried it might break the spell. The only sound was the crackle of the fire as it took hold. A very peaceful sound, if Aurora had to say so. At least Jiro seemed like he was going to be fine after his dunk in the freezing water. And she needed him to be okay. Because he had scared the shit out of her when he'd disappeared through the ice. The sight had transported her back eight years in the blink of an eye, to the lake near where her family had lived on the outskirts of Malmö. When her mother had died.

"I'm sorry if I scared you today. I shouldn't have run off like that," he said into the stillness. She could hear the contrition in his voice and almost recoiled away from him in shock. How had he known what she'd been thinking? Something about his remorse made her want to tell the truth, however. Something about the intimacy of them trapped together trying to get warm made her want to open up.

"You did scare me," she admitted. "Probably more than you'll know. When I saw you fall… I panicked. I almost forgot all my training. I just wanted to rush over and save you." She wasn't telling him this to make him feel guilty about disobeying her, and she hoped he understood this.

"I know," he whispered. "I put us both in horrible danger."

"You did. But it wasn't just that. I lost my mother in similar circumstances. And I was terrified I was going to lose you the same way."

"Holy fuck, Aurora, I'm so sorry."

"How could you have known?" she said, a touch brusquely, not really wanting his pity, more his understanding. And even if he had known, she doubted it would've stopped him from running in the heat of the moment. "But I wanted you to know, because those memories affected me too, affected the way I reacted. The eight-year anniversary of her passing is in a week, and she's been on my mind, influencing my decision-making process, probably for the worse. So maybe we're both a bit to blame for the debacle out on the ice. Maybe I should never have taken you that way." Maybe she should've followed her gut instinct and gone around the lake instead of the logical course of straight across it. But then that would've led them straight into the arms of the sniper.

Eight years ago, she hadn't seen her mother fall through the ice; she'd been too busy sulking by the edge of the lake because of something her father had said to her earlier that morning. She'd mentioned to him that the local community center was looking for volunteers, and she thought she might sign up now that she had turned eighteen. But he'd scoffed at the idea, asking her why she would want to work for free with a bunch of deadbeats and druggies who lived on the street. He was always dragging her down, telling her she wasn't good enough. Then he'd forced them all to go ice fishing with him, said that they needed to do more things *as a family*. Yeah, right, they only ever did *things as a family* that he wanted to do. It was always his way or the highway. Astrid had managed to disappear a few minutes prior, sneaking back to the house so she could go on her phone with her friends. Karl was always more lenient with Astrid; she knew she wouldn't get into real trouble for stealing away.

It was the sudden, strange silence that made Aurora look up from where she was sitting on a fallen log on the lake edge. Her father was standing like a statue, one hand on his fishing rod with the line still positioned over the hole he had drilled in the ice, the other raised halfway in the air, as if to make a point—he liked to talk with his hands and he was always making some point or other. But her mother was nowhere to be seen, and it took Aurora a few seconds to figure out why. When Aurora had last looked up, her mother had wandered away from where her father had set up the chairs in the middle for them all to sit and watch him fish, heading towards the opposite side of the lake. Karl always checked the ice first before they ventured out, and he gave them strict instructions to follow his footsteps, to make sure they stayed away from the thin patches. So, it was unusual for her mother to just wander off.

At first, Aurora had scanned the far bank, wondering if her mother had crossed to the other side and was now walking in the woodland. But she wouldn't have had time to make that distance since Aurora had last glanced up. So, her disappearance didn't make sense until she suddenly understood.

"Fader," she had screamed. "Where is Mamma?" But her father didn't move, didn't react to her screaming. So she ran out onto the ice, completely ignoring his instructions to stay in his footsteps. It took her precious minutes to run to where her father still stood unmoving, even as she yelled at him to do something. What was he waiting for?

Right before she reached Karl, he slowly began to wind in his fishing reel, placing it tidily on one of the chairs just as she skidded to a halt beside him.

"Where is she? What has happened? You have to go and rescue her!" she yelled, tears streaming down her face.

"You stay here," he ordered, face strangely devoid of all emotion. Then he began to walk—not run—in the direction she had last seen her mother go, his gait strangely robotic and awkward. Why wasn't he hurrying?

Unable to watch him dawdle anymore, she ran, meaning to rescue her mother herself. But her father had reached out and snagged her jacket as she raced past, jerking her backward, and shoving her to the ground. Then he leaned in and snarled in her face. "I told you to stay there. So you bloody well stay." He'd pushed her so hard that her head had banged on the ice. She'd lain on the ice stunned, tears running freely down her face, unable to fathom what was going on. Why her father was acting so strangely. She'd sat and watched as her father finally made it to where her mother had fallen through. He stood staring down for many, many moments, before he dropped to his knees, then began to commando crawl across the ice—just as she had done when she rescued Jiro. Aurora knew it was too late before he'd even reached down into the water and pulled up her mother's lifeless body.

Later on he said he'd been trying to protect her from the sight of her dead mother in the freezing water, but Aurora knew that wasn't the case. Something else had been going on, but she had never figured out exactly what. Had they had an argument? Whatever it was, she had a strong feeling that Karl had hesitated long enough so that her mother never got the help she needed. She also had a strong feeling that her mother may not have fought to live either. There had been no splashing, no yelling, no attempt to rescue herself that Aurora could see. The ice had broken beneath her feet, and she'd just let herself sink to the bottom. Of course, Aurora could never truly know what was going on in the heads of either of her parents, but she'd never recovered from that day. And had left soon afterwards, taking a job in Gothenburg at a non-profit charity for homeless kids, just to get away from her father. She'd never spoken of it to anyone except Astrid. And Astrid hadn't wanted to hear Aurora's theories; she was perhaps too young to really understand. Mårten knew the bare details—that her mother had drowned in a frozen lake— but she'd never let on her true suspicions to him. Never told him she thought her father had let her mother die.

"You didn't do anything wrong," Jiro insisted. "You did everything right. You were amazing."

His words of praise lifted her heart. Even if she didn't fully believe him, it was nice to know he had faith in her. Nice to know that he at least thought she had got it right. Another silence descended over them, but this time it wasn't awkward, as Jiro pulled her in even tighter, and she relaxed into him.

"What's going to happen to the man in the lake?" Jiro's question broke the silence, and she was strangely grateful for it, as it took her mind off the tumult of memories that were now cascading through her mind. As well as the tumult of sensations that was filling her senses because of Jiro's intimate closeness. They were so entwined it was almost as if they were in the afterglow of a lovemaking session. That thought had Aurora squirming with mortification, and so she concentrated on his question.

"We'll have to retrieve his body. We have specialized divers for that job," she replied. The image of the man floating face down in the frozen water would probably haunt her till the end of her days. It was her bullets that had killed him; she knew that much. But she had reached down and turned him over just to make sure he was dead. Pulling him out onto the ice would've cost her more energy than she had left. He would just have to stay there until she could call out a unit to retrieve him. The image of the dead man floating in the water was nothing compared to the primal fear she had felt as she watched Jiro fall through the ice, however. At least Jiro's story had a happy ending.

She knew she'd have to make the call to HQ soon, but she'd checked her own phone for reception before she'd taken off her clothes, and there had been no signal. She might be able to find another network she could connect to that would allow her to dial emergency services if she walked farther up the hill to the north, but that would have to wait until she was warm enough to make the journey.

"Do you think we're safe now? Was there only that one man after us?" Jiro asked the question that had been playing on her own mind.

"I can't be sure," she replied truthfully. "Especially because you won't tell me what's going on, apart from the fact it has something to do with the Yakuza, and frankly that scares the shit out of me." She wasn't proud of herself for that jibe. It'd just come out, but it was probably warranted. "But I'm gonna take a gamble and say that whoever was behind the phone call thought one sniper would be enough to take us out." The sniper could also possibly be the second person involved in the abduction of Kenichi, but that was just conjecture for now.

"Okay, that's good," Jiro replied, but she could hear thoughtfulness in his voice. Another silence settled between them, and she realized she was indeed getting warmer. The fire would be helping to take the chill off the air, but their bodies entwined was doing the job. Her eyelids felt suddenly heavy. Now that she was heating up, and the adrenaline had left her body, she was surprisingly fatigued, but she fought the growing lethargy. She was surprised when Jiro spoke again. "You're right; you deserve to know more. I've been a dickhead, keeping a promise to Taro because I thought I was helping him. But clearly, I'm not, because we haven't found him yet."

That surprised her. Was he about to tell her everything? Well, she wasn't going to argue because information was power, and right now they needed to scrabble back all the control they could get.

"No, we haven't," she answered carefully. "And I'm beginning to think we were never intended to. This whole thing was a distraction to keep us occupied and isolated and then eliminated. We were a problem they needed to get rid of."

"I can see that now," Jiro replied. As he spoke, his fingers began to trace circles on her lower back. It was clearly an unconscious move, but Aurora stilled beneath his touch. "I was hoping that Taro was somehow handling things behind the scenes, and I didn't want to jeopardize that. But I guess it's too late now."

"Yes," she agreed. "It was only sheer luck we both weren't killed. I'm sure he probably had some plan to put a bullet in both of us and then drop us in the frozen lake. Our bodies wouldn't be found for months, not at least until the spring thaw next year." It was a sobering thought, one that she hadn't allowed to fully take shape in her mind yet. If Jiro hadn't fallen through the ice, who knew how things might have ended. Perhaps in a way, it'd been a fortunate mistake. Because if they'd both been pinned down in the middle of the lake, the sniper would've been able to wait them out, and probably pick them off at his leisure. But when they'd separated so suddenly, and he'd lost track of them, it'd forced him to move location, which had given Aurora the few minutes she needed to reposition herself.

"Yep, it could have ended badly, and I'm so sorry for that,

Aurora. You have been nothing but supportive to me, and all I've done is keep secrets and put you in terrible danger." His hand on her back stopped circling for a second, and she could hear him grinding his teeth together. "I'm going to make you a promise that from here on in, I will not keep anything from you. I will be an open book." This was interesting and somewhat unexpected, but she would take it. He was right, she had helped him even against her better judgement, breaking her own personal rules, for reasons she still couldn't really fathom. It was about time he paid some of that faith back.

"I'll tell you what I know so far. You can ask as many questions as you need, and I'll try to answer them as best I can. Okay?"

"Okay." He started up the circles again, and she almost wanted to purr like a cat at the wonderful sensations. Instead, she tried to focus on what he was saying.

"Like I said, Taro was involved with a gang that is part of the Yakuza." She nodded against his chest, but didn't speak. "But I didn't tell you what his relationship was to them. He was smuggling weapons from the US into Japan for them, so they could wage their stupid gangland wars."

Okay, that was a little unexpected, but then she hadn't really had time to think about Jiro's revelation earlier that there was indeed a connection with the Yakuza. Sweden had no problems with these particular gangland mobs, especially not this far north, and so they were never really on her radar. Of course they had an Interpol division based down in Stockholm, which might well have had dealings with this type of thing, but in her limited experience, she had never come across anything like this before. She waited for him to continue.

"Taro told me it all started off rather tame, but then he got dragged in deeper and deeper, until he couldn't tell what was morally right or wrong anymore." Jiro was trying to defend his brother, but she didn't really need to hear that bit. If Taro was involved in gun smuggling, then he was a criminal, end of story. In her experience, most criminals had some sort of sad past or history they would use as a reason why they'd embarked on their criminal activities in the first place. But none of the sob stories mattered in the end. Mårten kept telling her not everything was black-and-white, there were shades of gray in every situation. And maybe later on in her career, she might soften her stance, but right now all she knew was that people who did bad things deserved to end up in jail.

"Things finally came to a head when they asked him to smuggle something big, something really big that scared him."

"What do you mean?" She lifted her head slightly, wanting to look him in the eye, but their silver cocoon wrappings kept her locked in place, so she rested her cheek back on his chest again. "Do you know what they wanted him to move?"

"Taro thinks it might have been nuclear material."

"Holy shit." That was big stuff; even a small-town constable like her knew that much.

"When Taro suspected that was what they wanted, he decided enough was enough. He was working on a way to get himself free of his commitments."

Commitments. Aurora nearly scoffed out loud. The guy had made his own bed, so how did he ever think it was going to be easy to stop once he'd started?

"But he had to make sure his family was safe before he did so. Which he did. He sent them to stay with an uncle."

Oh. Aurora had never considered the older brother might have a family. That added an extra dynamic to the situation. Why did the criminals never think about their families, think about the consequences of their actions when they first started down the path? Aurora had never been able to answer that question, but she decided that greed had a lot to do with it. Greed and power. And she would never say this to Jiro, but his brother was very firmly in the same boat.

"I think when the gang couldn't easily get their hands on Taro's wife and children, they decided to target my father instead."

"Let me guess, they didn't kill him because they just wanted to send Taro a message," Aurora interjected.

"Yes, that's what we suspect. But once Taro arrived in Luleå and knew Papa was safe, he was determined to go through with his plan. He didn't want this to keep happening. Didn't want to have to keep looking over his shoulder all the time."

"And his plan was?" she prompted.

"He was hoping to fly back to America as soon as tonight so that he could attend a meeting with an FBI agent. He believed a friend of his in the LA police department had set it up for him, and he was going to negotiate a deal."

Aurora drew in a sharp breath, and then pursed her lips. Her warm drowsiness disappeared. If only Jiro had been forthcoming with this all along, they might not be lying almost naked together, trying not to freeze to death. Then she stopped to consider that statement. Lying naked together, maybe it wasn't such a bad thing after all. But then logic overtook her carnal side.

"My partner, Inspector Viskten, has a friend, Jacob, who works for the FBI over in Seattle. If you'd told me this earlier, maybe we could've avoided this whole situation."

"Oh."

Was that all he could say? Why were men so annoying? She wanted to sit up and glare at him. But she was enveloped in this swaddle, and also found it extremely hard to stay angry at him when he continued to stroke her back so tenderly. So instead, she poked him hard in the chest.

"Ouch," he flinched away from her pointy finger, but his tone was amused.

"Jacob used to be Mårten's partner before he moved to Seattle last year. Jacob will do just about anything for Mårten, and vice versa. I'm sure he will sort something out. I just need to get hold of Mårten."

"Sorry." Again he sounded contrite, but she wondered if she could believe him. This was a complicated path they were treading. There were so many secrets and lies between them. He'd already held so much back from her, could she ever really trust him? Even though he said he was an open book now, she still had niggling doubts. She wasn't sure where this was going—whatever this was—or even if she wanted it to go anywhere. But one thing was for sure: there were certainly smoking-hot vibes like she'd never felt before.

"I know," she said on a sigh.

Talking about Mårten brought the email she sent him to mind. It was still a good six hours before he would receive it. What should they do until then? Should they wait here and stay warm? Or walk up the hill to find reception? There were so many things she should be doing right now, but her mind was becoming foggy. She hadn't managed much sleep last night, getting in late after staying up with Jiro and his father, and the exertion of trekking through the snow for hours on end, on top of the huge adrenaline burst during the shootout, she was fried. She was still trying to puzzle out what her next priority should be when she fell fast asleep.

CHAPTER FOURTEEN

Jiro knew the exact moment Aurora fell asleep. He felt her go limp beside him, arm heavy where it draped over his chest, all tension draining out of her as her breathing became slow and rhythmic. He enjoyed the sensation of her warm breath floating over his chest. Poor thing, she must be absolutely exhausted. He was feeling much the same way, now finally warm and drowsy in their little bundle, and he knew he would let sleep claim him soon too. If only he could get rid of all these recriminations jamming up inside his head. How many different ways could he be a dickhead? His actions today had been less than satisfactory. Jiro prided himself on his normally quick thinking, as well as his knowledge of the outdoors. All of that experience had fled at the sound of that shot firing across the snow, and now he was more than disappointed in himself. He was disgusted. With the way he had acted, as well as the way he had treated Aurora. But he was going to make up for all that; he made a solemn promise to himself.

Aurora's story about her mother's passing had hit him straight in the solar plexus. He had lost his own mother exactly eight years ago, almost to the day, as well. It was one more reason Kenichi had asked him to come on this cruise. So they could remember Deborah Nashimori. She hadn't died suddenly in a traumatic accident, instead slipping away ever so slowly, as leukemia drained her body. He had refrained from mentioning this today, however, not wanting to take anything away from Aurora's story. But it was an interesting connection that the two of them had. Both losing their mothers at a highly impressionable age. And then both being raised by a single father. They seemed to share the fact that they had issues with their remaining parent.

Aurora's admonishment that he should've told her sooner about to plan to meet with the FBI had also hit home. He'd kept the secret out of loyalty to his brother, but that loyalty was probably misguided, and now he was drowning in self-reproach. Perhaps if he'd insisted she stay in the room last night when Taro revealed the truth, she could've told them then about her partner's connection to the FBI, and all this might have been stopped. Now, because of his stupid pride and his brother's stupid stubbornness, everything had got away from them. Where was Taro now? Was he even still alive? Jiro liked to think so because without him the Kyodo-Kai gang couldn't continue their smuggling operation. So, a better conclusion would be they were holding him somewhere to force him to agree to their terms. Which meant he probably didn't know that Jiro and Aurora were supposed to be dead right now.

And then even after all of his bad behavior toward Aurora, a part of Jiro couldn't ignore how much he was attracted to her. Wanted to make love to her. Earlier, when Aurora had first stripped off and climbed in beside him, it had taken Jiro nearly everything he had to keep his lustful thoughts at bay; the last thing she needed was to feel him with a raging hard-on, when she was only trying to save them both from hypothermia. He even began counting backwards from one-thousand in his head, just to keep the blood from rushing to his groin. Her body had felt so good against his, ice-cold as they both were. When he'd suggested they get even closer on the pretext of sharing more body heat, he'd reveled in the feel of her long legs wrapped around his. He possibly would've kissed her if the opportunity had arrived. Perhaps it was better they were wrapped so tight in their survival blanket that they could barely move. He wasn't sure how to unravel his feelings toward this complicated woman. She had very quickly wormed her way into his heart with her feisty nature, quick wit, and formidable need to make sure justice was served at all costs. He certainly hadn't come here to fall in love. That was the last thing on his agenda. And yet…

He was in a bit of a pickle, he decided. But now wasn't the time to try to figure everything out. So he lay there listening to the fire crackling, just enjoying the feel of their bodies intertwined. Aurora's soft breathing finally lulled him into a calmer frame of mind, his eyelids becoming so heavy he succumbed to the effort of trying to keep them open and let them drift closed. If she was prepared to take an hour or so to recover, then so was he. Sleep was a form of healing, and who knew, he might have some answers when he finally awoke.

* * *

Jiro woke with a start when Aurora stretched beside him. It took him a few seconds to remember where he was. But when he did, he relaxed back down onto the hard bench. He was exactly where he wanted to be right now, snuggled up with a beautiful woman inside an isolated cabin. What could be more romantic?

But then she moved next to him again, and the spell was broken.

"How long have we been asleep?" he asked groggily.

"Not too long," she replied. "The sun is still above the horizon. An hour at the most. It's probably only mid-afternoon." At least they hadn't slept the whole day away.

But it meant they'd lose the light soon; these god-awful dark winters would drive him crazy if he lived here.

"Well, your plan worked. I'm toasty warm now," he said, moving his arm out a little from where it had been cramped into an awkward position wrapped around her waist—not that he would've had it any other way.

"Me too." As she said this, she stretched again, pushing her pert breasts against the side of his chest. The surge of lust was immediate. The sexual desire he'd forced away earlier came back with a vengeance. How could any hot-blooded male not react to having this gorgeous, almost naked woman beside him? Right then, he made a decision.

There were things they should be doing, phone calls to be made, and dead bodies to be recovered. They needed to get up and get moving, but suddenly none of that mattered. Jiro knew he was going to kiss her, and he hoped she'd respond the same way she had earlier. Their kiss back at the cabin had been a spontaneous thing, born of intense need and emotional adversity. This time he was going to kiss her properly, deep and incisive, an exploration that would let her know how much she had bewitched him. He wanted to taste her mouth again, set his tongue exploring her cute bunny teeth once more.

As she began to wriggle to get free, he snagged her around the waist and held her tight. With the other hand, he worked the silver blanket away from his shoulders, so he was free to then use his thumb and forefinger to reach down and tip her chin up and access her lips. He wasn't asking this time, he was taking. Her surprise at the touch of his mouth quickly turned to greedy hunger as she sucked on his lower lip. But he was determined to take his time, so instead of plundering her mouth with his tongue—as he so wanted to do—he swept it across her lower lip, gently tasting the corner of her mouth. Aurora made a noise, small like a lost kitten, and yet it shot straight through him, piercing him with a desire so strong he wanted to growl like a wild animal.

The hand that'd been wrapped around her waist drifted up to find the soft swell of her breast beneath the lace of her bra. He already knew the details of the black lacy bra; they'd been etched into his mind as she had stood in front of him, undressing. Had she worn this bra for him this morning? It was an enticing thought. Shimmying his fingers beneath the under wire, he found her nipple, which was peaked and plump, and he played with it, delighting in the way it hardened to his touch.

Aurora made another small noise, grinding her hips against him. At least he knew she was enjoying this. One of her hands was tangled in his hair, pulling his head down so she could get more of him, and the other was stroking his thigh from where it was trapped between their bodies. Soon, she managed to wriggle free a little and now the stroking was much closer to the junction of his thigh. Much closer to his…

He was burning up. "Holy mother of God, Aurora." Before he quite knew how it happened, he had worked his way on top of her. His cock was as hard as a rock, their underwear the only thing keeping them apart. He wanted to be inside her. She groaned and tilted her hips up to grind against his. It seemed she wanted the same thing. Then something occurred to him. He mentally double-checked himself, but came up with the same answer. *Shit*.

"No condom," he groaned against the corner of her mouth. He hadn't even brought one on the ship with him, that was how little he'd expected to hook up with anyone. Was it too much to hope that she might have one stashed somewhere?

"Me neither," came her muffled reply, confirming his worst fears. They should probably stop now then, before things became too heated, and he might not be able to. But then, he was nothing if not inventive, and they were many ways he could pleasure her without resorting to penetration. Why should he let this magic moment get away from them? Leaving her mouth, he wriggled his way down her body, shrugging the restrictive coverings away from his shoulders and loosening them from underneath her hips.

Using his tongue, he dipped into the contours of her body as he went; her collarbone, over the mound of her breast then down into the slight concave of her stomach, and up over her jutting hipbone. His actions dragged cool air in around their warm bodies, and he could see the skin of her torso pebbling; while the fire had taken the chill off the room, it certainly wasn't the ideal temperature to be naked making love in here. But she didn't seem to mind, as her fingers strayed to scratch long arcs down his back, then run up to tangle in his thick hair, her head thrown back in abandon as she relished his tongue on her skin.

He made his way, down and down until he found the juncture of her thighs, moving aside her panties, so that he could tease with his tongue until she was writhing on the bench, finally opening for him. Jiro had a skillful tongue; he knew this without being conceited. Many women had told him just how good he was. And now he put his skills to good use, licking and tasting, sucking and pressing until Aurora's hands clamped in his hair and she rocked her hips up and down with his rhythm. It didn't take long before she tensed around him, then called out his name, long and loud. He rode out her climax with his tongue, his own cock pulsing with need as he pushed her harder and harder until she collapsed, gasping onto the bench.

He moved back up to her head, so they lay panting, side by side, as she recovered, small shudders still wracking her body.

After many long minutes, she whispered into his ear, "That was…um… Let's just say that was intense. I'm usually a slow-burn kind of girl."

He levered up onto one elbow to look at her. Was she blushing? He wasn't sure exactly what to take from her comment, but he was pretty sure it was a compliment. If she didn't normally climax this fast, then he'd done a good thing. Perhaps she was even telling him she had never come on a man's tongue before, and if that was the case, then he needed to do it again, soon.

"But." She tilted her head coquettishly, the blush completely forgotten now. "I think it's my turn to find out a little about your preferences now." She pushed him down, and levered her leg over his body, so she was now the one on top.

"Oh, no," he protested. "You don't need to…Oh, God…" But it was too late, and he never finished his sentence, couldn't in fact speak any more, as she tugged down his boxer shorts and her lips descended upon him, her fingers typing out a tattoo upon his skin as she ran her hands up and down his body, and then expertly wrapped them around his cock. He'd always prided himself on his self-restraint when it came to controlling his own climax. But with Aurora…

All thoughts disappeared as he let his body's carnal cravings take over. It didn't take him long, he was almost ashamed at how quickly he came. He was consumed by the moment, crying out in ecstasy as he pulsed and writhed, completely losing control. But he had already been so hot and hard watching Aurora climax that it probably wasn't surprising. For the second time in only a few minutes, they lay side-by-side, panting and replete, Aurora with a small, smug smile hovering on her face.

"I like that I can make you lose it like that," she said, lifting her chin onto her palm so she could look down at him.

"I like it too," he replied, surprising himself. He'd been the commanding one in all his previous relationships. Not that he was superior to women, just that he liked to be the one to control the ebb and flow of sex. It was different with Aurora, somehow. He'd started off controlling the situation, but she'd taken over with such ease. She hadn't dominated him so much as encouraged him to be himself. He was surprised at how playful she was during lovemaking; almost the complete opposite of her everyday persona. Maybe taking off the uniform helped remove the constraint she had to keep in her professional life.

As she stared up at him, the glint of firelight reflected off one of her earrings, and he reached up a finger to touch it. Up close, he could see they were actually made of filigree strands of silver, intricately woven into a heart shape. "These are beautiful," he said.

"Thank you." An emotion that he couldn't quite pin down flittered across her face before she smiled and added, "They were a present for my eighteenth birthday. Jewelry is usually a no-no when I'm on duty, but these studs are small enough to pass inspection." So, it was as he thought; women in the force weren't really allowed to wear earrings, but these seemed special to her. Just as he began to wonder who had given them to her as a present, her features puckered, and her smile turned upside down. "But now I guess we have to get back to reality." Of course they did, but that didn't make him any less sad that this precious moment was coming to an end. "I'm not going to psychoanalyze this thing we did today. There's too much else going on in my life right now. I just want you to know that it was good," she added.

He reached up and gently laid his hand along the side of her cheek. "It was very, very good," he clarified, then kissed her long and deep, to seal their accord.

This time when she moved to get up, he let her go. She got out of their makeshift bed and went over to stoke the fire, which had died right down while they were otherwise occupied. Jiro stared at her body in open appreciation, admiring the way her lacy underwear highlighted her curves. One day he would get her completely naked, but today it was enough just to see her like this.

"Your clothes are not completely dry yet, but they'll have to do," she said, testing each of the garments she'd draped over the table and chairs next to the fire to dry. He wasn't looking forward to putting damp clothing back on, but if he hadn't been so stupid in the first place, then he'd still be warm and dry. Then again, if he hadn't been so stupid, he might not have just been intimate with Aurora in an isolated cabin in the middle of the woods, either. He knew which scenario he preferred.

Disentangling himself from the coverings, he got up with a groan. The rough floorboards were cold beneath his bare feet, and the chilly air pebbled his skin. Definitely time to get dressed. They climbed into their clothes in silence, and he went to stand in front of the fire to get warm again. He watched as Aurora ran her fingers through her hair, doing her best to untangle it, before tying it up in a complicated knot at the nape of her neck once more. Watching her was almost as intimate as what they had just done under the covers. He didn't think he would ever get tired of glimpsing that simple little gesture.

What would the owners of this cabin think when they came back to it? Would they be surprised to find someone had stayed here? Or was this a common occurrence? Aurora had said something along the lines that people up here left their cabins purposefully unlocked for just these types of scenarios. The benefit of savings someone's life far outweighed the risk of their cabin being ransacked, it seemed. But this would never happen in America; people there were way less trusting and way less trustworthy.

"What's the plan now?" he asked.

"I'm gonna walk up that hill behind the cabin and see if I can find some sort of reception. We need to call this in, and get units out here pronto to clean up this mess. But it would be better if you—"

"I'm going to come with you," he interrupted, knowing that she was about to tell him to stay in the cabin where it was warm. She narrowed her dark eyes in his direction, and he knew she was mentally debating whether to let him come with her or not. "Aurora, I know you think you have a job to do, and I know I've been really bad at following orders so far, but we are a team now. Whatever you do, wherever you go, I'll be right there beside you. I got you into this, and I want to get you out of it." He understood that if she told him to stay in the cabin and he was stubborn enough to refuse, he would still be just as *bad at following orders*, but he was hoping she didn't push the point. Logically, he knew that she was a trained police officer, and should be able to handle any situation she might find herself in; point in case, rescuing him and then bringing down a sniper all within the space of a few minutes. But if something happened to her out there, and he wasn't there to help, he would never forgive himself.

"Fine," she said at last. "You should know that if you come with me, I'm also going to try to call Mårten. If I get through, I want you to talk to him. Will you do that?" she challenged. The inspector would probably need to be convinced that the FBI should be involved in this case, and he should be the one to put his brother's case forward, so he willingly agreed with an emphatic nod.

For a few seconds he weighed up his next question, but it was important to their game plan from here on in. "What about finding Taro?" he asked. "I know we need to call in police backup, but what if the guy on the other end of those messages finds out? Will that put Taro in danger?"

"Not sure about that one yet," she admitted. "Now we've

turned your phone off, he can't track us that way. I believe he was probably using the sniper as his other method of shadowing us. With him gone, the kidnapper will probably be wondering what's going on, but will hopefully still be in the dark for a little while longer."

"Unless he had more than one henchman out there," Jiro replied darkly. Aurora merely shrugged at that, but it was one more reason that Jiro was determined to accompany her.

The next few hours were spent in the cold, first talking on the phone to Viskten and then waiting for the other police units to arrive, which took nearly two hours. Aurora insisted they wait down by the lake's edge, but periodically, they returned to the cabin to get warm—his clothes were now dry, but standing around in the dark as the temperature plummeted was not fun. Aurora told him they should be glad that at least it wasn't blizzarding, as that would make it very uncomfortable. Swedish people were nothing if not practical.

The first hint that this might turn into a bigger situation than he'd thought came when all the other cops arrived on their snowmobiles. It seemed like there were hundreds of them, but in actual fact they were probably at least fifteen, which felt a bit like overkill. It wasn't like there was a whole gang of Yakuza hordes to be vanquished out here; it was just him and Aurora, and she'd already neutralized the threat. He also hadn't realized that a cop discharging a gun was such a big thing—she was only returning fire, defending herself from a man intent on killing them. But as soon as Inspector Dalström arrived, he strode up to Aurora and officially relieved her of her weapon, which was then sent away for forensic testing, almost as if she was a suspect in a murder rather than an avenger of evil. He also advised her there would be an inquest into the shooting, and asked her to hand over her badge, placing her on desk duty until further notice, which shocked Jiro. But Aurora did everything she was asked without question, clearly understanding the formalities better than he did. Later, she confirmed that whenever there was a police-involved shooting, a strict protocol had to be followed. It was only then he realized this was the first time she'd had to follow that protocol; this was the first time she'd discharged her weapon while on duty, and again that sharp twist of guilt stabbed him through the gut. It was his fault she was going through all of this.

The frozen lake was then set up almost like a scene from a murder mystery movie, with bright lights, people milling around—some of them in white suits, which Jiro assumed were forensics. Once Aurora had walked the inspector through the whole sequence of events, she and Jiro were sent to the cabin, supposedly to stay warm. But he knew it was to keep them out of the way. At least someone had thought to bring them food and hot beverages, which helped to revive Jiro considerably—the chocolate bars Aurora had been keeping in her pocket were now sodden and inedible.

His conversation with Inspector Viskten had gone well. Aurora's partner seemed like he was a man who had his head screwed on right, because he said if Aurora believed Jiro's claims, then so did he. He was going to place a call to his friend in the FBI and get back to them once they returned to HQ.

Jiro was hoping to be allowed to visit his father in hospital once they got back to town, but he was soon disavowed of that notion when Aurora told him they would need to be interviewed—she called it giving a statement—before they were allowed to go anywhere. At least he'd been able to check in on Kenichi by calling the hospital, but the nurse he spoke to reported no change in the old man's status. Which meant he was still in a coma. Jiro's shoulders had sagged at that news, but then Aurora had reminded him that at least he was still alive, and that he needed to stay strong so that when his father did finally recover, he could be there for him.

Now and then he would catch Aurora's eye, and something would pass between them. Their little secret kept him warm, but they never spoke of it.

Afternoon turned into evening, and finally Dalström said he would escort them back to the car on a snowmobile—thank God they didn't have to walk out—and then follow them back to the police HQ in a squad car. Jiro again got the feeling they were being treated more like criminals than heroes, but he kept his mouth shut.

Then evening turned into night as they were firstly interviewed in separate rooms, and then brought together to sit around the conference table, explaining to Dalström and his partner, Constable Moreau, over and over what had happened out there in the snow and why they decided to go without telling anyone, which seemed to be the biggest sticking point for the detective inspector. Aurora continued to answer his questions calmly and directly, but Jiro found himself becoming increasingly frustrated with the merry-go-round of the same questions being asked in a million different ways.

At one stage, Jiro had stopped the proceedings, demanding to know if they had any news of Taro. The constable had been the one to tell him they were still looking for his brother, and he would be the first to know if any new information came to light. The disparaging side of Jiro wondered if this was actually true; were they really even working on finding his brother? Jiro itched to get out of here. He wanted to check in on his father. He wanted to look for Taro, although God knew where he was going to start. But doing something, anything, was better than just sitting around.

It was nearly ten p.m. when Aurora's phone pinged with an incoming message. Jiro had been doing his best to stay awake, but his eyelids kept drooping, and he knew he'd probably nodded off once or twice already. The conversation had mostly been in English, for his sake he presumed, but the droning voices were having a soporific effect.

"Oh, shit." Aurora shot up from her chair. "Sorry, I've got to go."

That woke him up. What was wrong? What message had Aurora just received?

"We haven't finished your debrief," Dalström complained.

"I need to get home. My father is… alone, and the lady I asked to check on didn't turn up as planned." Jiro had noticed Aurora had been getting more and more agitated as time went on, and now he understood why.

"Right then." Dalström's demeanor changed as she explained. "If you need to attend to your family, then you must go." Clearly, family was important to him, which surprised Jiro a little. Until now he'd found Dalström boorish and a by-the-book type of officer. Perhaps there was a soft side to him as well.

Jiro also stood. "I'm going with her." He wasn't taking no for an answer. Not from Aurora and not from Dalström. She was clearly worried about her father, and now so was he. He was also worried about her, but this was a good excuse for him to stay by her side. And it gave him a good reason to get out of this bloody room.

Aurora took her jacket from the back of the chair, and glancing at him once from under lowered brows, she exited the room almost at a run, with him hot on her heels.

"What's going on?" he asked, chasing Aurora down the hallway.

"That was a message from Millie. She only just got my text; she's been down in Stockholm visiting her family. Which means no one has been to check on my dad all day." There was a grim tone in her voice.

"I'm sure he'll be okay," he said, hoping it was true.

"If he is okay, he'll be starving and cranky as a bull. But my dad is not a very patient man. I'm worried he might try to do something…" She never finished her sentence, and it left Jiro to wonder what a man who was practically wheelchair-bound could get up to on his own that might cause a problem? He was about to find out.

CHAPTER FIFTEEN

"Fader," Aurora called as she burst through the front door, Jiro hot on her heels. Not bothering to stop and remove her shoes or jacket, she rounded into the living room and found the TV blaring but no sign of Karl. "Fader, I'm home. I'm so sorry I'm late." She would never live this down, her father would never let her forget her failings. But right now she was feeling very contrite, as if she really was a bad daughter, which was exactly what Karl was going to say when he saw her. But he wasn't in the living room.

Could have taken himself to bed already? Highly unlikely. If he'd missed dinner, he would be starving, and he would want to tell her all about it when she finally got home. She double-checked the living room, noting the Christmas tree still twinkled merrily in the window and nothing else seemed to be amiss.

She was just about to check the kitchen when she passed the stairway leading up to her bedroom and pulled up short. A crumpled heap of what looked like rags lay at the bottom of the stairs.

"Fader," she cried, kneeling down beside him. He was unresponsive and lying at an awkward angle. Her chest tightened, and suddenly she could barely breathe. What if he were dead? She couldn't bring herself to turn him over and check. It was Jiro who got down on the floor beside her, pushed her gently out of the way, reaching to check Karl's carotid artery.

"He's alive," he said, sitting back on his heels. "But I don't think we should move him." Aurora wasn't sure whether to agree or not. She suddenly had no idea what to do. Every coherent thought, every reasoned reaction fled in the face of her father's disaster. "I'll ring for an ambulance," Jiro said calmly. "You should find something to cover him and keep him warm."

"Yes, yes." But it took a few seconds for her legs to get the message that she needed to hop up off the floor. She was back in a flash with a throw rug from the couch, covering him gently. Oh God, she'd known something bad would happen, had felt it in her bones. She shouldn't be relying so much on Millie. The poor woman was upset to find that she'd missed Aurora's message, and terribly apologetic about not being there when she was needed, but it wasn't Millie's fault, not at all. It was Aurora's. She needed to work out a better care plan for her father. This wasn't working.

She reached out her hand to touch her father, but then withdrew it. She had no idea how badly he was hurt. Did he have broken bones? A fractured skull? Internal injuries. The list grew bigger and bigger inside her head. How long had he been lying here? He must've fallen down the stairs. But what was he doing trying to get up to her bedroom in the first place? She glanced up the tall staircase. She made sure the ground floor was wheelchair accessible. But never once did she say she thought her room might cause a problem for her father, because she never dreamed he would want to get up there.

The next half hour became a blur as the ambulance arrived and the paramedics carefully checked Karl and finally got him on a stretcher, making sure to mitigate any spinal injuries. Karl remained unresponsive throughout the whole procedure, and if it hadn't been for Jiro standing steadfastly by her side, Aurora wasn't sure she would've got through it all.

She told the paramedics they would follow the ambulance to the hospital, and she slipped into the driver's seat of her car just as the ambulance pulled out of the driveway. "Thank you," she said to Jiro as he got into the passenger seat beside her. "That's never happened to me before. It's like I was in a complete daze." It was a hard thing to admit. She thought she was tougher than that; she had to be tougher than that if she was going to be a good cop.

"It's called shock, and just because you're a highly trained police officer, it doesn't make you any less susceptible when it's your loved one who's in pain."

Funny, Aurora had never thought of Karl as a *loved one* before. Some days she even thought she hated him. But he was still her flesh and blood, and her reaction today proved that somewhere deep inside she still recognized him as her father.

They followed the ambulance all the way to the hospital, Jiro saying soothing words that she didn't really hear. Then they waited together, Aurora pacing across the waiting room, Jiro keeping step with her, until she told him to check on his own father, who was in another wing of the same hospital. He did so grudgingly but was back in half an hour, telling her there was still no change, and still no sign of Taro either.

She didn't want to comment on the irony of the fact that now both of their fathers were in hospital. What a pair they were. But he said it for her in the end, when she suggested he try and get some sleep on one of the chairs in his father's room—they were both exhausted, and he at least might get some rest—but he refused.

"You were there for me when I was distraught about my papa. I want to be here for you." She looked at him properly for the first time since she'd found her father lying on the floor. He stared back, dark eyes challenging, mouth quirked to one side. She traced his high cheekbones, watched that truant lock of hair fall over his eyes. She could smile and tell him he was being sweet, but that wouldn't be the whole truth. Because she could see behind his provocative gaze that he wanted to be here for her, to support her. It was an interesting revelation, because not many people in her life had actually been there for her.

Without asking, he stepped in and pulled her into his embrace. And she accepted it wholeheartedly, sank into his arms and let out a deep sigh, releasing some of the tension from tonight's events. After their intimate moments in the cabin today, there was a bond between them now. An ease and effortlessness that hadn't been there before. And now she felt safe in his arms too. Which again was a first for her. She was the one who was supposed to make other people feel safe. And earlier today she had done exactly that, kept him safe from the sniper. Perhaps tonight it was her turn to receive instead of always giving.

"Thank you," she said into his neck, accepting his sacrifice with grace. She seemed to be saying that a lot to him this evening. They stayed together for many, many moments, standing in the middle of the room, clasping each other, she drawing calm and resilience from him, him lending her his strength. There was nothing sexual about this embrace, and she was glad he hadn't tried to kiss her, because this was better; it was exactly what she needed.

A nurse bustled by the open doorway, the sound of her shoes squeaking on the linoleum finally breaking them apart. They separated, and she glanced up into his handsome face. He brought his hand up to wipe away a tear with his thumb.

She hadn't even realized she'd been crying.

"Does your little sister know what's going on?" he asked gently.

"Yes." Aurora tried not to sigh with exasperation as she stepped away from him. Astrid had been concerned of course when she'd called to tell her, but not concerned enough to leave her job and come up and see her father. In some ways, Aurora didn't blame her. But in other ways she resented the fact that she was left to deal with their father's problems on her own. And that resentment had boiled over, and she'd finally said some things she regretted. But perhaps they were things Astrid needed to hear, because in the end conscience had got the better of her.

"Astrid is catching the train up tomorrow. She should be here by late afternoon," she told Jiro. It was a good thing that Astrid was coming; it was time she saw how bad their father was getting. Until now, Aurora had been protecting her younger sister from the worst, but that was just delaying the inevitable. Their father was going to need more care than Aurora could give sooner or later. And she didn't know what she was going to do when that time came.

The doctor came into the waiting room, and they both turned to her expectantly—this was the same doctor Aurora had spoken to when they'd first admitted her father, Doctor Hessel. She was tall and extremely skinny, with sharp features, and short dark hair. "He's in recovery. You can come and see him now," she said brusquely. "He suffered a broken hip, a fractured wrist, and head trauma leading to a severe concussion."

Aurora clasped her hand to her mouth. That sounded awful. But then she quickly remembered who she was and where she was. She might not be in her police uniform, but in this small town where most people would know who she was, she was expected to act a particular way. Steeling herself, she squared her shoulders and nodded.

"At the moment, the head trauma is the most serious injury. We will need him to wake up before we can truly assess any impairments."

Shit. Aurora wanted to sag against Jiro, to have him hold her like he had just been doing. But she managed to keep herself steady. As if reading her mind, Jiro's hand stole into hers, and he squeezed her fingers, offering her support. It was enough to get her tongue moving again. "My father is tough, Dr. Hessel; he will pull through," she replied stoically, meaning every word. He was a tough old bugger, hard to kill, and she had every faith that he'd recover, even if it was just to be the bane of her life again.

"Good," the doctor said. "You can follow me. But he has to stay here." She pointed at Jiro. "Immediate family only."

Aurora shot him an apologetic look, but he waved her out of the room. "I'll wait. You take as long as you need." Her heart melted at those words; he was going to wait for her, and that might be the only thing that kept her going. She would've preferred to have him by her side as her rock, but she straightened her spine and followed the doctor down the long corridor. She could do this.

Hessel led her into a room, and she saw her father for the first time. Karl was lying in a hospital bed, surrounded by beeping machines and tubing. He was completely still, his face pale, but strangely peaceful, as if he were just sleeping. What should she do? A good daughter would go up and take his hand. But she seemed to be frozen to the spot. This man was just so… incompatible with the Karl she knew.

"Once he regains consciousness, we will be able to assess him better." The doctor broke the awkward silence, going up and taking the patient chart from the end of the bed. "There was no bleeding on the brain that we could see, just a slight contusion, which bodes well for his recovery. When he does wake up, it will be his broken hip that will become the big problem, however. Recuperation and rehabilitation from a broken hip can take many months, and he will probably have to stay in hospital for a long time. In a man of his age, this might not be such a problem, but I understand that your father suffers from Parkinson's disease."

Aurora nodded in reply, unable to tear her gaze away from her father in the hospital bed.

"This will add many complications to his recovery. He may never actually fully recover, and may even be completely wheelchair-bound. He will need lots of care." The doctor left her last words hanging in the air, as if she wanted to say more, and Aurora wondered what exactly she meant by that. Was she saying that Aurora wasn't capable of that kind of full-on care? She glanced over at Hessel, but found no discernible emotion on her face.

It almost felt like this doctor was blaming her for her father's fall. Part of her wanted to protest that this was all her father's doing—he was attempting to do something he clearly wasn't capable of, and he wasn't supposed to be up in her room anyway. But the larger part accepted the guilt, because if she had been home on time, this wouldn't have happened.

"Okay," Aurora replied, knowing her voice had lost that convincing air of authority. She wasn't going to get into it with the doctor tonight. So she forced herself to walk over to the bed and lay her hand on her father's arm. It was warm.

"I'll leave you with him for a while then," Hessel said after a few moments of silence. "A nurse will be in soon to check on him." This doctor's bedside manner left a lot to be desired, Aurora decided. But then she put that thought out of her head; she had much bigger things to think about now.

Karl was going to need a lot of care. Was she going to have to quit her job? It didn't seem fair, but how was she supposed to look after him as well as he needed and continue her demanding work? The job required her to be out at all different times of the day and night, and also some overtime. Would she have to get a normal nine-to-five job so that she could be there for him?

She stared down at her father, a jumble of mixed emotions rumbling around in her head. Regret, resentment, pity, worry, devotion, and finally acceptance. Acceptance of the fact that there was nothing she could do to change what'd happened. She would just have to accept whatever came next and deal with it day by day. She was usually Mrs. Fix-it. She liked being a problem solver. She'd also been called a bit of a perfectionist by more than one of her colleagues recently. She didn't like that term, but admitted that she liked things done a certain way, and they had to be done properly. Deep down, she knew the one aspect of her life that she was failing at was her father, because he wouldn't be corralled into a model parent. She now realized she would never be able to fix her father; he would never be the man she wanted him to be, and he would never fit into one of her perfect little boxes. Certainly not now. So if he wasn't going to change, then perhaps she would need to. Was it time to let go of her pedantic tendencies, and learn how to just let things be?

The door opened, and a rosy-cheeked nurse walked in carrying a tray of medicines. "Oh, hello," she said brightly. "I'm Nurse Rossi. You must be Mr. Karlsson's daughter." The woman spoke good Swedish but with a thick Italian accent. "You can stay if you like, I'm just going to check his vitals and top up his pain medication."

"Thank you." Aurora took the seat in the corner so she would stay out of the nurse's way, then watched without really focusing as the nurse flittered around her father's bed. The act of sitting down finally made her realize how totally fatigued she was. Tiredness crashed over her like a wave, and she had to rub her hand across her eyes just to keep them open. It'd been a big day. A huge day. And her father ending up in the hospital was the icing on the cake. She rested her head in her hands, giving in to the lethargy for just a moment. It was after two a.m., and she desperately needed sleep.

"There's nothing else you can do tonight, Constable Karlsson," the nurse said, surprising Aurora—how did she know she was a cop? The nurse gave her a sympathetic look as she returned her father's patient chart to its spot at the end of the bed. "He will be under sedation for the rest of the night. You should go home and get some rest. We'll call you when he wakes up." She said it in such a friendly way that Aurora couldn't take offense at being told to go away.

"Yes, I guess you're right," Aurora conceded. She would go and find a Jiro, and offer him the spare bedroom for what was left of the night. It was the least she could do. She was so tired she almost stumbled down the hallway, and it took her a while to find the waiting room again. But Jiro was still there, curled up and using his jacket as a pillow, trying to sleep in one of the uncomfortable chairs. She went and laid a hand on his shoulder.

"Come on, let's go to bed." Then she smiled to herself. That'd come out as more of an invitation than she'd meant, but he was still groggy and so hopefully hadn't heard.

"How's your dad?" he asked, unfolding his legs and rubbing bleary eyes.

"Sedated and as comfortable as they can make him. Pretty much the same as your papa," she added with a wry grin. Both of them walked like zombies to where her car was parked and almost fell into it.

She drove back to her house in grim silence, letting the car heater warm them up, making her even more drowsy. And so when they finally stumbled in the front door, all she could think about was climbing into her soft, welcoming bed. They stripped off jackets and boots without speaking, almost on autopilot.

There'd been no word from any of her police colleagues, so she assumed there was no new information to pass on about Taro's whereabouts, and she let the subject lie for now. She really hoped he was still alive, for Jiro's sake, but the longer he was missing, the less likely he would be found alive.

But as she went to lead Jiro down the hallway past her father's bedroom to the spare bedroom, she suddenly had an epiphany. The next best thing to climbing into bed alone would be to climb in and snuggle with another warm body. A hot, sexy, muscular body, to be exact. Not that she wanted sex right now, just the feeling of another human's arms around her.

"Would you…" She halted, unsure how to phrase it now. It'd sounded good in her head. "I mean, would you like to come up and…" Damn, why couldn't she communicate what she wanted?

"I'd love to," he said with a grin that told her he understood exactly what she meant.

"I don't expect anything to happen," she mumbled. "It would just be nice to have someone to hold, that's all."

"I'm willing and able to be of service," he replied, giving her a mock bow. "I will be as chaste and platonic as a best friend could be," he added. She glanced at him out of the corner of her eye, but was too tired to decide if he was pulling her leg or not. If he were willing just to hold her all night, then that would be enough for now. They turned as one, and she led him up the stairs, pausing only to flick on the bedside lamp before starting to undress. She stripped down her underwear and climbed under the covers with a heartfelt sigh. He'd already seen her in her lingerie—which she had put on this morning instead of her normal cotton underwear with him in mind, not that she would ever admit.

He was slower to undress, as if overcome by a sudden bout of awkwardness. But she was too tired to be embarrassed, and so she just stared at him, waiting for him to come to her. Eventually he shrugged and pulled his sweater over his head, dumping it on the floor at the foot of the bed. Something unexpected happened then. All the tiredness washed out of her body as she watched him undress. She couldn't remember having seen a finer specimen of a man. Not up close and personal like this, at least. And she suddenly wanted to run her fingers all over those bumps and contours, and feel the muscles flex beneath them. When they'd been intimate earlier today, they'd been wrapped up in a cocoon, and she hadn't been able to see him fully, only parts of him as she explored the length of his body. Now that she could see him in his entirety, it did something strange to her body. Something like a slow flip of her stomach, and then a rush of heat, pooling between her legs.

She lifted the covers and welcomed him into the bed, which she had now warmed with her body heat. At first, he did as she had requested, wrapping his arms around her in a most nonsexual way.

"Is this okay?" he queried, but she had other ideas.

"It's okay," she agreed. "But it would be better if we were closer, like this." She tugged him in, wrapping her long legs around his, and pushing her breasts into his chest, while letting one hand wander down over his washboard stomach to the waistband of his boxer shorts.

"But I thought…"

"A woman can change her mind, can't she?"

"Hell yeah," he replied with a grin that lit up his whole face.

Then they stopped talking altogether.

His skin was hot and silky, with the spring of toned muscles beneath her fingertips as she explored every inch of him. He flipped her over, so he was on top, then scraped his teeth across the swell of her breasts, and her belly turned to molten heat. Looking deep into her eyes, he brushed both breasts with his tongue and rolled the nipples between two fingers. Her eyelids fluttered closed as she gasped at the blast of desire that shot through her. He let one hand trace a meandering path through the soft curls between her legs, and she thought she might die from the pure sensations he was causing. She needed him inside her. And this time she had a condom handy.

"In the drawer in the left side table," she said through gritted teeth.

"Yep," he breathed. Not removing his hand from between her legs, he reached over in the direction she had pointed, and felt around until he gave a cry of triumph.

Then his hand was suddenly gone, and she let out a sigh of deprivation. But quicker than she thought possible, he was back, this time hovering over her body, his thighs resting on hers, his chest grazing her breasts, his cock rock hard and waiting for her consent. Which she gave by arching her hips toward him, almost begging him to enter her. And when he slid inside slowly, tenderly, she was transported. While his tongue had been magical, this was so, so much better.

They moved together in the age-old rhythm of love, and her climax built quickly; she was so close to the edge, but she didn't want to go without him.

"Jiro, I..." She never finished her sentence, her words ripped away along with any coherent thought as she surged over the edge, finding an orgasm quicker and more intense than she'd ever felt before. He wasn't far behind her. She was still breathing his name when he cried out, his body jerking reflexively as he climaxed as well.

They collapsed together, Jiro taking the time to remove the condom and wrap it in a tissue. Then they snuggled beneath the warm doona, foreheads resting together, arms draped over each other. He was asleep within seconds, and while Aurora wanted to do the same thing, she found her eyes remained stubbornly open.

The bedside lamp was still lit, and so she carefully propped herself on one elbow so she could study his face. Relaxed in sleep, his serious persona turned to boyish vulnerability. It was funny; she'd always assumed she would marry another Swedish man one day. Had never considered she might be drawn to someone from another culture. And while Jiro was definitely American in his mannerisms and speech, his looks were more exotic because of his Japanese heritage. She traced the line of his straight nose, and up to the curve of his almond-shaped eyes. Then up to his high forehead and thick, luscious hair, which now curled enticingly, hanging down over his dark eyebrows. He was so delicious; she wanted to kiss him again and again, but didn't want to wake him, so refrained. Just.

She'd known him for less than three days—they barely knew each other really—but already she felt so connected to him. Aurora was always the sensible one; she made decisions based on fact and lots of consideration. She rarely jumped into things feet first, especially not romance. She was a perfectionist at work, but that didn't necessarily translate into her love life. Although she made considered decisions about the men she dated, her men always turned out to be a safe bet, but not necessarily good for her. Which was why she'd never been in love before.

But with Jiro, things were different. She hadn't considered him as dating material, because he'd started out as a victim who needed her help. So he'd crept up on her, filling her senses so she could no longer think straight when he was around, and dazzling her with his sexy charisma. She'd crossed an invisible line she'd drawn for herself in the sand, not to date anyone she met as a witness or victim of crime through the job. It was distasteful, and slightly abhorrent in her eyes. And now…she didn't know what to think about him or how to feel. All she knew was that when he was around she buzzed with a strange kind of energy, and she wanted to kiss him all the time, wanted his body as close to hers as was humanly possible. What should she call this thing they had between them? Lust—definitely. Desire—hell, yes. Aching need—yep. A spark—unquestionably. But were they compatible? Were they actually good together? She had no idea how to answer that.

And there would be no time to find out, either. They couldn't start a relationship with all this uncertainty swirling around Jiro. Taro was a major thread in the tangled web of Jiro's life; the longer he remained missing, the more Aurora feared for his life. Would he ever be found, though? The possibilities were slim. If his brother remained missing, but his father recovered—she crossed all her fingers and toes that he would be fine—Jiro would most likely take him home to America; they couldn't stay here forever. And that would be that.

CHAPTER SIXTEEN

Jiro woke with a start to the sound of a ringing cell phone. Was it his? He fumbled around in the dark, unable to determine exactly where he was for a few seconds. He was definitely in a bed, snuggled deep under a cozy doona… Then a warm body moved next to him, the person emitting a low groan of frustration as an arm snaked out of the covers and reached for the side table. Of course, he was in Aurora's room; in Aurora's bed. Had done wonderful things with Aurora for most of the night.

"Hej, Aurora Karlsson talar," he heard her croak into the phone, even as she sat up and flicked on the lamp so that he had to shade his eyes from the unexpected light. He sat up as well, squinting hard and rubbing his eyes while trying to make out what Aurora was saying, but she was speaking in Swedish. Aurora flicked her gaze to his face, then quickly away again, but it was enough to let him know the conversation had something to do with him. He could see how tired she was even in the soft light of the bedroom lamp. She had large dark circles under her beautiful eyes, and lines around the corners of her mouth. He glanced at the digital clock on his side of the bed, confirming they'd only had a couple of hours sleep. It was just past six in the morning. But her hair was delightfully tousled, reminding him of how she'd thrown her head back in abandon as they'd made love, her long locks left free to fall over the pillow. She'd been magnificent. Giving and generous, but also greedy for him, taking everything he had to offer.

Suddenly, Aurora switched to English, and he brought his concentration back to the here and now. "We'll be there as soon as we can. See you soon." Then she hung up, turning to face him. "They've found Taro. Alive," she qualified, even before he could ask.

The relief hit him like a freight train, and he let out an *oof* sound of release. Thank the Lord. Taking Aurora into his arms, he hugged her hard. "Jesus Christ, Aurora, that's the best news." But then reality hit him. "Where is he? Can we go and see him?"

"Yes, he's in hospital. That was Tuckburg. He discovered your brother and the man who took him about an hour ago. The kidnapper is also in hospital. Tuckburg shot him. Those are all the details I have for now; we'll find out more when we get there," she said, the look on her face telling him not to ask silly questions that she had no answer for right now.

Okay, that was a lot of information to take in. But he was already clambering out of bed, eager to get going.

"Except for one more thing, Jiro." Her serious tone stopped him with one leg half-way out of the bed. "Taro has been tortured, and it's not a pretty sight."

"Shit," he breathed, the news bringing him back down to earth with a bang. "But he's going to recover. He's not going to die, is he?"

"No, I believe most of the wounds are superficial, aimed at causing the most pain, but not necessarily life threatening."

"Right." Jiro dragged in a deep breath. "I guess the quicker we get there, the quicker we find out how he is."

"Yep." But Aurora seemed to hesitate, not clambering out

of bed in a hurry as he had done. Instead, sitting propped up against her pillows, staring at him with those big brown eyes. It wasn't until later that Jiro figured out the cause of her hesitation; this was the last time it would be just the two of them together. She'd worked it out already, but he hadn't yet. She was despondent because she knew she was probably going to lose him, and he was acting like a complete imbecile, only thinking about one thing—his brother. He wished he hadn't been in such a rush, had taken the time to thank her for the night they'd spent together.

Instead, he'd asked, "Are you coming?" as he searched the floor for his clothes.

"Yes, yes," she sighed, moving more slowly than he'd hoped. But by the time he was fully dressed, she'd picked up speed and was pulling on the shirt of her police uniform and doing up the buttons; she was going to be an official cop today.

"I need to grab something to eat quickly," she said, leading him out of the bedroom. He was starving as well, and welcomed the hunk of dark rye bread and slice of cheese she pushed into his hand. The last thing they'd eaten was a couple of sandwiches and some hot coffee back at the cabin while they'd been waiting for Dalström to finish his inspection.

Then they were in the car and driving to the hospital, a route that was becoming familiar to Jiro now. Jiro had to hand in his phone to the inspector as it was now considered evidence, so he had no means of communication. The plan had been to get a new phone this morning, but that would have to wait.

"Have you had any messages about your father?" he asked through her mouthful of bread.

"No. And nothing about yours either." She'd given her phone number to the nurse as a contact if anything changed about Kenichi.

That was not good. It was now coming up to three days that his father had been in a coma. The doctor said the longer he stayed unconscious, the worse the potential prognosis. Karl was also in a coma, but it was an induced coma so they could monitor his fractured hip and worrying concussion. Jiro wondered absently whose father would wake up first. It was a touch ironic that both of their paternal parents were in the hospital together, only a few rooms apart.

They made it to the hospital in record time, Aurora not breaking the speed limit, but flying close to the maximum, negotiating the icy roads with skill. She led him into the building, asking at the front desk for Senior Constable Tuckburg, and they were shown down the long corridor and into a private consultation room, where three other officers waited for them. Aurora greeted them all, and then did the introductions for him.

"Senior Constable Andreas Tuckburg, this is Jiro Nashimori." He shook the man's hand heartily. He'd never met Tuckburg, but right now he wanted to take him in a huge bear hug and thank him over and over again. He refrained, however. Tuckburg didn't look like the sort of man who welcomed hugs from strangers. He was about the same height as Jiro, heavyset, but with the once-straw-colored hair —now going gray—and Slavic cheekbones of a Swedish local. Aurora had said he was close to retirement and preferred to spend most of his days behind the desk. But he had done her a special favor by following up on her requests. It seemed like the old guy still had it in him when it was needed.

He'd already met one of the other young constables in the room; Moreau had been at the initial search for his father on the reindeer farm, and so he shook his hand in a warm greeting as well. Lastly, he was introduced to Poliskommissarie Runar Staaf, who was built like a bull, bald, with a thick neck and very large biceps. This case must be bigger than he thought if the commissioner was involved, and judging by Aurora's face, she hadn't expected him to be here either. He noted with interest that Dalström was missing.

"I don't know how to thank you," Jiro said after all the introductions were made, looking longest at Tuckburg. He was itching to get in and see his brother, but it seemed there was more to be said first.

"We were just doing our jobs," Tuckberg finally answered with a modest shrug.

"Well, you did a great job," Jiro confirmed.

"Hmm." The commissioner made a sound that had all eyes turning to him. "Inspector Viskten will return to Luleå later today. And we will organize a video linkup with Agent Utsi soon after. As long as you are agreeable?" Staaf said, getting straight down to business while peering at Jiro from behind round glasses, which he kept resettling on his nose.

Jiro looked to Aurora for confirmation that this was the FBI contact she'd mentioned. When she nodded, he let out a stream of relieved air. "Of course I am," he acknowledged. "I hope he can help us. I know Taro is in a lot of trouble, but anything the US government can offer us has to be better than possible death." Jiro mentally noted that he'd just said *us*. Taro was the one in trouble, but Taro was also family, and he would stick by his brother for as long as he could. He'd draw the line at going to jail for him, but he'd do everything in his power to make sure Taro received as much leniency as possible.

"Yes, he's in a lot of trouble. It seems you have brought a very large problem here with you. We take gun-smuggling very seriously. Even if the crime didn't originate in our country, we are a global force when it comes to trafficking of weapons or explosives," Staaf replied gruffly, his tufted eyebrows waggling solemnly.

Jiro wanted to argue that tarring him with the same brush as his brother wasn't fair, and that he and his father weren't responsible for any of it, but held his tongue. The commissioner didn't want to hear it. Instead, he turned to Tuckburg and said, "How did you find my brother?"

Tuckburg gave a wry smile. "It was Constable Karlsson's suggestion that gave us the clues we needed."

"Oh?" He turned toward Aurora, but she just shrugged to show she was as much in the dark about how they'd rescued Taro as he was.

"She asked me to follow up with an eyewitness. A staff member at the farm who remembered seeing your father sitting with another man."

"Yes, that was Tory. We never got around to interviewing her," Aurora chimed in.

"No. But yesterday morning, I managed to track her down, and she gave me a very good description of the man she had seen. So good, it led us to one of the tourists who was on the same cruise ship as you."

"She did mention he was wearing a cruise-branded jacket," Jiro commented.

"Well, when I checked with the ship's captain, we discovered he never re-boarded the ship either. The captain didn't report him as missing, because he left a message with the purser to say he would be remaining in Luleå for the time being, and may catch up with them later on. While this is unusual, it's not unheard of for a passenger to re-board at another port along the journey."

"So who was he?" Jiro asked, racking his brain trying to come up with anyone who looked suspicious while they'd been on the ship. No one came to mind, but suddenly Jiro had a memory of the morning his father went missing, and how his mood had gone from upbeat to downright grumpy.

Had something happened that morning that Jiro had missed? Had this guy tried to contact him or threatened him in someway?

"His name is Liam Kenzo, an American national, but with Japanese heritage. We're diving into his criminal history now, but it might take a while to get the answers we need from the US authorities. It seems as if he was here alone, hiring the sniper locally to carry out his plan. The sniper was ex-military, he's been on our radar for a little while as a possible gun for hire, but we didn't have enough evidence of his criminal undertakings to do anything about it. Until now," Tuckberg continued.

There had been quite a few Japanese tourists aboard the Le Commandant Charcot, but none of them had rung any alarm bells for Jiro. This guy must be a bit of an amateur though, if he hadn't covered his tracks well enough to keep the Swedish police from finding him eventually. He wondered if this man had a plan in place, or if he'd just taken the first opportunity to get Kenichi alone? Jiro's blood ran cold when he thought about what could've happened to his father. This Yakuza thug could just have easily caught his father alone at the edge of the boat, and tipped him over the railing into the freezing ocean so no one was any the wiser. But it seemed the message was meant as a warning to Taro, and the guy had never meant to kill Kenichi. But he had come close; may yet even succeed if Kenichi didn't wake up soon.

"I did some serious research into this man's movements over the past few days. Searching up CCTV footage, checking credit card usage, and looking at all the accommodation bookings in the area, I finally had a hit."

"It's one of Andreas' strengths," Aurora confirmed. "He's the best at finding someone who doesn't want to be found."

Tuckburg gave Aurora a quick grin of thanks as he continued. "I found a charge on a credit card in his name for rental of a house on the outskirts of town. Then, I confirmed it was the same man using CCTV cameras on the street, which showed him parking a hire car out the front and entering the house the night before last."

"Good, good," Jiro nodded enthusiastically. This was good police work. This was what Dalström should've been doing all along.

"I won't bother you with the details, but we managed to get a warrant to search the place late last night, and we went in early this morning. Unfortunately, when my officers breached the building, they had to use lethal force when they were fired upon. The offender was shot twice, once in the leg and once in the stomach. He's still in surgery, and we haven't been able to speak to him yet."

"Okay." It seemed as if Jiro wasn't going to get all the answers he needed right now, but at least his brother was safe and they had the kidnapper in custody. One day soon he hoped to be allowed to talk to this joker, to let him know exactly what he thought of the little game he'd forced Aurora and himself to play. And to find out exactly what his plans for them had been. Had he really been prepared to have them both murdered in cold blood? Jiro could understand why he might be a target, but to kill Aurora when she was an innocent bystander begged belief.

"So can I go and see my brother now?" he asked.

"In a moment." Staaf held up his hand. Until this point he'd remained silent, letting Tuckburg give them the details, but even Jiro could tell this man wasn't happy.

"I'm not sure you understand the ramifications of everything that's happened over the past few days. You led one of my officers astray, coercing her into breaking procedure for your gain." His words held a cold edge of fury.

Jiro stilled at the commissioner's words, but he wasn't about to be intimidated by this man.

"And while she should've known better," the commissioner shot Aurora a sideways glance, "she is not wholly to blame for the way things turned out."

"I couldn't agree more," Jiro said, squaring his shoulders and standing to his full height, which was many inches above the police commissioner's head, forcing him to look up. "And I'm prepared to deal with any ramifications if they come about." Jiro purposefully didn't look in Aurora's direction.

"Hmm." The commissioner narrowed his eyes behind his glasses, his steely stare unnerving, but Jiro refused to give him any sign that he was uncomfortable. He would protect Aurora with all he had, and if he had to take the blame on himself so that she remained safe, then that was what he would do. It was ironic really; he wasn't prepared to go to jail for Taro's sins, but if he had to go to jail to protect Aurora, then so be it. But he had no time to dissect that strange instinctive response, because Staff continued speaking, "You're also a prime witness in a police shooting, and as such you may be called upon to give testimony if required in the internal investigation, as well as in a court case if it gets that far."

"But I'm not under arrest?" Jiro asked, needing clarification.

"No. But we'll hold on to your passport until we have had time to look at things from all angles."

Jiro didn't reply, not wanting to show that his insides had begun to tremble. The relief he'd felt when he heard Taro was alive was now replaced with unease. He hadn't even considered that he would be in any sort of trouble; he'd been so fixated on his brother sand his problems. But he wouldn't change a thing, even if he could, and he was prepared to account for his actions if he were called to do so. He just hoped that Aurora didn't get dragged into the mud with him.

The commissioner's beady gaze swapped to Aurora,

almost as if he could read Jiro's mind. "And as for you, Constable Karlsson, while you broke procedure by contacting Andreas after you'd been explicitly ordered off the case..." Staaf paused, fixing Aurora with his laser-like gaze. "Without your interference, we may never have caught this criminal. I am very unhappy with your conduct, and there may be disciplinary action," he added. "But you have a solid champion in your corner. Inspector Viskten speaks highly of you, says that even though you might be a little undisciplined now, you will make an excellent police officer one day." The commissioner's glare said that he wasn't sure he agreed with the inspector.

Jiro gave Aurora a sideways glance. Her face remained impressive, but he could see how hard she was clenching her jaw together; she was just as displeased with the commissioner's unforgiving manner as he had been. But if he was reading it right, it sounded like she might get away fairly unscathed from this whole debacle. Jiro guessed it could've been a lot worse. Aurora could be in real trouble for disobeying a direct order. The two of them stood side-by-side facing down the commissioner, waiting for whatever would come next.

Jiro noticed Tuckburg behind Staaf's left shoulder wink surreptitiously in Aurora's direction. It seemed she had more than just Mårten on her side. Moreau had said nothing throughout the whole conversation, but he was looking decidedly uncomfortable in his spot beside the door. None of the men in the room would admit it, but Moreau's presence confirmed it for Jiro; Dalström had fucked up, and Moreau was here to make amends. Moreau had been the one who had tried to talk Dalström into continuing the search on the night his father had gone missing. Had he been promoted to cover this case now?

"That will be all for now," Staaf said at last. "You can see your brother. But we need to know your whereabouts at all times. Understand?"

Jiro inclined his head. "Yes, sir." He decided that discretion was the better part of valor at the moment.

"Constable Karlsson, you are required back at the office. You can help Inspector Viskten with the logistics of the FBI meeting."

"Yes, sir." Aurora echoed Jiro's words. They both turned on their heels and exited the room, Jiro's stomach tied in knots. But he refused to let the feeling sink him. They strode down the hallway together, eager to get as far away from that room as possible.

"I'm not sure if we came out of that unscathed or not," Jiro finally said once they were out of earshot.

"I think we came out of that fairly lightly," Aurora replied. "Mårten is one of the police commissioner's favorite officers. He hates to admit it, and we all joke about it, but I think without him in my corner I might be in real trouble." She shrugged. "And I think in protecting me, he is also protecting you. But that remains to be seen. We'll just have to wait and see over the next few days as they inspect the evidence to make sure we won't be prosecuted."

"Wow." Jiro let his shoulders drop now that they were out of sight. Then he grabbed Aurora's arm and spun her around so they were face-to-face. "I know I've said this too many times before, and I am beginning to sound like a broken record, but I truly am sorry I dropped you in all this shit, Aurora."

She looked up at him, brown eyes wide and appraising. "I came into this shit with full knowledge of the risks," she replied, a half-smile filling her face. "And of my own free will. All the choices I made were mine and mine alone, and whilst some of them might have been stupid ones, I stand by them." Then she did something completely unexpected. She stood on tiptoe and brushed her lips across his. It was a tender, unguarded kiss, but there was also something like regret in the touch of her mouth.

Before he could do or say anything in return, the sound of footsteps squeaking on the linoleum approached down the hallway and forced them apart. Aurora's eyes shuttered as she turned away. "Could you please point us in the direction of Mr. Taro Nashimori's room?" she asked the advancing nurse.

The woman took one look at Aurora's uniform, and said, "Yes, of course. He's being kept in a private room at the end of the east wing." The nurse pointed to a hallway branching off to the left.

"Thank you," Aurora replied stiffly, her cop mask firmly back in place. He had lost her for now. But he really needed to see his brother, and he would continue this conversation with her later.

Aurora took the lead, turning down the hallway as he followed the clack of her boots. There was a guard outside the door to Taro's room, and Jiro faltered for a few steps when he saw him. On the drive to the hospital, Aurora had warned him that a guard would be there, as much to keep Taro safe as to also stop him from leaving, but it was still a shock to see the man in the dark blue uniform standing to attention at the end of the hallway.

"This is Jiro Nashimori, the victim's brother," Aurora said to the guard, assuming a formal tone. "He has permission to enter."

The guard nodded. "There is a nurse surveilling him in the room; she will give you all the information you need," he replied. Jiro wondered about the nurse's purpose in staying in the room with Taro. Was it because he was so badly injured he needed constant monitoring? Or was it more security, making sure he couldn't leave? Probably more of the latter, he decided.

"Do you want me to come in with you?" Aurora asked. Jiro knew she'd been ordered back to HQ, and as much as he'd like her company, he didn't want her to get into any more trouble than she already was.

"No, I'm good," he said, trying to sound like he meant it.

"I'm going to pop my head into my father's room on the way out. I'll check on Kenichi as well. If there's any news, I'll get a message to you somehow."

"Good idea." He leaned in and gave her a quick hug, conscious of the constable watching their every move. "I'll check on my father too, once I finish here, but that could be a while." After she left, Jiro pondered how she was going to get in touch with him when he still didn't have a phone.

He wasn't looking forward to going into this room for many reasons. The large part of him that'd been overjoyed to hear that Taro was alive was now being crowded out by misgivings and fear. Taro had been tortured, but Jiro had no idea how bad his injuries were, and he wasn't looking forward to seeing his older brother vulnerable or in pain. He also wasn't looking forward to the many discussions they'd have to have regarding his brother's future, and how Jiro— and indeed, his father—would factor in all of that.

But for now, he plastered a smile on his face, nodded at the guard, who stepped aside for him, and pushed open the door.

CHAPTER SEVENTEEN

Aurora was sitting at her desk, glumly staring out the window when the call came in. Her father was awake. Her heart rate accelerated as she pushed her chair back and stood, grabbing her jacket from the back of the chair. She needed to get to the hospital as quickly as possible. Mårten would understand that she was leaving. But the thought of seeing Karl gave her mixed emotions. What sort of mood would he be in? She feared the worst.

It was now late afternoon, and she'd spent the past few hours talking to Mårten, who'd returned from Malmö at lunchtime. Mårten was now up to speed on everything that'd occurred, grilling her for all the tiny details that even she could barely remember. He was now ready to hold the meeting with Jacob. They were going to do a video linkup at seven tonight, which would be mid-morning Seattle time. Mårten was going to head over to the hospital so they could do the call from Taro's room. Aurora had wondered if Taro was up to it—not having seen what condition he was in herself—but Jiro had assured her when he'd spoken to her on a borrowed phone that Taro was adamant they get it done today.

Astrid would be arriving by train soon, but she could

always catch a taxi to the hospital. Aurora needed to get in and see her father, make an assessment of his well-being for herself, and it'd be better if he was awake and lucid before Astrid saw him. Earlier this morning, when she'd checked on him, Karl had looked pale and small in his hospital bed, still surrounded by beeping machines. But the nurse had told her that things were positive and the swelling on his brain from the concussion had subsided, so he should be awake within the next twenty-four hours. It looked like the nurse had got it right.

She poked her head into Mårten's office as she passed by, saying, "I need to get to the hospital, my father is awake."

"Oh, right." Mårten looked up at her, but she could tell he was distracted. "Yes, yes, you have to go and see him."

"I'm still hoping to be there for the interview at seven," she replied. Mårten wanted her to sit in on the discussion; she might have some valuable information to add, technical stuff Jiro wouldn't be able to tell them. She would be at the hospital anyway, she'd just need to excuse herself for half an hour. "Astrid should be here by then, so she can sit with Fader while I join you."

"Oh, I didn't realize she was coming up. That's good. Great actually. You're going to need help with Karl when he gets out of the hospital, and I was worried about how you were going to cope alone."

Aurora didn't tell him she doubted Astrid would stay that long. Instead, she plastered a smile on her face and said, "Yes, a big family reunion. Great." Mårten wouldn't miss the sarcasm behind her tone.

Just as she turned to leave, he called to her. "Aurora, you know I'm here for you. Both Summer and I are here for you. If you need anything, need help with your father, you just have to let me know." Aurora turned and looked into his familiar ice-blue eyes. There was compassion and kindness, but no pity; she wouldn't accept anyone's pity, and Mårten knew her well enough to understand that. He was a good man, and she knew his offer was genuine. But she wasn't going to let Mårten anywhere near her father if she could help it. Mårten had met Karl only once, when she'd been having car trouble and he'd dropped around to pick her up for a shift. Karl had been civil throughout the short meeting, but she didn't want to chance it again. It was hard enough that Jiro had seen how fractured their relationship was. For some reason, she hadn't minded so much letting him see her family issues.

On the drive to the hospital, she went through the things she might say to her father when she saw him. Her first instinct was to apologize; it'd been her fault he fell because she wasn't home in time to care for him. But then Jiro's words came back to her as they'd been lying in bed and she'd been lamenting her failures. He'd said, *"While you might be Karl's carer, you're not responsible for him every second of every day. He is his own man, who still makes his own decisions, be they good ones or bad ones, and you're doing the best you can, trying to juggle a full-time police career and care for him as well. You're not to blame because Karl took it upon himself to climb the stairs to your bedroom."* Repeating that mantra over and over in her head helped a little, but the guilt still sat like a stone in her stomach.

All the way up the stairs and down the hallway to her father's room, Aurora's mind churned with silent apprehension, wondering what she was going to find when she went in through that door. Pushing aside all her misgivings, she brought up a good approximation of a smile and entered the room. A nurse in green scrubs was bent over her father's bed, readjusting a cannula in his arm. And there was Karl, sitting up in bed, hair all askew, a dark frown hovering on his brow as he squinted at the nurse in contempt.

Aurora got a bad feeling—he definitely wasn't in a good mood—but she couldn't turn back now.

"Hello, Fader," she said, quietly approaching the bed, one eye still on the nurse who had finished fiddling with a dial on the IV bag, and looked up and smiled.

"You!" Karl pointed a shaking finger in her direction. "This is all your fault. It's your fault I'm trapped in this bed. Trapped in this jail cell. Look at me. I'll never walk again, and it's all your fault." Aurora took a step backward. The nurse glanced at Karl, startled at the old man's torrent of vitriol. "Get out of here. Get out of my sight. I don't want to see you ever again," he demanded hotly. Aurora was used to Karl's sometimes witless eruptions of fury; he got angry a lot over the smallest thing. But this was something different, and the look of betrayal he gave her speared right through her heart. Sudden tears sprang to her eyes. She'd expected him to be cross, but nothing could've prepared her for this hysterical outburst. All of a sudden, she couldn't handle his unfounded hatred anymore. Without another word, she turned and fled from the room.

Walking a few paces down the empty hallway, Aurora leaned back against the wall and sucked in a few deep breaths, trying to regain her equilibrium. This hadn't gone at all as she'd planned. She was going to be firm but fair, ready to withstand his accusations. But now… Suddenly, the nurse bustled out of the room, turning toward Aurora when she spotted her down the hall.

"I'm so sorry about that," she apologized. "He's been… quite agitated since he regained consciousness. Perhaps it's a side-effect of the pain medications, as well as his waking up and being disoriented by his surroundings. Maybe just leave him for half an hour or so until he's more himself." Aurora loved that the nurse was trying to explain away her father's hostility. She glanced at the woman's name badge.

"Thank you, Ulrike." Lifting her chin, she regarded the other woman levelly. "I'm sure you're right." She wanted to add that he wasn't normally like this, but the lie wouldn't come this time. Instead, she merely lifted one shoulder in a half-hearted shrug.

"It's not true what he said, that he won't walk again, because he will, even though it'll take lots of rehab," Ulrike continued, probably hoping to lift her spirits. "He's just not listening at the moment. He's feeling like his world has been shattered, that's all."

He and she both, Aurora thought. "I'll give him half an hour, then I'll try to talk to him again," she assured the nurse, even though she wasn't sure if she would indeed make that attempt.

"Good idea." Ulrike patted her arm on the way past as she headed down the hall towards the nurse's station. "Call me if you want some support when you go in again."

Aurora didn't know how the nurses did it. How they remained sympathetic and compassionate in the face of openly hostile patients like her father.

Aurora was still leaning against the wall five minutes later, contemplating her shoes, when the sound of running feet alerted her to Astrid's arrival.

"They said he's awake," she puffed, dropping a large suitcase at Aurora's feet. Her surge of pleasure at seeing her little sister died before it even had a chance to rise properly. There was no sisterly hug hello, no questions about how she was holding up. It was always Aurora's place to play the role of caring sister; she always gave and Astrid always received. But in Aurora's deflated emotional state, she had no reserves left to give. So instead of plastering on a look that said she was happy to see her sister, she simply said, "He's in there. He doesn't want to see me. Perhaps he'll talk to you instead."

"What? Why?" Astrid looked surprised, almost as if she

wasn't aware of how bad her father's relationship with Aurora had become. And maybe she wasn't aware, because Aurora hadn't told her.

"I'm sure he'll tell you everything. I'll stay here and watch your bag," she added, waving Astrid towards the door to their father's room. Her little sister hadn't seen Karl in over two years, but she didn't seem the least bit worried about how he was going to receive her, or what she was going to say. Astrid was lucky; she seemed to have a thick skin, laughing off anything mean or rude Karl might say. But then she'd always been his favorite, and so had never really endured the sharp edge of his tongue. Maybe today might be different. But Aurora wasn't going in with her to find out.

After Astrid disappeared through the door, Aurora stood pondering the large suitcase. Astrid had clearly come straight from the train station. She'd been wearing sweats, and her hair was tied up in a messy bun. But she'd looked good, face unblemished and smooth of any worry lines and brown eyes —the mirror of Aurora's—bright and clear. Working at the newspaper seemed to agree with Astrid, and Aurora was glad about that. At least one of them was happy and carefree, and perhaps that was the way it should stay. Perhaps it was Aurora's duty to shoulder the burden of their father so Astrid could lead a normal life.

Glaring at the suitcase as if it could give her all the answers, she finally decided she would leave it behind the desk at the nurse's station until Astrid emerged from Karl's room. And she should probably get back to work, especially if her father wouldn't see her. But she couldn't raise the energy to lift one foot in front of the other, let alone lift the suitcase. So she sat down on it instead. What was she going to do? How were they going to solve the problem that was Karl?

Aurora was so lost in her own thoughts she didn't hear the person approaching until a hand landed on her shoulder. She looked up into Jiro's wonderful, handsome face.

"You okay?" he asked carefully.

She just shook her head, unable to form the jumble of emotions inside her chest into words.

"Come here." Strong arms came around her waist and dragged her to standing. Then he pulled her into the solid wall of his chest, wrapping her into his embrace. She laid her cheek against his collarbone and they stood, unspeaking. The flood of sensations that filled her at his touch washed away all the miserable feelings. It was like he was a balm to her wounded soul. Like he understood what she needed.

This. This was what she had yearned for. This was where she felt safe. Wanted. Perhaps even loved. That thought made her pull up and mentally kick herself. He didn't love her; he hardly knew her. But right now he was the thing she needed most, and she didn't even care that she was a cop in uniform with a job to do. She accepted what he was giving wholeheartedly and sank into it.

After many, many long moments, Aurora felt strong enough to lift her head and look into his eyes.

"I heard Karl was awake," he said, brushing a strand of hair gently away from her face. "I take it things didn't go well."

"Nope." She didn't want to talk about it. Wanted to be anywhere but here right now.

"Okay." He stroked the side of her cheek. "Well, I've just had some news. Papa is also awake."

"Wow." Aurora drew back. "That's great." And a tad ironic, both their father's waking up within an hour of each other. She wasn't superstitious, but if she were, she might read something into that.

"I was on my way to see him, but I wanted to stop by here first. Do you want to come with me?" he offered.

Why not? There was nothing for her here right now, so she

nodded in agreement. "I'll just see if I can store Astrid's luggage behind the nurses' desk," she said, grabbing the handle of the suitcase.

"I've got it." Jiro took the bag from her, raising an eyebrow as if to ask if she was going to argue with him? Not today. She turned the bag over to him with a smile of gratitude. "So Astrid has arrived then?" he asked as they ambled down the hallway.

"Yes, I'd introduce you, but she's in with Fader, and I would guess now isn't a good time to interrupt them." That was probably an understatement. But then again, Astrid might be happy with an interruption around now, if Karl was giving her even half as much grief as he'd given Aurora. She didn't want to go back into that room, however, and so she kept walking forward with Jiro by her side, away from all that pain and anguish, toward the light.

"Do you have to go back to work?" Jiro asked.

"Not really." She shot him a sideways glance. "I was going to sit in on the meeting with you, Taro and Jacob later tonight anyway," she added by way of explanation. Mårten couldn't really disapprove of her abandoning her father to her sister's tender mercies and heading to see Kenichi instead. She was technically still working, as Kenichi was one of their key witnesses, and it would benefit them all for her to find out his condition, and see how soon he could be interviewed.

They dropped the bag off with the nurse and headed down the next hallway. This area was a much busier section of the hospital, with nurses and doctors striding down the hallways, and visitors coming and going from patient rooms. As they walked, Jiro slipped his hand into hers, as if it were the most natural thing in the world to do. And it was natural. It felt so right that Aurora left her hand linked with his, just enjoying the sensation.

Kenichi also had a guard stationed outside his private

room, which brought more than a few stares from passers by. But if the meeting tonight with Jacob went well, hopefully this extra protection would no longer be required. Aurora surreptitiously dropped Jiro's hand—but not without a large dose of regret—and identified herself and Jiro to the guard, who stood aside to let them in. But Aurora quailed before she stepped through, suddenly unsure.

"You should go in by yourself," she said, taking a step backward and almost colliding with the guard in her effort to slip away.

"No." Jiro's denial was absolute. "I want you with me. You deserve to be in here as much as I do."

Did she though? Aurora wasn't sure, but she let Jiro lead her in through the door anyway. Once inside the room, Jiro made his way to the bedside, where Kenichi was sitting propped up by many pillows. It was good to see that the old man looked very different from when they'd rescued him from the freezing cabin. Lips no longer blue, and skin no longer deathly pale, his cheeks were pink and warm, his eyes alive and bright. Kenichi's face lit up when he saw his son, and he held out both hands toward him, which Jiro took reverently, bowing his head as he did so. She stood in the corner of the room, not wanting to intrude on this intimate family reunion.

"Papa." Aurora heard the catch in Jiro's voice. Then he said something in Japanese that Aurora didn't understand, but she got the gist of it. Tears glistened and Kenichi's eyes as he hugged his son to him. How different her and her own father's meeting had been from this one. For a second, Aurora wished she could have a father like Kenichi. But then she remembered Jiro had implied all was not perfect in their relationship either.

Aurora wanted to slip out of the room, and leave these two men to it, but as she took a slow step sideways, Kenichi raised an interested eyebrow in her direction. "And who is this?" he asked in perfect English.

Jiro turned, but his smile for her turned to confusion as he opened his mouth, but no words came out.

"I'm one of the officers who helped rescue you," she replied simply, stepping forward, so she now stood beside the bed. She understood Jiro's hesitation. Because what exactly was she to Jiro? Even if they could explain it, the complicated story of her and Jiro would be too much for the old man to take in at this time. It was easier if he thought she was just a police officer doing her job. But a small part of her, a very tiny, but very poignant part, cried out in anguish. She wanted Kenichi to know the truth. Wanted to tell him that his son was an amazing person whom she'd become very fond of over the past few days. Wanted to hear Jiro say that she was special to him in return.

Instead, she shook the old man's hand, and said, "All of us are so glad you've recovered. Now I'll leave you and your son to catch up. I'm sure you have lots of questions."

Jiro grasped at her hand, but she subtly evaded him. "Wait," he called to her, but it was too late; she already had her hand on the door.

"I'll see you tonight," she confirmed to Jiro with a tight smile, and then left the room.

CHATPER EIGHTEEN

The meeting with the FBI agent was going well as far as Jiro could tell. But the fact was, he kept losing focus because he was spending most of his time trying not to be distracted by Aurora, who sat directly beside him. They were seated in two plastic chairs at the end of Taro's hospital bed. Someone had placed them close enough together so that every time she moved or gestured, their knees would touch and he would be transported back to last night in her bed. Which had been a revelation, and he was desperate for a repeat of that amazing intimacy. But Inspector Viskten was pacing back-and-forth as he spoke to the computer screen, talking to Agent Utsi in his office back in Seattle, and Jiro needed to concentrate. He could think about running his tongue down the length of Aurora's thighs later.

Taro was sitting up in bed, his face strained with pain, which he was trying to hide. But he answered all the questions the agent asked him directly and concisely. He made it clear that he was not playing games, and he'd happily give up all information if they would help him protect his family.

Jiro had not been able to hide his shock when he'd first seen his brother earlier today. Tuckburg hadn't been wrong when he said Taro wasn't a pretty sight. His face was a myriad of cuts and abrasions, as if he'd been beaten and then systematically sliced open. He was missing part of his left ear, and the tip of his pinky finger, among many, many other injuries. When Jiro had seen how badly his brother had been treated, his first reaction had been that he was going to find the man who'd inflicted these injuries and kill him; it'd taken a while for his brother to talk him down. Jiro already knew the guard outside the door would never let him into the kidnapper's room anyway, but that didn't stop him fantasizing about what he would do to the man if he ever got the chance.

Taro had told him that the kidnapper—the man they now knew as Liam Kenzo—had wanted assurances that he would continue the partnership with the Kyodo-kai gang and go along with the new conditions as well. Taro had made it seem as if he was putting up a bit of a struggle—even though he knew he was going to pretend to agree in the end—because he didn't want the man to think he'd caved too quickly. But then even after the man removed part of his ear and Taro had finally agreed to his demands, Liam continued his sadistic torture. His brother wasn't sure if it was to make sure Taro got the message, or if he just enjoyed inflicting pain. Jiro had felt as if he was going to throw up as Taro recounted the time spent with the Yakuza thug. These men had a fearsome reputation, and perhaps this guy was merely upholding that renown.

The meeting was winding down now. Inspector Viskten was asking if Agent Utsi had enough information to put Taro's family into witness protection while they confirmed all the details Taro had just related. Jiro liked Mårten. He seemed to be a good partner for Aurora, treating her as an equal rather than the rookie. He was solid as a rock, caring, but also not without a tough side when it was needed. Jiro was a little envious of the man. He got to spend at least eight hours a day in Aurora's company. Got to talk to her, watch those pretty eyes wrinkle up every time she smiled, encourage her sharp mind to come to the correct conclusions, laugh along with her at her witty jokes.

Jiro wanted to be able to do the same things. But he was leaving.

Of course he'd have to take his father home; there was no choice in the matter. It was his duty to make sure Papa was healthy and settled peacefully back into his old life once more. But part of him didn't want to leave Sweden. Didn't want to leave Aurora. The realization didn't shock him as much as it should have. She'd been creeping up on him steadily over the past few days. Creeping into his heart without him really comprehending, until it was too late. Their physical attraction was unquestionable. He'd started more than one relationship on less. But attraction wasn't everything, and while this was the strongest he'd ever felt, was it enough to make him form a dependable connection? He didn't know. But he did need to find a time when they could talk alone. Needed to find out how she felt about him.

If she felt the same, perhaps he would tell her that if she wanted him to, he could come back to Sweden after he'd settled his father and sorted out Taro's affairs. But that would mean leaving his perfect job. Could he do that? There must be wolf projects in northern Sweden he could work on. But he loved living in San Diego. With his family close by, why would he leave all that for something he was unsure about?

Jiro shook his head. There were just too many ifs and buts. With too many balls in the air, he had to juggle. He needed some time alone to process his feelings. And he needed some time with Aurora to talk about those feelings.

It bothered him that he still hadn't had a chance to replace his cell phone yet. The police probably wouldn't release his old one for many weeks yet, as it formed a crucial part of the evidence against this Liam fellow. Without it, he felt disconnected from everyone. Disconnected from the world. It meant he couldn't get in touch with Aurora either, and that thought bothered him more than anything else.

Aurora's shoulder brushed his as she got to her feet. The meeting was at an end, and he'd almost missed it. Agent Utsi was saying his final farewells, assuring Taro they'd do everything in their power to protect his family. Which was one good thing to come out of this meeting, and the main item on Taro's agenda, at least. The other wrecking ball that was hanging over Taro's head would be much harder to dodge. The question of how long he would spend in jail hadn't been mentioned. But he'd been formally charged with weapons smuggling by Inspector Viskten and was now handcuffed to the bed. He'd be extradited back to America to face the charges as soon as he was well enough to travel.

"Thank you, Inspector Viskten." Taro extended his hand as far as the handcuffs allowed for the police officer to shake. Even though this was the man who had chained him to the bed, he was also the man who had engineered this meeting and was working to protect Taro's family, as well as Taro himself. Viskten was just doing his job, and Jiro was glad to see that Taro held no grudge against him; he'd accepted his fate.

Jiro also stepped forward to shake Mårten's hand. "Yes, thank you. For everything you and your officers have done for me and our family." He meant every word, and he could tell by Mårten's firm grip and the way he looked him directly in the eye, he was glad to accept that approval.

Mårten gathered up his computer, and everyone prepared to leave the room; Jiro was desperate to talk to Aurora, hoping he could get a few minutes alone with her in the hallway. But just as he was about to follow her through the doorway, Taro called him back.

"Hey bro, I need to talk to you. You haven't told me how Papa is yet."

Shit. Jiro glanced at Aurora's retreating back, catching a glimpse of her smooth, dark hair as she ducked around the corner. He'd confirmed their father was awake and seemed to be recovering okay when he had first entered Taro's room, but there'd been too much going on for him to elaborate.

"Can he stay for a few minutes?" Taro's question was directed at Viskten, who turned, hesitating for a moment.

"Yes. That should be fine. I'll let the guard on the door know." The inspector lifted his chin in the brother's direction and gave them a rueful look. "But no more than five minutes. Now you're formally under arrest, all your visitors should technically be approved by the commissioner and accompanied by an officer."

It looked like Jiro was staying whether he wanted to or not, because this might be the last time he got to talk to his brother one-on-one. And they had a lot to discuss.

He could no longer see Aurora. She'd already disappeared through the door and was probably waiting for Viskten in the hall. It was on the tip of his tongue to ask the inspector if Aurora might be able to wait for him, but then Taro started talking and the moment was lost. He'd have to catch up with her later, although where and when that might be was anybody's guess. Even as Taro asked again how Kenichi was faring, Jiro's mind was only half on his answer. The other half was with the woman who was probably walking down the hall, blue uniform on, shoulders straight and head held high. The woman he might be falling in love with.

* * *

"Is this okay for you, Papa?" Jiro hovered beside his father's armchair, making sure he was comfortable. He'd made a traditional pot of green tea, and now poured Kenichi a cup and set it on the small table beside his chair, still lingering.

"Stop treating me like an invalid," Kenichi snapped, but there was no heat to his words. Then in a milder tone, he added, "Yes, I'm fine. Thank you for the tea. Now sit down and stop clucking over me like a mother hen."

Jiro did as he was told. Both the armchair and the couch faced a large floor to ceiling picture window, through which they could view the Hollywood Hills and beyond. As he sipped his own tea, he contemplated the amazing vista of the hills bathed in the soft orange light of a California sunset. Kenichi's LA house wasn't exactly a mansion, but it was pretty damn nice. Filled mainly with Japanese antiques—Kenichi wasn't an antique dealer for nothing—it was the epitome of grace and luxury. Jiro's mother had been the one to decorate the house, but Kenichi had changed nothing since her death. Jiro had grown up here, taking most of it for granted, until he'd become old enough to realize that most people didn't live this way, and he was one of the lucky few. That's when he'd also begun to perceive how much his father coveted status, and from that power, and he'd rebelled against the whole idea of the importance of social standing, finally moving to San Diego when he was old enough to escape his father's oppressive ideals.

He hadn't visited his father in over two years, and he'd suffered some trepidation about coming back to this place. But this time, things were different. Kenichi's attitude towards his youngest son had softened considerably since they'd returned home. He no longer criticized every little thing Jiro did; instead, he'd become almost excessive in his approval. Although Kenichi never said the words out loud, it was becoming clear that he understood how much he owed his life to Jiro. He'd also stopped comparing Jiro to his older brother. Indeed, their roles now seemed to be reversed; Jiro was the golden child now that Taro had fallen from grace.

It'd been a week since Jiro and his father had returned to the US. He was staying at Kenichi's house in LA, caring for the old man as he recuperated. The Swedish police had handed Jiro back his passport after five long, torturous days of endless rounds of questioning when they could find no reason to keep him in the country any longer. By that time, Kenichi had been declared fit to travel, and so they'd left in a hurry before anyone could change their mind.

Christmas would be here in two days, but Jiro was barely aware of the upcoming holy day; he'd been so focused on getting his father repatriated home. This would not be a Christmas they'd want to remember in a hurry, with the specter of serious jail time hanging over Taro's head, and his brother's family hidden away in witness protection. He should do something about getting a tree and decorating it, he supposed, but there was also the shadow of his mother's death looming in early January. For the past eight years, Deborah's passing had cast a pall over the Christmas season. The year she'd died, he, Taro, and Kenichi had spent the holidays in hospital, watching her slowly slip away, so Christmas had been swept to one side and Jiro had never really had the heart to celebrate ever since. But maybe this year, he should make the effort. It might help to lift Kenichi's spirits and help him recover more quickly. Perhaps it was time to bring some light back into this family. And Jiro could definitely do with something a bit fun to look forward to. His mind drifted back to the beautifully decorated tree in Aurora's house. With everything else she'd had on her plate, she'd found the time to bring some festivity into her house, so why couldn't he? Yes, he would do it. He would go out and buy a tree today. The thought lifted his mood, and he sat a little straighter in his chair.

The doctors back in Sweden had warned that Kenichi might suffer some aftereffects from the coma and hypothermia, and would need twenty-four-hour monitoring for a while at least. Mainly cognitive issues, such as memory loss, confusion, difficulty expressing thoughts and emotions, and disruption of sleep cycles. But there were also physical things to look out for, such as fatigue, higher risk of infections, including pneumonia, and general weakness in the muscles, especially factoring in Kenichi's age.

Kenichi seemed to be recovering just fine, however. Stoicism in his generation of Japanese men was a cultural trait, and his father was one of the most unflappable people Jiro had ever met. It was important to Kenichi that he not lose face, especially in front of his son. Or that was the way it had been until recently. In the past week, his papa had opened up more than Jiro had ever seen before; he'd even cried once, when Jiro confirmed Taro would be spending time in jail, possibly a long time—jail sentences for gun smuggling could be up to twenty years in a federal prison. Even if Taro managed to cut a deal by giving the FBI all the information they needed to bring down the Yakuza gang, his children would still most likely be teenagers by the time he got out.

He and his father had talked a lot about the past and how this had all transpired; about Taro's bad choices. Kenichi had not gone so far as to accept blame for Taro's ceaseless need to increase his social status or the way he coveted money, always needing more. But he had admitted that he'd sometimes been worried about Taro's business ethics, as well as the lack of consideration he gave to the products that he sold. Kenichi might be a hard-nosed businessman, but he also respected the old furniture and held it in esteem, keeping back the most special items for the people who deserved them, and would care for them appropriately, rather than whoever could pay the most.

Soon, Jiro would take Kenichi into the city to visit his older son in jail. He was being held at the Metropolitan Detention

Center in the centre of town while he awaited his trial. Kenichi had only seen his older son once since he'd woken from his coma. Again, it'd been Inspector Viskten who had engineered the visit. allowing Kenichi to be taken in a wheelchair to visit Taro in hospital before they deported him. Jiro had accompanied him, and this time there'd been a police officer in the room with them. Jiro's only regret was that the officer hadn't been Aurora. She had returned to her duties and had been reassigned to a new case, Inspector Viskten had told him. He hadn't known it then, but he wasn't to see Aurora again before he left Sweden. If he had, he would've tried harder to get in touch with her. Much harder.

During the short meeting with his father, Taro had begged for forgiveness, would've even got down on his knees and prostrated himself on the floor if his handcuffs had allowed it. Kenichi's stony countenance had been shattered then, his face lined with grief when his son had broken down in front of him. Even though he shed no tears and told Taro that he was the biggest disappointment of his life, eventually Kenichi had forgiven his oldest son. Because what choice did he have? He either disowned him completely or accepted his failings and moved on. The meeting had been emotionally charged, and his father had been clearly drained by the whole thing, his face pale and drawn as Jiro wheeled him back to his room.

Now they were back in the US, they talked about how best they could help to support Taro. Kenichi desperately wanted to see Thalia and the two children, but they weren't allowed to visit the small family, as they were being kept in witness protection, and they might not be able to see them for many, many months yet to come. Kenichi raged at the injustice of it, but Jiro understood the reasons behind the embargo. The FBI was working behind the scenes to quietly build a case against Hiroshi Kiyota, Taro's conduit to the Yakuza gang. Viskten had kept news of Taro's arrest as quiet as possible, hoping to keep the Kyodo-kai gang in the dark until they came up with a scheme to bring them to justice.

Even though Jiro wasn't privy to the FBI's plan, he understood it must be a highly delicate undertaking as they attempted to collaborate together with Japanese authorities and keep the gang under surveillance without giving away their presence. Taro's trial date had not been set yet, but Agent Utsi had intimated these things often took many months, and it all hinged on how swiftly they could get the evidence they needed to bring down the gang. Jiro wondered exactly what *swiftly* meant in FBI terms, but decided not to dwell on it as he had no authority in that capacity.

Kenichi would most likely be a key witness at the trial. And his testimony regarding his kidnapping by Liam Kenzo would hopefully help to demonstrate the link back to Taro's dealings with the Kyodo-kai. In the days after his father had awakened from his coma, Jiro had helped him to piece his memories back together so they could trace the story of his abduction.

Kenichi had confirmed it was the phone call on the night before they'd visited the reindeer farm that'd started the ball rolling. He hadn't known it at the time, but the menacing voice on the other end of the phone had belonged to Liam Kenzo. Liam had demanded that his father meet him in the barbecue hut the following day, and to make sure he was alone, and if he didn't follow instructions then Jiro's life might be in danger. Kenichi had no idea at the time what the threatening call had been about, but he'd done as he was told to protect Jiro. And then for the same reason, Kenichi had willingly followed Liam out of the hut and into the forest, where he'd hidden a snowmobile behind a large stand of birch trees. That was when Liam had injected Kenichi with something, and he could remember no more until he woke up in the hospital.

When Jiro asked him if he suspected the phone call had something to do with Taro, Kenichi had nodded sadly, admitting he'd had the same gut feeling as Jiro about his oldest son's dodgy dealings, but would never lose face by acknowledging it at the time. Jiro was both disappointed in his father for his stubborn adherence to his own ego, and proud of him for seeing through Taro's veil of lies at the same time. Perhaps if his father had been able to profess his thoughts aloud when Jiro first brought up his own misgivings, all of this might've been averted. But the past couldn't be changed, and so Jiro let go of his frustration with his father's pride so that he could move forward. A small part of Jiro was surprisingly pleased with how brave Kenichi had been; putting his son's welfare above his own, aware that he might be putting himself in danger. He now looked at his father with a little more respect, and indeed admiration. It was a good start toward mending their relationship, perhaps for good.

On the subject of mending the rift that was separating them, Kenichi had also revealed that was the reason he'd asked Jiro to go on the cruise with him in the first place. In his own way, he realized he was the reason his son would no longer visit, and with his suspicions that Taro was wandering into perhaps criminal territory, Kenichi was determined not to lose both of his sons. Again, while Jiro couldn't really applaud his father's tactics, the sentiments behind his actions were good. At least now Kenichi was coming to realize the benefits of being able to sit down and just talk things through instead of bottling it all away.

"When are you going to visit that nice police lady back in Sweden?" Kenichi's sudden question shook Jiro out of his reverie.

"What?" He coughed, nearly choking on his tea. The query

had come out of the blue. Was Papa referring to Aurora? And if so, how did he even know something had developed between them? Jiro had never mentioned the fact that they'd become close. Whenever Aurora came up in the conversation, he behaved as if she'd been very helpful in finding Kenichi, but they were no more than acquaintances.

"I know the look of someone who is lovesick when I see it. And you, my son, are pining severely after that young lady." Kenichi's sharp observation shocked Jiro. The old man had never mentioned anything like this over the past week. Why was he bringing it up now?

"I…ah…" He didn't know what to say. Even if he wanted to, he wasn't free to return to Sweden anytime soon. His responsibilities were here, looking after his father and making sure Taro got a fair trial, as well as doing anything he possibly could for his brother's family. Once the trial had taken place, and hopefully the FBI rendered the Yakuza threat to Taro's family null and void, they'd need a lot of support to get back on their feet without the man of the house around. Jiro couldn't see himself being able to leave the States for at least the next six months, if not even a year. It was a hopeless case. He was a hopeless case. And he should just forget about her.

He drew in a deep breath. There was no point in beating around the bush with Kenichi anymore. "Aurora was a special lady. But she understands as well as I do that there is no chance for us to be together. We both lead very separate lives, and she's not about to move to America, so we just need to forget about each other." Although they'd never had the chance to have this conversation in person, Jiro had had it plenty of times in his own head. He'd gone over and over the various scenarios in which he and Aurora could be together.

"It's actually not that hard, my boy. If she doesn't want to move, why don't you relocate? If it's true love, then anything is possible."

"It's not love," Jiro argued. "We barely knew each other. And besides…" He stopped right before he said, *"And I need to stay here and look after you,"* because he knew that would get his papa's hackles up. Kenichi would argue black and blue that he didn't need anyone to take care of him, which clearly wasn't true. Instead he said, "I have a good job here. And my family is here; I don't want to leave all that behind."

"Hmm," Kenichi looked at him askance. "The heart wants with the heart wants," he said cryptically. "I think it's pretty clear what your heart wants, but how do you know what her heart wants unless you ask her?" When had his father become so philosophical? He wasn't having this conversation right now. It was impossible, end of story, so he changed the subject to one that he knew would distract his papa.

"I think I might have found a lawyer who's willing to represent Taro. I sent him an email yesterday, and I got his reply today. Do you want me to read it to you?"

Kenichi stiffened in his chair, his knuckles going white around his teacup. This was always going to be upsetting to their father, but it was a process that Kenichi was determined to be a part of. Papa would be paying the legal fees, as all of Taro's assets had been frozen, even his bank accounts, which were considered to be ill-gotten gains and the proceeds of crime. Jiro had been tasked with the job of finding a good lawyer they could afford, who'd help them try to get Taro's sentence down as far as possible. This guy had actually been recommended by Agent Utsi, who'd told him his suggestion was strictly off the record as the FBI might see it as a conflict of interest on his part. Which it blatantly was, and Jiro wondered if Jacob might get in trouble if anyone found out. He also wondered if Aurora had had anything to do with Agent Utsi's recommendation? She could conceivably have asked her police partner—supposedly Jacob's good friend— to help him wherever he could.

There he went, thinking about Aurora again. He just couldn't seem to get her off his mind. Perhaps his father was right when he said he was lovesick, because he'd never felt anything like this before. Like he was an empty vessel, and nothing could refill him. He was floating through every day almost on autopilot, doing the necessary things to care for his father, filling out paperwork, making phone calls and sending emails, making dinner, taking his father to doctor's appointments, completing more interviews with the FBI, all while a little piece of his mind was somewhere else.

Every time he closed his eyes, an image of Aurora would form uninvited. Her face as she glanced up at him, brown eyes wide and thoughtful, wisps of escaped hair floating around her face right after they had kissed in the snow that first time; vulnerable yet not afraid of him. Not afraid of what'd happened between them. Aurora crouched down in the snow, weapon held at the ready, intense gaze fixed on the sniper as she'd returned fire; a warrior goddess ready to serve and protect. To protect him. Aurora laughing, her delicious mouth turned up at the corners, as her eyes twinkled with mirth; witty and intelligent. Everything he loved in a woman. Everything he wanted in a woman. The only problem was he couldn't have this woman. And it was driving him quietly insane.

"Go on then," his father prompted, interrupting Jiro's thoughts. "Tell me about this lawyer." So Jiro put away the images of a very special woman and tried to concentrate as he pulled up his email on his phone.

This was his life for now; he just needed to accept it. Without regrets or recriminations. He had to get his father through this Christmas with as much cheer as possible, so he couldn't allow thoughts of Aurora to get him down. He decided he needed to be more present, and just put her out of his mind once and for all.

CHAPTER NINETEEN

Aurora yawned, closed the morning newspaper, and put down her empty coffee mug. She was still in her pajamas, but knew she should get changed and perhaps take a wander down to the lakeside, just to get out and about. However, a more enticing thought was that maybe she should just stay inside and enjoy her day off. All this newfound freedom was a little disorienting, something Aurora would have to get used to again. Yesterday had been a harrowing day, and she was still emotionally exhausted from the whole thing. But staying in her pajamas all day wasn't a good idea, especially because it was Saturday with midsummer in full swing outside, and she should go out and celebrate some of the pleasures she'd missed out on recently. Yep, she would get dressed.

As she walked past the mudroom door on her way to climb the stairs to her bedroom, her gaze caught on the two pairs of snowshoes still hanging on a rack on the wall. She should have put those away in the storage shed months ago. But something had stopped her. One pair were hers, but the others were her father's; the ones she had lent to Jiro on the day they'd walked out onto the frozen lake. Sudden realization dawned upon her. Surely she couldn't be that sad person who was leaving them there as a reminder that Jiro had been real? That she hadn't just imagined him. She stopped in her tracks and huffed out a frustrated breath. Right, that was it. The snowshoes were going back in the shed right now, and that would be the end of her foolish mooning after a man who probably barely remembered her.

Snatching the shoes off the wall and shoving them under her arm, she marched straight through the kitchen to the back door, grabbing a key off a hook under the countertop, then heading out to the small shed at the rear of the garden. A beautiful, warm sun beat down on her bare shoulders from above, and a sudden, unexpected yearning hit her. A desire to show Jiro what this place looked like in the summer. So green and lush, and so completely different from the white world he'd encountered. He would love it; she just knew it.

She stopped walking and stomped her feet on the concrete pathway. Why was she continuing to do this to herself? She thought she would be over him by now. Funnily enough, Jiro was still in her thoughts, even after six months had passed since he and his father had left Sweden. She'd never even got to say goodbye. But that was for the best, and it was the way she'd wanted it; not allowing herself to go near the hospital until she knew the Nashimoris had left town. When she'd seen Jiro with his father in the hospital room that night, the realization had begun to dawn on her. Jiro had a duty to Kenichi, just as she had a duty to Karl. If anything, Jiro took that duty even more seriously than she did. He would not stay just for her, and she decided she wouldn't ask him to do so. It wouldn't be fair. So she'd managed to avoid him for days, asking Mårten not to put through any calls from him at work, until he got the message and left, even though her heart felt like a lead block inside her chest the whole time.

And the pain hadn't subsided one bit, even after all these months.

The only person she'd talked to about her feelings surrounding Jiro was Mårten's fiancé. Summer had laughed at her confusion, telling her, it didn't take a genius to figure out what that pain meant. She'd fallen in love with Jiro. Aurora had shaken her head and raised a wry smile for Summer's benefit, telling her that nothing could be farther from the truth. How could she be falling in love with someone she'd only known for three days? Summer hadn't let it go, however, and continued to encourage her to contact him; she was a strong believer in love at first sight, just look at how she and Mårten had got together. Secretly, Aurora had contemplated it. But in the end she'd been a coward, deciding that her pain would fade eventually, and that he was too busy with his own life back in America to care much about a girl he barely knew back in the wilds of Sweden.

Just once she'd fantasized about what she would've said to Jiro if things had been different. What if Jiro had told her that he loved her before he left? What if he'd asked her to wait for him? Would that have changed anything? She could just imagine the conversation in her head. Her reply would've been something like, "I'm in love with you too." But that would've been where the fantasy ended. Because then she would have to say, "But I don't know what to do with that feeling. I'm in an impossible situation. My life is taken up with caring for a man who is the bane of my life. I don't have the bandwidth to carry out a relationship. And I don't have the time to devote to a love affair. I don't have the time that you deserve. It's impossible for me to leave to move to a different country, so what's the point."

He would've understood that, of course he would, because he was in very similar circumstances. But would he have argued? Would he have fought for her, nonetheless? Would he perhaps have suggested he could come to Sweden instead? She would never know because it was all just one big fantasy. And for the past six months she'd tried to push it all as far back in her mind as she could as she dealt with the everyday complications of caring for her father, who once he came out of hospital, needed daily rehab sessions, and had become increasingly difficult to deal with.

But now, all of a sudden, she did have time on her hands.

Yesterday, she and Astrid had moved their father into a care facility.

It'd been Astrid who'd finally convinced Aurora that she couldn't continue to live the way she was. Astrid had stayed with Aurora for a week after Karl's fall. Together they spent time with Karl every day in hospital, and it hadn't taken long for Astrid to work out how abominably he treated Aurora. After the fourth day, when Karl still refused to even acknowledge Aurora while she was in the room, let alone speak to her, Astrid sat her down at her kitchen table as soon as they got home.

"Why do you put up with him?" she'd asked.

Aurora had stared at her sister for many long moments, wondering how best to answer that question.

"Because he has no one else. Because it's my duty as the oldest daughter. Because he asked me to," she'd replied, trying to keep the defensiveness out of her voice. They were all valid reasons, and each one swirled through her head on regular rotation. She didn't mention that it was also guilt that made her stay. Guilt mostly engineered by her father, but guilt was a very strong motivator.

"Yes, I get all that. But he has no right to treat you that way." Astrid laid her hand over Aurora's on the tabletop. "Look, I know he wasn't the best father when we were young. And I guess I did a good job of trying to block it out most of the time. I know now that you took the brunt of his bad temper, and I know I let you, which I'm not proud of."

Aurora opened her mouth to speak, but Astrid held up her hand.

"Let me finish," she implored. "But at least when mother was around, she seemed to soften his bad moods. It was only after Mother died that I really began to understand what an awful man he was. Which is why I was happy when you moved to Gothenburg. I didn't say it to your face, but I understood you were escaping."

That made Aurora sit back and take another look at Astrid. Her sister hadn't been totally oblivious to all of her pain after all. Aurora wasn't sure if she was happy with this revelation or not. After all, she'd done everything in her power to shield Astrid. But perhaps her façade hadn't worked as well as she thought.

"You can't keep putting your life on hold just to care for a narcissistic, ignorant old man. I know he's our father, but you deserve so much better," Astrid added, when Aurora still didn't speak.

Aurora didn't want to admit that she'd been having the same thoughts recently, and so she squirmed in her chair. "But what is the other option?" she asked eventually. "Do we get a full-time nurse? I don't think I can afford that."

"No, because that doesn't really solve the problem. He's still here, living in your house, still injecting his poison into your life." This was the most candid conversation Aurora had had with Astrid in probably forever, and she felt a little shamefaced that she'd believed Astrid to be totally impervious to everything that was going on up here. But could Aurora begin to entertain the idea of finally getting her father the care he needed? Because that would give her back her freedom, but it'd come at the cost of her father's misery; she knew he'd hate to be put in a home with a vengeance.

"Let me be the bad guy this time," Astrid said, locking her

gaze with Aurora's. "There're plenty of care homes both here and in Malmö we could start looking at. He talks to me, he'll listen to me. I know he won't like it, and might try to shut me out as well, but he needs to hear this." That Astrid was now prepared to take some of the burden onto her shoulders made a lump form in Aurora's throat.

The conversation had shaken her to the core and given her a lot to think about. But with Karl in the hospital, it was no time to start talking about what might happen in the future. So she'd asked Astrid to leave it for now. Before his fall, Aurora would never have even considered moving Karl to a care home; he wouldn't have stood for it, and she wouldn't have had the capacity to fight back. But with Astrid in her corner… she began to have a little hope.

Her younger sister had gone home to Malmö, and Aurora thought she might not see her again anytime soon. But Astrid had returned every month or so since then to see how things were going. Checking in on Aurora as much as she did on her father. She was the barometer for Aurora's emotions, because Aurora was so caught up in caring for Karl, she was too close to see how he was affecting her. And Astrid could see Aurora was starting to suffer, was being dragged down by the constant stress and the duties that were pulling her in every direction.

Astrid finally went to speak to Mårten, recruiting him to her cause. Mårten had already commented once or twice to Aurora that he was worried about her—she was often late to shift because she had to take her father to rehab sessions, and she was always late with her paperwork now, which'd been unheard of before. Her perfect standards were slipping at work, and while it killed her inside that she might lose the job she loved, she couldn't bring herself to ask anyone for help. Karl had alienated Millie to the point that the poor old lady felt incredibly sorry for Aurora, but even she had stopped coming around in the evenings to help out.

Astrid, Mårten, and Millie had all descended on her house one Saturday morning and said they were holding an intervention, whether she liked it or not. Karl had been home too, and they told her they purposely wanted him included in the conversation, just so he knew how much he was hurting her. He seemed not to care, however; he'd ranted and shouted, swearing that he'd rather be dead than live in some stinking, shitty care home. It was Karl's frenzied reaction—and his complete lack of concern for Aurora's life that was in a downward spiral—more than Astrid and Mårten's determined, compassionate faces that'd forced her to see what was really going on. She'd never forget the stony look on her father's face when she'd finally agreed they should start looking for somewhere else for Karl to live. He'd refused to participate in the conversation after that, even calling Astrid a traitor, just as bad as her sister. But both sisters stood shoulder to shoulder facing their father and told him this was the way things were going to be from now on.

Then, yesterday, an ambulance had come to move Karl to his new assisted care home. Her father had refused to speak and remained as stony and implacable as a statue as the paramedics helped him into the back of the van. Aurora had almost changed her mind then, but Astrid had taken hold of her hand and together they'd watched as Karl was driven away.

Nordic countries had some of the highest care regimes for people with disabilities in the world, and most of what was being provided would either be free or very low cost. Karl had been assessed, and was eligible for full-time nursing care in a retirement home come nursing facility on the outskirts of Luleå. Aurora didn't envy the nurses who'd be looking after her father. One more reason for her to feel guilty, that other people would be bearing her burden now.

Guilt would always be her constant companion when it came to Karl, but she was beginning to realize that a toxic relationship with anyone, even if they were your only surviving parent, wasn't good for her mental health. It was time to start putting herself first. Perhaps the one good thing that'd come out of this was that she and her sister were now closer. Astrid had returned to Malmö on yesterday evening's train, and Aurora had actually been sad to see her go. They promised each other they'd visit regularly, and Astrid would come up to see her father more often too.

Aurora unlocked the shed and hung the snowshoes up on a hook on the back wall. There, now she had put the shoes back where they belonged and would no longer think of Jiro every time she walked past the mudroom. Perhaps it was time to take Erik up on his offer. The IT consultant hadn't stopped asking her out—never seeming to register that she was holding a candle for a certain American tourist—telling her he realized she was dealing with a lot with her father but when she was ready, he'd love to take her to dinner one time. So now her father was receiving proper care, should she give in to his gentle pressure and go out with him? She didn't want to stay single and alone for the rest of her life, did she?

She sighed and gave the shed a discerning glance. It needed a good cleanup. It was stacked with boxes, mainly full of Karl's stuff that wouldn't fit in her house when he'd moved in. Perhaps she could start this task today. After she'd been for a walk to the lake, she'd come back and begin clearing it all out. Yes, that would be good—another step in creating a new life for herself.

As she relocked the shed, she thought she heard her voice calling out her name. It sounded strangely familiar, but… "I'm around the back," she shouted, then suddenly remembered she was still in her brief summer pajamas. Shit. It was too late, however, as a figure appeared walking down the small pathway between the side of the house and the fence.

Aurora stopped in the middle of her garden and stared. Was that…? It couldn't be.

"Jiro?" It was as much a question as it was a statement. She could barely believe her eyes. But it was definitely him, even though he was dressed in shorts and a T-shirt this time, rather than the bulky jackets and long pants she remembered him in. The small part of her brain that was still functioning saw he had a pair of mighty fine legs beneath the hem of his shorts. Long, tanned, athletic. And strong biceps bulged from beneath his short sleeves. That unruly, curly hair still hung over his forehead. Tantalizingly cute.

"What…?" It was as if she'd lost the ability to speak.

Then he smiled, and something in her heart cracked wide open.

"I hope I'm not intruding," he said, stalking closer to her. "Mårten told me you had the day off. So I thought…"

What? He thought he would do what? Just come around here unannounced and set her heart beating so fast she thought she might be having a heart attack? And he'd talked to Mårten? What was that all about? Part of her wanted her to act cool. Stay distant. Be a little wary even. But another part—the biggest part—wanted to jump for joy. Suddenly, she didn't care why he was here. She just cared that he was. She'd been dreaming of him, and never let the idea of him go completely, and now he was, in the flesh. So what was she going to do about it?

She took a few precise steps toward him. "No, you're not intruding," she announced. Then, in a most un-Aurora-like-manner, she flung herself at him, wrapping her arms and legs tightly around him, crushing him to her as if wanting to make sure he was real. He let out a kind of *oof* sound as she collided with him, staggering a little but managing to stay on his feet as he took her full weight.

"Good to hear," he whispered in her ear. "I was afraid you might turn me away." He lowered her slowly so that her feet hit the ground, and she looked up into his face, suddenly shy, merely shaking her head. Of course, she wouldn't turn him away. She hadn't seen this man for six months, and she had no idea what she was supposed to do with him now. He solved that dilemma for her by dipping his head and dropping his lips onto hers. They were soft. Gentle. Undeniable. And it felt like her chest had suddenly exploded.

She'd been so worried he'd forgotten about her. But his lips told the opposite story. He remembered her. He wanted her. He worshipped her. Her mouth became greedy for his, and she stood on tiptoe, pulling his head down closer. She needed him closer. Was this even real? Or was he a figment of her imagination? Something she'd conjured from desperation. Then he picked her up in his arms, and she knew he was really here. The physical strength of him as he wrapped his arms around her echoed through her body, and she remembered his touch, how good it felt. It was still there. The chemistry was like touching dry tinder to a match and watching it flare. Immediate and intense.

She didn't want to speak. Words sometimes didn't tell the full story. She wanted action. Wanted to let her body tell him how much she'd missed him. Everything else could come later. Explanations, justifications, reasons. She didn't want to hear any of them right now.

"Upstairs," she demanded through her kisses. Jiro obliged as quickly as he could, his mouth never leaving hers as he negotiated the stairs up into the kitchen. But the stairs to her bedroom were a much greater obstacle, and for the sake of speed, she motioned him to put her down, then dragged him by the hand up to her bedroom.

God, she hoped she still had a spare condom in her

bedside drawer. She was no longer bothered that she was still wearing her pajamas—there was no bra or panties to impede their progress this time—or that her bed remained unmade. They were undressed in seconds.

Jiro almost threw her onto the bed and then dived after her. Her heart was hammering so hard as Jiro lay the length of his body against hers. One hand slid between her legs, while his other grasped the back of her head as he fastened his mouth to hers, leaving her speechless. Not that she had anything to say, she was pure physical form right now. Besides, she didn't trust her words. He was here, and she was reacting to him as if he'd never even left.

Desperate to feel him inside her, she bucked her hips, sucking hard on his bottom lip, hoping he would get the message. He did. A condom appeared in his hand as if by magic—had he come prepared this time? He slipped it on and then levered himself so that he was hovering over her. Aurora stared deep into his beautiful brown eyes as he slowly entered her. Then everything became fuzzy around the edges, but yet also so sharply focussed as he began to move. Her hands slid up and down his body, whispering across his tanned skin, reacquainting her with his strong back, broad shoulders, and taut thighs. How could he make her feel like this so fast? She was hanging on by one tiny thread, her whole body taut with her need to orgasm. Before she could even warn him, a deep shudder started low in her belly, rising like a crescendo that she couldn't control.

"That's right, baby, come for me," he whispered in her ear.

And she did just that, as wave after wave of ecstasy crashed over her until she felt almost entirely drained. Then Jiro orgasmed almost as hard and fast as she had, his whole body going rigid as he gasped out her name, over and over.

Afterward, Jiro pulled her into his arms, and they spooned, draping a sheet over their naked bodies as a warm breeze floated in through the bedroom window. They slept peacefully together for a few hours before Jiro stirred beside her again and this time they made long, languorous, middle-of-a-summer's-day sex which was just as satisfying but proved beyond a doubt in Aurora's mind that they were as sexually compatible as two humans could possibly be.

But this time, Aurora couldn't fall asleep afterward. Her mind had begun to function again, and there were a million and one things she needed to know.

Eventually, she could stand it no longer, and she rolled over and lifted up onto an elbow so she could look down into his handsome face. "When did you arrive?" she asked, voice still raspy. She didn't ask the other question on her mind, *"And how long are you here for?"* because that was skating too close to the edge of the abyss. Was he here to stay? Or was this just a quick visit? A roll between the sheets a few times before he headed back home. Not that she'd regret what they'd just done, but her heart was hoping for so much more.

"I got in late last night. I booked a room at the Scandic Hotel. I wasn't sure if you would even see me." He reached up to brush a strand of hair away from her face.

"Okay." It wasn't quite the answer she was looking for.

Before she could phrase another question, he got in first. "How's your dad? I mean, he's not here, so is he out at an appointment or something?"

Aha. So Mårten had told him she had a day off, but hadn't mentioned the other momentous thing that'd happened in her life. She wasn't sure where to begin or how to tell him about Karl. Her happy mood began to evaporate. It'd been six months without any contact, and now he just reappeared as if not a single thing had changed. He knew nothing about what'd occurred in the past few months because he hadn't bothered to stay in touch. She was confused, to say the least. But if anyone were to understand what she was going through with her father, then it would be Jiro.

And she shouldn't be the pot calling the kettle black, as she hadn't enquired after him or his family either. While Jiro hadn't tried to contact her once he'd returned to the US, she hadn't followed him up either, even though she'd been tempted more than once to ask Mårten for his address. But she'd been kept updated by her partner as to what was going on with Taros' case, even though she hadn't asked, so perhaps she had an unfair advantage. She knew that after Liam Kenzo had recovered from his bullet wounds, he'd been tried down in Stockholm and found guilty of unlawful deprivation of liberty and serious aggravated assault. He would be spending most of the rest of his adult life behind bars.

She also knew that Taro's trial had recently been held, and he'd been found guilty on multiple charges of gun-smuggling. His sentence was yet to be handed down, however, so that must still be hanging over Jiro's head. Hiroshi Kiyota, the man who'd first coerced Taro into working for the Kyodo-Kai gang, had been arrested after months of undercover work by the FBI and been charged with multiple smuggling charges. His trial had been postponed, however, as they tried to get more information out of him about the inner workings of the gang, so they could dismantle the American faction. Jacob managed to collar two of the leaders of the gang in a well-orchestrated raid, but soon after, most of the other members fled back to Japan and went underground. Mårten and Jacob both knew that even though the Japanese authorities were hunting them, they'd probably just re-group and come back in a newer, better configuration in a year or three. This was one of the frustrating parts of policing—sometimes you never fully eradicated the vermin.

Jiro was still looking up at her, gaze gentle as he waited for her answer.

"Astrid and I made the decision that Karl needed more care than I could give. So yesterday, he was moved to a care home down by the harbor." At least Karl would be able to see the big cruise ships come in, if he ever stopped sulking enough to actually go and look.

A sympathetic frown wrinkled Jiro's forehead, the wayward lock of hair falling into his eye as he got up onto one elbow as well so he could look her straight in the face. "Oh, Aurora, I'm so sorry. I didn't know. That must've been hard for you."

"Hmm." Yes, harder than most people would ever know, except perhaps Astrid. And now Jiro. She nodded, suddenly unable to speak past the lump in her throat. In many ways she pitied her father, having to live a life that wasn't his own anymore, in a situation against his will, with people looking after him he'd already decided he hated. He'd been the architect of his own downfall, however, and while Aurora was desperately sad for him sometimes, she knew she could no longer be responsible for his actions.

Thinking about her father in the care home reminded her that she was now free to do as she wished. Date whomever she liked. She was unencumbered. Her life was now her own again. The fantasy of having Jiro all to herself could now become a reality because she had no excuse for not being able to love him. The idea terrified her and excited her in equal measure.

But there were still so many questions that remained unanswered. Things she needed to know. "What about your papa?" she countered. "How has he recovered from his ordeal?" And more importantly, how was he coping with his older son being sent to jail? But she left that one for now.

"He's doing really well." A smile lit up Jiro's face. "Physically, he's recovered completely. He's a tough old bird." Jiro gave an affectionate laugh. Then, his face turned thoughtful. "And he's also a determined old bird. I thought that seeing Taro charged with those horrible crimes, he might never recover. I think I told you that Taro was always the golden child; the one who could do no wrong in Papa's eyes."

Aurora nodded, letting her hand that was resting on his arm move up and rub his shoulder soothingly. Jiro had mentioned that his relationship with Kenichi was complicated, and he'd never been able to please his father, no matter how hard he'd tried. They both had difficult fathers to overcome.

"Well, after many discussions, Papa and I have come to some understanding. He's adjusted quite well to the idea that he can no longer control the paths of either of his son's lives. Especially mine. I think it helps that he's found a new lease on life; he's dating a lady he met while he was attending a doctor's appointment one afternoon." Jiro shook his head as if wonders would never cease. "He was actually the one who encouraged me to come here and find you."

"Oh." Aurora felt some of the wind go out of her sails. So Jiro had come here because his father had told him to? Shouldn't he have come because he wanted to? Because he loved her? But he still hadn't said those three little words.

CHAPTER TWENTY

Jiro saw the exact second that Aurora's heart closed over. Her face changed, losing all animation, going strangely blank instead. Her lips closed over her cute bunny teeth, and her mouth became serious. What had he said? Something wrong, obviously. But he'd come here to declare his love, and he couldn't give up now. She'd been so open seconds before, so receptive, he needed to find that girl again, and quickly. And the only way he knew how was to say those five simple words.

"Wait, Aurora, you don't understand. I'm in love with you," he blurted. "That's why I came to find you." He swallowed hard, hoping he wasn't too late. Hoping she felt the same way. "You're everything I've ever wanted, and I was stupid not to see that before. I was stupid to let duty and responsibility drive me away from you."

Daring to look up into her eyes, he was surprised to see a sheen of tears appear suddenly in those beautiful brown depths. Then they filled with so much love it nearly took his breath away. She didn't need to say the words; he could see her emotions all laid bare for him.

"Oh, Jiro, I was hoping you'd say that. I'm in love with you too." She reached up and stroked his face. "I was worried that perhaps you hadn't come here for the right reasons. And I'm still a little worried about how this is all going to work. But there's no denying how good we are together."

He sat up and pulled her into his lap, and she snuggled into him, setting his heart aflame again.

He cleared his throat. "Well, I knew the future would be an obstacle we'd need to address if this was to work. So, for the past few months, I've been researching Sweden's wolf population. Did you know they were hunted to extinction and were completely gone by the 1960s? Then, in the early 1980s, three wolves migrated from Russia and Finland and started up a new colony?" His research had been fascinating, and he'd been surprised to find out the wolf population of Sweden was now thought to be around four-hundred and fifty, a fairly robust number. So much so, the government even allowed some minimal hunting of the animal to keep the numbers under control. Jiro had been shocked when he heard this, as wolves in America were highly protected; numbers were still so unstable. But here in Sweden, the wolves seemed to be doing well, which was highly encouraging and made Jiro wonder if he could be part of their continued existence.

"No, I didn't. And that's very interesting." But he got the feeling she was more interested in what else he had to say than in the scientific details of Nordic wolves.

Instead of putting her out of her misery straight away, he cheekily went on to say, "Not only that, they're genetically isolated from every other population and completely unique." Again, a fact that'd piqued his interest. So much so that he'd started asking around. His best mate at the Wolf Center had put him onto a contact here in Sweden, who'd led him to a researcher, Lucas Nygård, at the Norwegian Institute for nature research, NINA, which worked across all countries incorporated in the Lapland area, including Norway, Sweden and Finland, running collaborative research projects on wolf populations.

Lucas believed that the Swedish wolf population was becoming dangerously inbred and required a genetic rescue if they were to continue breeding successfully. He had plans to introduce individuals from nearby countries to help rescue some of the smaller, more isolated populations, especially in northern Sweden, which had excited Jiro immensely.

"Riiight. And this has something to do with us because…?" She tilted her chin up and raised an eyebrow in his direction, a shaft of sunlight glinting off the heart-shaped studs in her ears. He really needed to find out who had given them to her; they were clearly very special to her, but that question could wait for another day.

He gave a wicked smile, but knew it was time to stop tormenting her. "It has everything to do with us, because I've been offered a job with NINA, an institute in Norway, but which runs projects all across Lapland."

"Oh?" Aurora sat up very straight now so she could look him directly in the eye.

"And I came here to see if you would like me to accept the position. It would mean quite a bit of fieldwork, but I could be based anywhere up here in northern Sweden. Even say… Luleå."

Aurora threw her arms around his neck. "Holy hell, Jiro, you know how to keep a girl on edge. Yes, yes, yes. A thousand times, yes."

Her answer had been what he'd hoped. It would be hard leaving his father back in the US, leaving Taro to face his fate in prison alone. But now that the trial was over, and the instigator of all the gun smuggling, Hiroshi Kiyota, had been arrested, and the Kyodo-kai disbanded, the FBI were going to release Taro's wife and kids from witness protection. Straight into the arms of Kenichi, who had offered for them to come and live with him in his large mansion-like house. It was a good solution for both of them. Kenichi would have the company and be able to enjoy his grandchildren, and Tamika would have the protection that the Nashimori name could offer. Plus, now Papa had a love interest, who kept him more than well-occupied. Jiro had never thought to see his father with another woman after their mother died. And at first, he'd been a little taken aback, and worried that she might've just been after his money. But Yuki was a traditional Japanese woman of substance, and Jiro was coming to respect and like her. There might even be wedding bells on the horizon. Wouldn't that be funny if his father got married before he did? That thought didn't scare him at all now. He was sure Aurora was the perfect woman for him. Of course they'd need time to work each other out. But he could feel it in his bones that he was going to marry this woman.

"Hang on." Aurora drew back from him. "I thought you hated the snow. I distinctly remember you wondering, *How could anyone live in this god awful weather?* She crinkled up her nose at him in a cheeky grin.

"I guess I'm going to have to get used to it," he replied with a sigh. It was perhaps the biggest drawback of moving to Sweden. But he had to acknowledge how beautiful the place was, no matter the weather, and if Aurora loved it, then he was sure he would learn to cope.

"Are you sure about this? I mean really sure?" Those dark chocolate eyes speared him with an intense gaze. She was right to ask, and she was right to have doubts. They had only truly known each other for such a short time. And now he was back six months later, declaring his love for her. How could he prove to her how committed he was? It would have to be firstly by his words and secondly by his actions. It would take time, but he needed her to trust him right now.

"I'm deadly serious about moving here," he replied. "I've

given up my rental place in San Diego, and quit my job at the Wolf Center." Some people might call him crazy. He'd come here on a whim, not really knowing what kind of reception he'd get from Aurora. But he had spoken to Mårten on the phone before he came, and her police partner was only too happy to confirm that she wasn't seeing anyone else, and was still in fact pining for Jiro. The words had shocked Jiro, sounding a little alien coming out of the normally earnest inspector's mouth. But Viskten was a good guy, and didn't seem to hold any grudges against Jiro for the way he'd left Aurora and Sweden. In fact, he seemed rather happy to hear Jiro would be coming back to Luleå.

"I missed spending last Christmas with you, and it nearly broke my heart. I want to spend this Christmas with you, helping you to decorate your beautiful tree. And every Christmas after that, if you'll have me." He hoped she could hear the sincerity in his voice. "I want to see this Aurora Borealis you are named after with my very own eyes, even though I know it won't be nearly as beautiful as you."

Her face went a delightful shade of pink at his bumbling attempt at a compliment. But he meant it. He was yet to see the northern lights, and would love to do so while holding her hand. Nothing could compare to her beauty right now, however.

"I missed you last Christmas too," she replied softly. "More than you'll ever know." He had been such a dickhead leaving her like that. Leaving her to face Christmas with a father who was still in hospital. But he'd had his own family dramas, and perhaps they both had to sort out their problems alone before they could finally come together and be the incredible couple he knew they could be.

He placed his lips on the back of her neck, landing soft butterfly kisses. After that, they stopped talking for a long time. And he used his body to show her exactly how much he adored her. He knew he would never tire of worshipping her this way. At last, they lay entwined together, twisted in the bedsheets, panting and sweaty and ecstatically happy.

"We should probably retrieve your bag from the hotel at some stage," she said, a raspy note still in her voice. "I'd like you to move in with me, if that's what you want too." He'd been planning on finding a place to rent nearby, not wanting to impose too much on her too early on. But if she wanted to jump in feet first, then why not?

"I'd love that," he replied, kissing the tip of her nose.

"And after we've done that, I might drop in to HQ and tell Mårten I'm taking a few days off. He'll understand," she added. "We've got a new rookie on our team. He can take up some of my slack while I'm gone." This time she gave a wicked smile. It was good to hear she was no longer the newest kid on the block. She'd earned her stripes.

Then something occurred to him. "Whatever happened to Dalström?" he queried. "Right before I left Sweden, I heard rumors the detective inspector had been put on suspension, but I never confirmed exactly why."

"Hmm." Aurora screwed up her nose. "Yes, Dalström still isn't my favorite person. But he's back working with us now. The commissioner had no choice but to suspend him when it became clear the detective inspector was indeed intentionally mishandling the case."

"Oh, wow." So Jiro hadn't been wrong when he'd felt the other man had something against him.

"It turned out that the sniper, Liam Kenzo, who was hired to kill us, was actually an old friend of Dalström's. They went to primary school together and had been very close at one stage." Jiro had never found out the sniper's name, but wondered now if it was even important. "The sniper was feeding Dalström false information. He told the detective inspector that your father was mixed up in dodgy dealings and had actually disappeared to fake his own death to get money from a life insurance policy."

"And Dalström actually believed him?" Jiro was aghast.

"For a while, I guess he did." Aurora grimaced as she thought about the officer who'd been a thorn in their sides and let his allegiance to a friend color the way he viewed the case. "He had a severe conflict of interest and was trying to hide it. But when the sniper attacked us, he obviously changed his mind. He felt very guilty about the whole thing. Especially when the commissioner removed him from duty." She gave a wry smile at that. "But it seems he's been forgiven, or at least allowed back to work. He's on probation and has to adhere to strict rules and regulations, and he'll probably be watched like a hawk for the rest of his career."

Jiro didn't feel the least bit sorry for the man. He'd made the job of finding his father a whole lot harder, and Jiro would never forgive him for that. They sat in silence for a few moments as Jiro digested the information. "Perhaps I can't forgive him, but maybe I'll just forget him instead," he said at last, putting the man from his mind.

"Good. Are you hungry? Shall I go and fix us something for lunch?" Aurora asked, stretching her arms above her head and revealing her delectable breasts as the sheet fell away.

The only thing he was hungry for was her. Without answering, he pulled her back down onto the bed beside him and showed her what he really wanted for lunch.

They could talk more about the future later. About hope and love and even having a family. But right now, Jiro was going to savor every second he spent with this amazing woman. His move to Sweden was going to be the best adventure in the world. With Aurora by his side, they could achieve everything they dreamed of.

Also by Suzanne Cass

NEW
The Three of Hearts Series
Nordic Romantic Suspense
Books can be read as stand-alone
Winter's Heart
Summer's Heart
Aurora's Heart

Women's Mystery Romance Fiction
Single Title
Finding Kait

Dark Tides Series
Mystery and Romance collide.
Books can be read as stand-alone
Into the Rain
Rain Washed
The Clearing Rain

Stormcloud Station Series
(A Stargazer Spinoff Series)
Small Town Romantic Suspense
Books can be read as stand-alone
Clear Skies
Starlit Skies
Crystal Skies
Dawn Skies
Tangled Skies
Outback Skies

Stargazer Ranch Romance Series
Small Town Romantic Suspense
Books can be read as stand-alone

Combustion: Prequel Novella
Wildfire
Firelight
Snowbound: Christmas Novella
Snowfall
Cloudburst
Silverstorm

Island Bound Series
Mystery Romance (on an Island)
Books can be read as stand-alone
Bound by Truth
Bound by Silence
Bound by the Stars

Colors of the Earth Series
Small Town Romantic Suspense
Books can be read as stand-alone
Shadows in the Dust
Shadows in Deep Blue
Shadows of Red Earth

Romantic Suspense
Single Title
Island Redemption
Glass Clouds
Chasing Bullets

Love in the Mountains Novella Series
Small Town Short Romance
Novellas can be read as stand-alone
Rain on a Tin Roof
Lost and Found
Rescue his Heart

Please Leave a Review
The greatest gift you could ever give an author is to leave a review. You will
be helping other people to discover this book and making a difference to me

as an Independently Published Author. If you liked this book and want other people to read it too, please leave a review.

About the Author

Suzanne Cass is an Australian author who writes rural romance and romantic suspense abounding with passion and danger.

Her debut novel, Island Redemption, won the Romance Writers of Australia Emerald Award in 2016. Suzanne was also a finalist in the 2019 Romance Writers of Australia RUBY award.

She had always had a fascination with the tough resilience of people who live in our amazing red-dirt outback country. When not writing about the characters that inhabit her head, Suzanne can be found roaming the Perth beaches with her border collie, or encouraging from the sidelines as her two sons play sport.

Or you can stay in touch via my website
www.suzannecass.com
Or

www.ingramcontent.com/pod-product-compliance
Lightning Source LLC
Chambersburg PA
CBHW051255210726
48287CB00002B/512